Shredded: A Sports and Fitness Body Horror Anthology

Edited by Eric Raglin

Cursed Morsels Press

Contents

Note from the Editor

Many stories in this anthology deal with intense subject matter. A list of content warnings is available at the end of the book.

Foreword

Steve Stred

Hey, it's the foreword, that part of the book that everyone loves because you get a sneak peek into what's about to come, but also—

Whoa, whoa, whoa—hold up... were you... were you going to skip this? You were, weren't you? Ah, you jerk!

Ok, give me a sec, gotta shake it off, reset, get my head back in the game.

Back in the game. See what I did there? That's right—a sports pun in a foreword for an anthology based around horrific sporting events.

You are welcome.

So, just why the hell am I the one writing this?

Back from about 2006 to until 2013 I was busting my hump in track and field, specifically as a shot putter. You know us. I was 350 pounds, hurling a 16-pound lead ball as far away from my body as I could after spinning in a tiny circle. I loved it. My body did not.

As this is a horror anthology, and people love brutality—the two worst things I ever saw as a thrower:

- A javelin thrower who was repeatedly warned not to throw his javelin into the ground did just that, only to jump towards it after it stuck. He sailed forward and landed on the end of the javelin. We thought he'd impaled himself, but luckily he only sliced open some skin.

- At an indoor track meet at Western Washington University, one thrower wasn't paying attention and a shot put sailed through the air, striking him in the back of his leg. It made a horrendous sound and dropped him to the ground, but somehow nothing was broken.

Now, as I mentioned, my body didn't hold up to throwing, and after blowing my throwing elbow out at an indoor meet, I knew I was done. But as fate would have it, my athletic career wasn't. After a chance meeting at the Calgary Airport, I tried out and was invited to compete for a spot as a brakeman with the Canadian Bobsled Team. Over the course of the following year, I lost 100 pounds to meet the weight limit criteria and focused on becoming faster. I suffered some injuries—notably a borderline hamstring tear. Somewhere on my Facebook page is a photo of me at one of the sprinting camps, tensor wrap having busted off my leg and flying behind me like an attached length of discarded toilet paper.

For those who don't know what Bobsled is, it very well might be the craziest sport out there. I can safely say it is the toughest sport. Depending on if it's 2 man/woman or 4 man—you start at the top of a long icy tube, run on ice as fast as you can while pushing a 200 kg sled, and then jump in. The pilot steers it down a bunch of crazy twists and turns as you fly along at around 85 mph/140 kph. It is exhilarating and exhausting both mentally and physically. Because there is a maximum weight limit (adding the weight of the sled plus the weight of the crew), the inside of the sled is very minimally padded and the sliders themselves wear next to nothing. Helmet, speed suit, and spikes. I also wore a burn vest because if you crash at those speeds, the ice will literally melt your skin off. Hell, even with the burn vest on, the ice can still melt your skin.

My first week of training in Whistler, a.k.a., the fastest track in the world, I was with an Olympic slider who was switching from brakeman to pilot. We had some great runs, and then on our third day, we crashed in a notorious corner called 50/50 (named because it was such a tricky spot and pilots had a 50/50 chance of crashing). We hit the roof of the track at about 85 mph. We slammed back down and then slid on our sides until we finally stopped. Damage to Steve—separated left shoulder, shard of material from the sled cutting my leg, and a destroyed index finger nail. On top of that, numerous bumps and bruises and ice rash. It was close to a month before I could get back in a sled.

It's interesting—parts of Bobsled are similar to writing. When I understood my chances of making the Olympic Team were all but completely gone after numerous spinal compression fractures, Achilles strains, and hamstring injuries, I returned to writing to fulfill that part of me that wanted to create, achieve, and chase dreams.

During my time training for the team, I was always someone who cheered and supported everyone. This is the same approach I've taken in my writing and reviewing. I'm a huge, huge fan of the idea that we need more WE and less I in the world. This applies to the writing community and the reading community as well. Be happy and celebrate others achievements, but also share and shout when you read a great book or a stunning story!

When I saw Eric share this anthology news, I reached out to him and mentioned if he was ever looking for someone to provide a foreword to keep me in mind. Never in my wildest dreams did I expect he'd take me up on the offer. Thank you, Eric, truly honored.

Now, I know in many forewords the writer of said foreword will share a bit about the stories. But I've decided to take a different approach. Whether you love, hate, or feel indifferent towards sports, we all have a sports memory. A moment that you can recall where you were, who you were with, and what you were doing. It could be a specific goal, a team win, an Olympic triumph, or an amazing play.

For me, the first story in this anthology is a perfect example of the nostalgia sports can bring. I spent a lot of time with my grandparents growing up and they were diehard WWF (now WWE) fans. We watched it every Saturday morning and it fostered my love of wrestling for many, many years. My first dog was named, Jake, after Jake 'The Snake' Roberts. I lived and breathed wrestling and that was a direct reflection of my time with my Poppa and Nanny. And wouldn't you know, the first story in *SHREDDED* by Nikki R. Leigh focuses on 'the dark side' of wrestling. I was smiling from ear to ear. Also, "Let's take these bones to the graveyard" is a phenomenal promo line.

I suspect many of you readers will have a similar experience while reading this phenomenal anthology. You'll come across a story and it'll take you back to a time in your life and make you smile, even while the characters within are crushed, maimed, bludgeoned, or beaten.

That's the beauty of sports—and fiction—when you can be transported to another place, during another time, and it can make you both happy and horrified.

I'd say that's a winning combination. Yeah... another sports analogy to wrap this up.

You're welcome.

Steve Stred, Splatterpunk-Nominated Author of *Sacrament* and *Mastodon*

I Am the Ring, My Heart Is the Mat, My Bones Are the Ropes

Nikki R. Leigh

Wrestling families are cursed families.

So cursed, that we've attracted the eyes and ears of you, right? This little docuseries trying to dig deep into what exactly happened at WrestleMassacre last year?

I'll tell you all about it. The whole backstory, too, because it's really, really important you understand why we turned our bones to rubber and packed our muscles with stone.

What you saw that night was a miracle of science and magic come undone. What you saw that night wasn't a show, but a chaotic battle between tradition and change. I promise, it's just as dramatic as it sounds.

Hold that camera steady. Make sure you don't cut a damn thing from this.

You're going to have to hold that mic up to my face for quite some time. Skeletal structure's kind of fucked these days.

When Dem Bones Deb speaks, you listen.

I'm about to spill what guts I have left. Turn up the sound.

"Let's take these bones to the graveyard."

I can hear it every day, rattling throughout my head. My dad first uttered those words in the eighties. Our family hasn't stopped saying it since.

Dear ol' Pops, God rest his soul. Colton Coffin. The man who started it all. He got my family into this business when he started wrestling some of the biggest names around. Giants in stature and fame. He vowed to be one of them, and I like to think he made it. Made his career when he took out the biggest face of the industry at WrestleMassacre 1995.

He wasn't "the bad guy". Wasn't just some heel looking to crush the American hero. Colton Coffin was a star. He had made it the hard way: exercising day in and day out. A little help from some steroids. Protein by the gallon. Rinse, repeat. He trained high-flying professional stunts until the gym lights turned off so that he could turn heads on live television.

He had to. Train with every waking moment he had. Any slip-up could cost you a limb. Could take your life.

And one day, it took both.

In the early 2000s, Colton Coffin and my older brother Skull Nasty were a pop and son tag team force to be reckoned with. Their careers were at a peak, and they were up against their long-time rivals: The Big Bad Bears. Triple B were breaking all kinds of records with their win streaks, and all kinds of stereotypes about what wrestlers could be, seeing as they were a big bag of flamin' hot gay-tos.

There it was. Tradition and change. Dad and son facing off against two of the baddest motherfuckers around. They walked right to the center of the ring and gave Triple B a little *doink* on the tips of their noses. I remember seeing the glimmer of laughter welling in their opponents' eyes, which they quickly turned into stage anger. These guys all loved each other. Wouldn't have wanted what happened to my dad to have happened at all, and certainly not by their hands.

But those two tag teams, they squared off. Fought like hell. Big brother Skull Nasty was cut open from an exposed turnbuckle, and they had Dad on the ropes.

He said it for the last time, then. Colton Coffin, father of two and wrestler extraordinaire let out one last, "Let's take these bones to the graveyard," before that tag team rushed at my dad with their own battle cry.

Needless to say, you put four-hundred pounds of pressure, splashing him against those flaccid ropes over and over again, eventually, they'll break. And when they do, and both men—both giants—topple over the edge and land on you, you're as good as dead.

I could hear my brother and his chorus of "no, no, no" coming from my fuzzy television I was knelt in front of, carpet fibers digging into my knees. I still feel that sensation, my skin grinding into itchy fibers as I watched my dad die on live television.

To say that his body looked like some kind of flesh pretzel is an understatement. Every limb was splayed in a different direction, and my dad was no longer Colton Coffin, my father, or alive. The cameras didn't cut away in time, and when those two wrestlers climbed off my dad, tears already in their eyes knowing full well what they'd done, my eyes snapped a picture that would never be erased.

Arm underneath his back. Legs in the wrong direction. Eye blown from the impact with the ground.

That shit fucks you up. I was eighteen, just starting to get my feet wet in the wrestling business. So far my feet were only getting wet with the sweat of a hundred men before me, slamming into that mat, all while telling me I couldn't do it. Tradition and change.

After watching my dad almost explode under the weight of that tag team, I decided I was going to do it, and I was going to do it better.

With a little help from a ritual and ancient alchemy, of course.

What's that you just asked? Am I joking?

No, honey, I'm giving up the kayfabe.

———◆———

I hit it big a couple of years after my pops died and my brother fell into an alcoholic tailspin. I guess being there, sprayed with blood that shot out of my dad's meat tubes will stick with you in the worst ways.

I always feel a little guilty, knowing that the worst thing that happened to my family led to my rise in stardom. Something about me being associated with one of the most startling deaths in the ring that made me desirable under the camera's eye. It also made me angry. Angry at the company for not taking proper precautions, preferring cash flow over safety. Mad at the crowds for always wanting more. And really, kinda frustrated with my dad for giving it to them until it killed him. I took that anger and turned it somewhere else.

I took it all, bottled up and ready to burn, and I finally found a mentor, except it wasn't exactly the typical kind of trainer you'd find in the wrestling federation.

I found my mentor in the form of a girlfriend who was a big fan of the sciences and arts, and as it turned out, the mighty sport of wrestling. We met at a bar where I was trying to catch up with my brother in terms of drinking myself to death. We hit it off real good, and just like the start of a match, I heard that *ding ding ding* of the bell in my head. We began a match of our own, one of a blistering pace and throttled with passion.

My girlfriend, my partner, and my mentor. I told her my gripes, and she set to work, figuring out a way that I could right the wrongs of my dad's death. Vickie was like that, you know? Giving. Inquisitive. Driven.

And that's where it *really* started. Vickie and I would lie in bed all night, naked and sweaty, and she'd whisper husky alchemical secrets in my ear. I fell in love with her a little more every night because she didn't just want to be famous, or be with the famous lady wrestler. No, she wanted *me* to achieve my dreams. Even if it meant turning my bones to the equivalent of calcified rubber bands.

You heard that right.

Dem Bones Deb. Might as well have been Dem Rubber Bones Deb.

Vickie had figured it out after hunching over her workstation for hours.

"Say, Deb, isn't it always the really bad bone breaks? Neck injuries and stuff like that that takes you all out?"

"Sure," I said. "If not the concussions or drugs and heart attacks."

"We can tackle that later, sweetie," she said, and then hunkered back down with her arcane symbols.

"We're gunna fix dem bones, Deb," she said with her corniest grin.

God, I loved her. And Jesus did she do me dirty.

———◇———

My first match with Vickie's special concoction, I was nervous as hell. Here I was, five foot eight and just enough muscle mass to hit 185 pounds. I was going up against Boom Chakra Laka, some beast of a blonde haired, blue-eyed woman who had at least fifty pounds on me and ten years experience. I was supposed to be the fall gal to push her win streak forward.

That was all fine and well, but I knew the head exec of the federation had it out for me, thinking I was trying to sully ol' Colton Coffin's legacy. It wasn't going to just be me acting out the role of a jobber. He wanted to see blood.

I'd give it to him, but I was gunna make it look gruesome as fuck to make my own name. Sometimes, it doesn't matter if you win or lose. Sometimes, the crowd loves you when you take a good beating with your chin held high.

I held the potion that Vickie made in my hands, and I drank that shit down. Tasted like licking a sweaty asscrack, but I stomached it and felt its magic working almost immediately.

It was weird. It felt bad.

When the last drop went down my gullet, my stomach started to bubble. I watched myself in the mirror, noting no outward changes, but holy crap was stuff happening on the inside.

I could feel my bones melting themselves down. What was hard and strong and very, very breakable, started to warm, a heat flowing through my body. They started to feel heavy, like they'd sag right out of my skin if I thought about it too much.

Vickie, the little scientist she was, figured that since the bones are usually what hold the rest of the body up, something else would have to do the work. That's where all the bulking up came in. Stronger muscles to hold the bones.

A real mess of the framework, but as I stayed upright, I knew it had worked.

"Chop my arm with all your might," I said to her. She laughed at first until she saw my dead serious face. Walked right up and chopped the shit out of my forearm.

It still hurt. Still felt that muscle give way and my nerves light up. Skin started to bruise shortly thereafter. But when she smacked me with the blunt of her hand, her hand sank, ever so slightly into my flesh, and where I would have usually felt it hit my bone, it simply... bounced back.

My body realigned itself quickly. Could have almost missed that strange valley she dug into my arm if you blinked just right.

My beautiful woman had done it.

And now, I was ready to take her alchemy for a test drive.

I stood in the ring, my stomach full of chemicals and my bones of magma. Boom Chakra Laka menaced me from her corner in the ring.

I was ready to take her beating. I took it all, and I sold the shit out of her moves.

Threw me against the ropes, and my body bent and bent until the back of my head nearly kissed the middle rope. I could feel my bones elongating within, sliding through me like snakes in a hole. Boom stared at me, eyes wide at the flexibility I was showing. I resisted the urge to smack her cultural-appropriating face.

But I *did* resist, because I knew my place. And I was writing my own legend.

She hit me out of the ring. I splashed to the floor just like Colton Coffin had done a few years earlier. The audience couldn't see it, but I sure could feel it when the back of my skull hit the ground and just kind of flattened against the rubber-matted cement. Kept me from breaking my head open, but I was sure I was concussed.

I stood up, a bit wobbly on my feet, only to see Boom lunging out of the ring in a tope suicida and I knew I was fucked.

She hit me, head and shoulders to chest, and I flew like a drunken bird into the metal railing holding the crowd back. She hit me so hard that I felt my body inverse and swan dive in on itself, my head going lower and lower, and my spine curved and kept curving in its rubbery state. I think my head was damn near my own lady parts when my ass hit the barricade and I sandwiched in some twisted version of me.

The crowd gasped. Inhaled as one before letting out a collective holler at what my body had done. Every ache and pain that was already beginning to show its ugly head was worth it.

It went on like that for the better part of twenty minutes. A fixed job match where I was supposed to lose in five minutes carried on despite the network's time capacity because what people were seeing was incredible. Magic.

I lost with my ass exposed. Boom had beaten the shit out of me, and I was cut open because despite my malleable bones, my skin was still fragile. There I was, bleeding from my forehead, with Boom on top of me, pulling my legs up and around so that I was almost pinning myself. She may not have understood at the time what was happening, but she sure worked it for all she was worth.

The ref's hand slammed into the mat three times, vibrating my worn body. I could feel my bones buzzing as the alchemy began to wear off, and I was thankful that my body would be normal again soon. I remember feeling the unrelenting fear that the potion would be done while Boom had me folded up, and I'd break in half.

So that was that. The match that catapulted my career into the spotlight. I'd broken myself over and over again in that ring since then, even if I looked like a cross between Gumby and gumbo when it was over.

After that, the network knew I needed to be in the spotlight, with my incredible flexibility and physics- and biology-defying stunts. They kept asking what kind of yoga I was doing, hoping to get some other wrestlers involved so they could replicate my style. I just gave them the finger and carried on, shouting from the rooftops that I was one of a kind and I should be treated as such. I kept winning and losing matches—the federation couldn't decide which was more exciting.

Vickie and I... we fell in and out of love over and over again over those years. She kept making my special fitness drink. We got engaged, but to be honest, it had gotten to the point where I wasn't sure anymore if Vickie wanted to be with me, or with my career. I knew I needed her in both capacities, but I don't think she cared about the intimacy of our relationship as much as she used to. She grew more distant, spending less time at home and more at her lab. It wasn't until last year's WrestleMassacre that I learned why.

So, let's get there. This is what you came here for, right? Trying to figure out if what you saw was all some gimmick or pretend "death" and injury?

I mean, I hope by now you'll believe what I'm about to say. That this all goes beyond some stupid kayfabe. It's real, and my broken body that your perfectly aligned arm is holding the mic up to should be enough proof.

Alright, sorry. Look, it's hard not to be a little bitter thinking about this day and what it meant. It's not just my body that broke, but also that little vessel in my chest too, okay?

Over the last few years, I worked my body and soul to get into that ring as the women's headliner for a title match to rule the television. I finally got it, heading up against the wrestler that kickstarted my career—Boom Chakra Laka. She had the belt, and the network had finally decided that it was my turn to take it, and I just *had* to take it from her. I think it was the first time that the network had billed a women's title match as the main event. I was as proud as I was disgusted by that fact.

She was mad. Rip-roaring angry I could tell. Despite holding that championship belt, she had always played second fiddle to my ever-evolving display of death-defying stunts.

Like always, I drank my special juice backstage, not thinking twice about the fact that it tasted a little different and the buzzing in my bones was a bit more pugnacious than usual. I shook it off, thinking that maybe I was already getting a little too old for this business, and entered the stadium.

I stood in the middle of the ring, the challenger with the world at her feet. Boom's entrance music played, an antagonistic swirl of guitar and piano that featured aggressive sounds of meditation, playing off her spiritual persona. She raised the ropes, stepped in with her white knee-high boots.

We threw insults back and forth. She had brought a literal soft pretzel into the room, which had become something of my symbol over the years, what with all the bending, and took a big bite out of it. I told her I was going to realign her chakras and advised her to nama-stay away from me. We had something of a white hot rivalry that over the years had shifted. I think she really hated me.

Boom cracked her knuckles, and a panic struck me. They didn't just crack, they ground together, loudly, like the sound of rubbing rocks.

I felt fuzzy. Something different than usual. The starting bell rang and it echoed in my head like some church bell gone insane. I didn't get a chance to figure out what was going wrong before Boom was across the mat, and my body went into auto-pilot.

She hit me with a chop across the chest, and that's when I knew I was fucked.

Her hand hit like a rock golem and my chest caved. It didn't shatter like it might have, had I not had the bone altering serum weaving through my body, but it hurt and probably looked like something out of a cheesy kung fu movie. Her hand slammed into me, I felt her rock-hard fingers cleave a wedge in my chest.

Every time I was hit before, my bones would give way, stretch and bounce right back like a rubber band. It didn't happen like that this time.

Her hand wedged a four-inch cleft in my chest, and when her fingers receded, that divot was left behind in plain sight. I wheezed with every breath after that one.

Boom smiled at me. Fucking smiled with her perfectly straight white teeth and twinkling blue eyes and that was when I knew. I suspected that she had done something to make her muscles and bones hard as a rock. And even more, that something had been done to mine to throw off their rubbery state.

Another chop, another wedge in my chest. They lined up little canyons, until I held my hand up to block them. She took that chance to launch a super kick, which made a right angle out my arm.

The crowd was used to my body doing oddly flexible things, but when the limb didn't bend right back and realign, I heard more than a few gagging sounds from the audience.

I stared at my forearm, folded like a collapsible straw, and Boom grabbed me around my midsection. I felt her own rocky limbs then, beyond muscle and tendon and bone and now igneous rock, sharp and blunt and unbreakable.

I was plenty breakable though, and she knew that. She suplexed me into the mat, and sent a shock through my bones that landed some of the vertebra into others, scrunching my neck like an accordion.

Pain and more pain rippled through me as nerves were trapped between immovable swaths of rubbery bone. Never felt it like this before. I lashed out, trying to get her away from me. Didn't care about losing anymore, was only terrified that my body was going to be stuck like this forever.

She didn't stop though. That damn gleam in her eye as she got real close to me on the ground, putting a show on for the audience who wasn't sure what to think. Those greedy wrestling federation bastards were just letting it play out, figured our waivers should cover this.

Boom came in to lick my face, a classic taunt of hers, and what I saw scared the shit out of me. Her tongue, no longer soft and pink, looked like it was made of bulbous, coarse minerals. She licked me with whatever it was and grated some of the skin off my cheek.

That hurt, but it didn't hurt quite as much as what I realized I had smelled when she leaned in: Vickie's aromatic hair wash, blended with rosemary, lemon, and something she called her "secret scent." She wouldn't have given that alchemic secret away to just anyone, and that's when I knew she was in cahoots with Boom.

Betrayal flashed across my features, and I could see Boom relish in it. She picked me up and threw me towards the ropes. All I could think about while I sailed towards those ropes was that my darlin' had committed the ultimate sin against me in a two-in-one of cheating with Boom all while collaborating on a potion that would change her body. What better way to keep bones from being broken than to turn everything to rock?

Boom ran toward me, with my back against the ropes, and the maniacal look in her eye told me that her heart was a muscle too, and that must also have turned to stone.

She hit me with a rock hard lariat, catching me in the chest. I spun around the ropes, my top half rolling with the force. My rubbery bones kept spinning, and turning, and twisting until it felt like Boom had tied me into a literal knot around the ropes.

I heard the gasps from the crowd even though my senses were failing. I was dizzy from looping over myself so many times. Blinded with Vickie's treachery.

Boom whispered in my ear and my blood chilled.

"Let's take those bones to the graveyard."

I was as good as dead.

She ran to the other side of the ring, bounded off the ropes and collided with me like a freight train.

The ropes broke with me still tied around them, stuck in my twisted position thanks to whatever Vickie had done to my drink.

I landed on the ground, in a heap of myself.

With my face crunched somewhere between the cement and the weight of my own body, tangled in the ropes, I saw it all for what it was.

No medicine could figure out a way to untangle me from myself, so whatever Vickie and Boom had done to me was permanent.

You want to know my thoughts about last year's Wrestle-Massacre, and why I can no longer do anything other than simply exist?

This is the last thing I'll say about, and then I'm going to have myself tucked away in a dark room with alcohol sent directly into my veins to numb this away eternally.

Fuck tradition. Screw change. That night, the one thing we were was Vickie's playthings, caught in her chaos. We weren't rivals. We weren't just pawns of the federation.

We weren't heel and we weren't face. We were fucking undefinable.

Unfortunately, at the point it all went to hell, so too were our bodies.

Undefinable.

Couldn't tell if that quivering thing in the corner was a pile of arms or a lump of ass.

It was us, and that other hardened mass of flesh was them. And we'd just put on the show of a lifetime.

The Swish Heard 'Round Central Nebraska

Tim Meyer

The orange globe hits nothing but net, the sweet whip-crack of the nylon music to the crowd's attentive ears. Before the ball touches wood, everyone in the gymnasium shoots out of their seats, arms raised, screaming until their lungs and throat burn with that good burn—the heat of victory.

Kenny London is still standing beyond the three-point arc, right arm extended toward the basket, wrist bent, savoring the moment, when the bleachers empty, when the students and teachers and parents cheering for Millpoint High rush the court, howling their heads off. Kenny feels his body elevate, his feet leaving the hardwood too quickly for his brain to process. Arms on shoulders and thighs, hoisting him, higher and higher—

———◦———

"Earth. To. Kenny," says Dell Roberts as he claps his hands in front of Kenny's eyes, a clap for each word—*clap, clap, clap!* "Yo, London!"

Kenny snaps to. Instead of the Millpoint gymnasium, he's outside, in the woods somewhere, somewhere dark, somewhere he wasn't and maybe never has been. It's an odd feeling, this baffling sense of temporary displacement. Not so far away a campfire burns steadily, and a group of teenagers is chatting the night away, laughing and cackling at jokes he cannot hear.

He faces Dell, who's tilting his head sideways, ogling him like Kenny's face is stuffed full of actively oozing pimples. "Huh?"

"Yikes, dude." Dell puts a hand on his shoulder, glares at him with rheumy, *I've-had-way-too-many-Buds* eyes. "You were drifting."

"Drifting?"

"Like... in outer space." Dell's finger traces a wide arc over his head as he mimics the sound of a rocket ship blasting off into the stratosphere. "Like, you were sailing."

"I was?"

"How many beers have you had tonight?"

There's a half-empty light beer in his hand, but he can't remember picking it up, let alone drinking it. The last thing he remembers is the high school gym, the basketball game, the game-winning shot—and even that stuff seems blurry, a fractured memory of something he may or may not have done. Other than this strange sense of self-separation, he feels good. Better than good—great, even. Like he could head into the weight room right now and bench one-and-a-half times his weight, more than he's ever done. Gosh, the strength he feels coursing through veins. The power.

I feel invincible.

"I don't know actually," he replies because he needs to say *something*. Dell's waiting, continuing to eyeball him.

"You're acting weird, man. Starting to think that comet hitting your old man's farm is affecting you. Not saying the two things are related, but last week that thing wrecks your pop's barn, this week you're scoring forty-two points off the bench and hitting the game-winning buzzer-beater. Seems to me like some of that floaty dust is giving you superpowers or some shit."

The comet. The floaty dust. These are all events he recognizes. Things he's stored in his head, *memories.* He remembers, of course he does. Last week, Tuesday he thinks, when the London family was fast asleep in the middle of the night, a crash from Hell roused them. It literally sounded like the world was ending, the focal point of the apocalypse being the barn and silo. Both were destroyed, smashed to rubble, a doomsday collection of splintered boards and pebbled glass and torn shingles. The silo came down like a boxer taking perfectly placed knuckles on the chin and getting knocked out cold. It now lies in a long pile of debris that will take a cleanup crew several weeks to haul away. Big Ed London, Kenny's father, doesn't seem in any rush to clear the area, especially since the insurance company is dragging their feet on cutting the check.

The floaty dust. Ah, yes. That. Since the comet hit and buried itself a good twenty feet beneath the surface, the Londons have seen floating particles all over the property, almost a mile in each direction. It's more concentrated near the point of impact, the aquatic-green luminescent material more noticeable at nighttime, looking like magical fireflies from a fairy-tale book.

"Yo, London!" Dell shouts again, smacking Kenny's left cheek, hard enough to sting. "Snap out of it, man."

Kenny does. He comes back to reality, leaving behind the images of those flitting, glowing embers. "Sorry."

Dell puts an arm around his neck and walks him back over to the bonfire, where the rest of Millpoint High is celebrating the big upset. "You need to focus if we're going to beat West-haven next week in the finals. Need some more of that freaky magic shit."

And they'd get it.

Or so the conscious voice swimming through Kenny London's veins tells him.

Oh yes, they will get the magic.

---❖---

In the mirror he looks like himself, but also different. His biceps are swollen, puffed like they sometimes get after a good workout, only... bigger. Much bigger. As he rotates shirtless in front of the bedroom door's mirror, he sees every muscle is slightly inflated, noticeable versus yesterday. And yesterday he didn't even lift.

A part of him likes these results. A part of him is worried that Dell could be right—the floaty stuff is affecting them—all of them—the whole family.

When he goes downstairs, his family is sitting in the kitchen, huddled around the circular tabletop, eating breakfast. They pay him no mind when he enters the room; they continue to shovel heaps of eggs and bacon into their mouths, eating greedily, like they haven't eaten in days. Which isn't true. The Londons haven't skipped a meal since who-knows-when. Kenny sure doesn't. In fact, they've added two meals to the daily eating schedule. A meal between breakfast and lunch, one between lunch and dinner.

He raids the fridge for the jug of milk, then grabs the protein powder off the top. Heading over to the counter, he catches his father watching him. Wait, not just his father. His entire family. His mom and sister too.

"Six days," his father reminds him. Of what, he doesn't know.

"Six days," his mother repeats, low, monotone. Zero enthusiasm going into this announcement. Her eyes are not looking at the same things he can see.

"Six days," his sister, Cheryl, follows. Same voice. Like they practiced it this way.

One scoop of protein powder goes into the empty glass. The right amount of milk splashes on top of it, mixing, a thick concoction he can taste upon scenting it—a chocolaty goodness that will coat his throat and stomach oh-so-perfectly.

"Six days," he agrees, though he's not exactly sure why. Whatever it is, it's true.

Six days.

———◆———

Outside. Nighttime. The green embers dancing in the dark, lighting up the sky, a calming collection of flittering orbs. Kenny, arms spread open, fixates on them, his eyes darting back and forth, his soul absorbing the unseen energy that's being emitted from each particle. His mouth is open, catching air. After a few minutes, he glances over and sees his father next to him. His old man's mouth is also open, sucking in deep breaths, allowing the energy around them to infiltrate his body, his arms stretched wide as if he's trying to hug the entire property. Mom is next to Dad, and Cheryl is next to her—both in the same position. Their breathing is rhythmic, synced with one another. They are one with the night, the embers, the stars, the universe, the—

———◆———

Cardinal on the end of a tree branch is cleaning its wings, its triumphant chirps echoing throughout the misty-gray morning. Kenny stops to observe its routine, drawn to the creature. He stares for a moment, then drops his book bag on the dirty ground. He checks over his shoulder, makes sure his mother and father aren't watching him, but the house is silent and still, and the rubble from the comet's impact doesn't judge him on what time he gets himself to school. He focuses on the cardinal, and the cardinal notices him. It takes a break from bathing its wings to stare back. Kenny sharpens his gaze, obsesses over the cardinal, the tiny creature covered in red, red the same color of fresh blood, the—

———◇———

"Three days," Dell says, slamming his locker door, so hard the lock doesn't catch and the door bounces back at him. A second, more gentle approach shuts the door just fine. "You ready to whoop some Westhaven ass?"

Kenny barely hears him, nods anyway. A few of the other players come over, still riding high from the upset victory in the semifinals. They treat Kenny like he's already cemented himself as a Millpoint legend, a legacy that will never be forgotten.

It's so true, he thinks to himself, though that voice that speaks is hardly his own, but that doesn't matter, not yet.

"What's up, beefcake?" Arron Leake says, pinching Kenny's biceps. "Shit, you're getting ripped, my guy."

"You juicing?" Ricky Howe asks, laughing behind his hand. "You gotta be juicing. Last week, you were looking like a barn cat scraping for dead mice."

"Not juicing," Kenny tells them.

Dell wraps an arm around his shoulder. "Lay off the merchandise, fellas. Give the kid some room to breathe, all right? Kid's not juicing. My boy doesn't need to fuck around with that shit."

"Yeah, okay," Ricky says, still laughing, giggling like a hyena, his mouth open, perfect white teeth in a line, exposed, and all Kenny can think about is how good it would feel to knock them down the prick's throat. A fiery, temporary rage fills him, and he thinks he might explode—like, *actually* explode—from the combustible ingredients that boil inside him, his muscles, his face. He balls his fist, but before he can strike, the feeling passes and he's calm again.

"What's your problem?" Ricky asks, losing his smile at once. "It was just a joke."

"Yeah, London," Arron says, adding nothing to help Kenny's nerves. "Relax. You're wound too tight, guy."

"Fellas, just lay off, okay?" Dell leads him away from the pack of (now) concerned varsity basketball players. "The Legend is feeling a little under the weather. He needs his rest before Friday night, okay? Ain't that right, London?"

"That's right," Kenny says, swallowing the rage, pushing it down, deep, to where it cannot touch his actions, to where it will remain until—

"One day," his father says, then stuffs a piece of meat in his mouth. The bloody juice runs down his chin, a watery trickle staining the paper bib fixed to his collar.

"One day," Mother says, cutting herself a slice of raw beef. It's still dripping when she puts the slaughtered animal in her mouth.

"One day," Cheryl confirms. The lower half of her face is stained a dirty, dark red. A squirrel with its abdomen shredded open sits on her plate, butchered innards hanging over the torn flesh like this is amateur surgery hour.

"One day," Kenny says, but what happened to the—

—cardinal? It free-falls from the branch as if it contacted an exposed telephone wire, electrocuting itself dead. It hits the ground with a soft, feathery thump and lies motionless on the dusty pathway. Kenny thinks: Did that just happen? Did I just mind-kill that bird?

Yes. Yes you did.

But how?

You're changing.

We are changing.

This is good.

Collect your reward.

In a few blinks he's kneeling over the dead bird, picking it up by one of its wings. He sinks his teeth into the joint bridging the wing and the body, feels the bones break between his bite, his teeth snapping them like twigs, and blood wells to the surface, and he con—

————◇————

—sumes as much as he can before the bell rings. He's eaten three slices of pizza, six celery canoes stuffed with extra chunky peanut butter, and downed three twelve-ounce bottles of chocolate milk.

"Damn, dude," Dell says, dropping a used napkin on his cafeteria tray. "No wonder you're bulking up. Got any room for dessert?"

Kenny doesn't say so, but he has plenty of room for dessert. And, honestly, he's got room for more lunch too. His stomach feels bottomless, in constant need of satisfaction. Like there's a monster at the end of his lower intestine, greedily gobbling up whatever he puts down there.

"What's..." Dell's face changes, his brow pushing up, forming lines in his forehead. "What's that on your neck?"

Kenny doesn't understand, not at first, thinks his friend is speaking to someone else. But Dell's eyes are glued to his neck and there's no one else at the table.

"Dude..." Dell snaps a pic with his phone. "Look."

Dell shows him. Kenny glances down at the photo, sees an abnormally large knot attached to his skin. As he looks, he applies his fingers to the spot and probes the area. The knot—about half the size of a golf ball—isn't hard but filled with a thick fluid, a jellylike mass that seems to have sprung up overnight. *Or during the day.* Dell is the first to mention it.

Kenny pokes the soft extension of himself, testing its bouncy nature, hoping to—

"You better get that checked out, man," Dell tells him. "Better before—"

"Tomorrow," Dad says. He's in Kenny's room, standing over his bed, along with his mother and sister. The three of them have come to tuck him in, kiss him night-night. Their eyes are dead-black, reflecting rings of moonlight, and the room is filled with the floaty embers that used to remain outside exclusively but have now infiltrated every area of the house, clinging to the walls and ceilings, making nests in the drywall. They're extra vibrant tonight, pulsing and glowing a Halloween emerald.

"Tomorrow," the three of them say in unison, and in that scary green glow, Kenny can see the growths on their faces, the swollen clumps of flesh pushing outward and he—

—pops it in front of the mirror. A creamy explosion of some infectious fluid spills down the side of his neck, getting the left shoulder strap of his game jersey wet. He cleans himself off with a towel, then removes the excess broken skin around the wound with his fingers, tearing whatever is left of the sick boil. He wipes down the sink, then disposes of this evidence in the trash. He can't force himself to ignore the other ones growing on his face and arms and legs, the raised puffs beginning to swell with the gross liquid, but he can't do anything about it now because the game starts in—

———◇———

"Five minutes," Coach says, tapping his watch. Everyone's huddled in the locker room, getting themselves pumped up, flooding their bodies with the adrenaline needed to overcome the huge disadvantage—Westhaven is favorite by double-digit points, and no one expected Millpoint to reach the semifinals, let alone *win* that game. But they're here now, and they have Kenny London, and he's going to start at the two-spot, may even have to run point, but he's up for the challenge, ready to score, ready to win, ready to kill—*no, not kill*—ready to sacrifice his body and leave everything he has out on the court because that's what winners do and they don't—

———◇———

"—give up," Coach says. It's halftime, they're down by twelve. Not a big deficit, but when you're playing Westhaven, it might as well be thirty-five points. "Never quit!" he tells them in his Marine-*oorah*-battle-cry voice. "Get out there and leave it all on the court. There's no tomorrow, boys!"

Everyone cheers, the speech doing its job to rally the troops, even if the war is already lost and the enemy is knocking on the door of certain victory.

Kenny hangs his head. He checks his arms, notices the pockets of bubbling flesh becoming highly visible now, and he hopes no one else will see them—but how can they not?

He hides in the background, hoping to—

———◇———

Scoop up the loose ball and streak down the court, lay it in for an easy bucket, but the Westhaven guard gets between him and the open court. Kenny grabs the ball after poking it free from the offense, zips toward the basket, cuts it laterally, hoping to shake the defender. The Westhaven guard—number Thirty-Two—adjusts nicely and squats, arms out and ready to swat any attempts at a pass. But Kenny isn't dishing the rock, not on a breakaway one-on-one, not this close to the basket.

"Come on, comet freak," says Thirty-Two, between heavy breaths.

Kenny doesn't know why, but the comment enrages him, fuels him to do something he might not have ordinarily done. He's never been aggressive when it comes to driving the lane, part of the reason he's spent most of the varsity season riding the bench, but now, in this moment, things are different. Clearer.

He knows what to do.

He lowers his shoulder and steps to the left. Thirty-Two steps to meet him but he's too slow to the mark, and Kenny squeezes past him but not without shoulder-checking him. The contact slides past the official, who seems to be calling this championship game fairly loose, so the play continues and Kenny speeds toward the basket, jump-stops underneath the rim and pump fakes, sending Thirty-Two into the air, his strong attempt to block the layup sailing past. Once Thirty-Two's attempted block fails, Kenny squares up and uses the backboard for an easy two.

This cuts the Westhaven lead to six points. Only ten minutes left. Plenty of time.

"You're not winning shit, comet boy," Thirty-Two says as he trails Kenny back down the court. "You hear me? You hear—"

———◆———

Me.

Hello?

I'm in you.

Let's do this. The time is now.

Ten seconds left. Down by two. The bleachers are packed with standing attendees, everyone's knuckles in their mouth, watching as Millpoint inbounds the ball.

Now.

Before the ref blows the whistle, Kenny looks to the bleachers, sees his parents and sisters joined by their hands, their eyes tilted to the roof, glazed back, showing all-white. Their flesh moving like something beneath the surface is trying to poke through. He glances down at his own arms and legs, sees the boils starting to move on their own, pulsating to the rhythm of some unheard chant, swelling and decompressing in incessant succession. In the air a cloud of shiny-green embers collects near the ceiling, twinkling like celestial stardust.

"I'll kill you before I let you take this last shot, comet boy," Thirty-Two says, then seems to finally notice the boils on his opponent's skin, the way they're moving with the moment. Thirty-Two's face sours, and he elevates his shoulders from his crouched, defensive position, opening himself up to losing not just one step—but several. "What the fuck, man?" he mutters, backing away.

The ref blows the whistle.

Kenny bolts to the spot Coach marked out on his dry-erase playbook. Dell's inbound pass is on target, hitting Kenny in the hands.

Two seconds on the clock.

Thirty-Two can't recover in time. He steps and jumps, extending his arm, trying to shield Kenny's vision. But Kenny's already squared up behind the three-point arc. He's jumping, shooting, following through, his wrist bending toward the rim.

The ball, sailing through the air. The buzzer sounding, the crowd gasping.

The crack of the net as the ball hits nothing but nylon.

The crowds leaping and stomping and cheering.

Thirty-Two doesn't even seem mad, just... disgusted. He retreats as if he knows what's coming next. But there's no way he can know. No way anyone can.

The bleachers clear, and the students and parents and teachers rush the court.

Now.

As the people crowd around him and yell in his face, congratulating and hugging him and putting their sweaty palms on him, Kenny feels the numerous bubbles on his skin pop at once, explode outward in a messy detonation of thin skin and creamy mucus. No one seems to notice, not even as the liquid brushes their own skin; they're all too busy getting caught up in the game's crazy aftermath, celebrating as if this is the biggest moment of their lives, *their* accomplishment—not Kenny London's.

Kenny looks to his parents and Cheryl—their meat suits have opened too, flowering long ropes of fleshy stems. At the end of each extension, three talons. There're a hundred stems between them, leaving their body, seeking homes in whatever body they can get their claws on. Again, no one seems to notice or care that the Londons have transformed into something of a cosmic nightmare.

They keep on cheering. Even as the butchering starts.

Kenny watches as a long stem, thick as a solid oak tree branch, slides out of a hole on his thigh. Dell's in his face, screaming about how they won, how much of a hero he is, how this night will be remembered forever. The stem's sharp end meets Dell's throat, shears open a sizable throughway, and slips inside, silencing Dell forever.

People start to notice now. They start to panic, start to run.

But it doesn't do them any good.

The floaty green embers fall from the ceiling, covering them in the fantastic glitter.

The rearranging of human flesh is louder in the panicked cacophony than the game-winning swish was in the breathless silence.

I'm Gonna Make You A Legend

Brandon Applegate

Nathan swipes a hand across his face and it comes away streaked with crimson. He's sick of seeing his own blood. The ache in his cheekbone flares white-hot.

Not much he can do about it.

Hiding seems to work. He's packed himself into the sliver of space between the school and the massive blue dumpster. The smell of rotting cafeteria waste hovers around him like a prophecy. He spends enough time back here that the scent sticks to him, which doesn't help his situation.

A flash of blue and yellow passes by. A letterman jacket. Nathan tries to fold himself deeper into the crack. Ribs burn where they kicked him. *God, don't let them see me.*

"You okay back there kid?"

Nathan clamps his jaw shut on a scream. He opens one eye and looks up. The smiling face isn't one he knows.

"You okay?" the jock repeats.

Nathan doesn't answer. Best thing to do with football freaks is to keep your mouth shut and hope they go away.

"Come on, kid, it stinks back here. I ain't gonna hurt you."

"I don't know you," Nathan says, voice hoarse, shaking.

"What, you like it in there? C'mon."

This has to be a trick. But if he wants to get at Nathan, all this guy's got to do is call his buddies to move the dumpster. And he's right—it stinks.

Nathan struggles to his feet. Now that they're standing in the sunshine, the jock looks different. His face is gaunt, eyes droopy like he's missed sleep—for a while.

"There," the jock says. "Better?"

Nathan skitters over to the wall. Tired or not, the guy is big and he wants some space between them.

"Hell of a shiner you got there."

A "shiner" is what Nathan's dad calls a black eye. "Is it?"

"Yeah, it's really turning purple." The jock smirks.

"Great." Nathan grimaces. Visible bruises are like an invitation to add more.

"Why do they do that to you?" The jock's head is cocked, eyebrows scrunched.

"Man, you'd know better than me." Nathan gestures to the jock's jacket. The blue and yellow letterman jacket, the official uniform of violent psychos since time out of mind.

"Do you want them to stop?"

The question doesn't make sense. Kyle and his friends are like a natural disaster. You can't stop them; you just hope to survive and clean up when it's done.

"Dude, I don't really like repeating myself. Do you want them to stop or not? If you do, you need to say it."

Voices approach. Nathan's blood freezes. They're close—around the corner, laughing like hyenas, full of bloodlust and arrogance. "Where'd you go, crybaby?" Kyle shouts in mock sing-song. "We weren't done with you!"

Nathan turns back to the dumpster. He's got to hide. He takes a couple of stumbling steps, like walking through syrup. No way he'll make it.

"Dude, you have to tell me that you want my help," the jock whispers.

What's he going to do? Take on the whole gaggle of bullies himself? Even for a guy that big, it seems unlikely. But Nathan's out in the open. No choice.

"Okay, yeah, help me." *Fuck, they're gonna kill us both,* he thinks. He pivots to look at the jock but he's gone. Nathan's alone. *Oh god.*

Kyle's first to round the corner, followed by his cronies. All of them have identical expressions, toothy grins too wide. Kyle's fists ball at his sides.

"There you are," he growls.

A whisper in Nathan's ear. "Hold still." Strong hands grab his arms, pin them to his sides. A body presses against his back. At first, he thinks the jock wants to hold him down while the others beat him. But the sensation turns strange like he and the jock are occupying the same space. Nathan feels like he is being pumped full, swelling, ballooning. His head burns. A shout catches in his throat.

A bright white flash, then—he's in a car at night. Everything spins. The world buzzes past. He wants to puke, but holds it back. If he hurls, Bobby will kill him, or make him pay to have the seats cleaned. The road disappears. Bobby screams, then laughs, high and frantic. The car judders as it forsakes the asphalt. Grass and limbs tick and scrape. "Here we go," Bobby shrieks. There's a tree—

Nathan lands back in his own mind. Nothing's changed. Three massive jerks stalk toward him like hungry panthers. Only now he can't move. He sends frantic signals. Run. Hide. Scream. *Do anything.* They all die in his brain stem.

But there's something else here.

Watch this, a voice says. It's not his. The tone is gleeful, confident.

Everything that happens next is without Nathan's input. He steps forward, squares his shoulders. Kyle's friends stop. Faces turn from predatory to confused, but Kyle's grin widens.

"About time you grew a pair of nuts. Won't help, though."

Nathan and Kyle crash into each other. Kyle swings and catches him on the side. Pain flairs. The rib is bruised or broken. Nathan's body doesn't stop. His hand wads into a fist around the front of Kyle's shirt and shoves him, lets go, sends him staggering. Kyle lands on his ass. Nathan leaps, lands in front of him. Kyle's face drips with terror. Nathan's fist lands like a medieval mace against Kyle's cheek. Head jerks sideways. Blood and spit spray. He falls backward, skull *thonks* on asphalt like a hollow gourd.

Nathan's legs straddle the bully. His weight drops on the big guy's stomach. Kyle chokes out a lungful of air; eyes bulge from their sockets. Nathan swings. Skin splits over Kyle's cheekbone. Blood drizzles from the gash. Kyle screams, tries to pull free, but Nathan's knees pin him down.

Nathan's not doing any of this, but he's enjoying the show.

The other fist arcs down, catching Kyle's temple. The meat-head sobs, lets loose a guttural choke. His eyes roll, unfocused. Then another blow, and another. Bone cracks under Nathan's knuckles. Kyle spits out bloody teeth. The flesh around his eyes swells green and purple.

Footsteps drag Nathan's attention upward. Kyle's cronies sprint back around the building. Gutless sycophants.

Nathan's body stands, backs away. Kyle curls into a fetal position on the ground.

What the hell was that, he thinks.

Just a taste, says the voice. Nathan recognizes it now—the jock. *Stick with me, kid, and you won't have any more problems.*

———◆———

"Here we go!" The look on Bobby's face is jagged lightning. His eyes glow. Everything moves in slow motion. Branches whip at the passenger window.

Sobriety hits just in time for the big tree to come into focus. Before the crunch. Before the black.

Nathan sits bolt upright, sweating like a runner. The room is dark. His sheets are soaked. Sweat or piss? He grabs tight to the blanket and winces—knuckles ache under their bandages. He split the skin on every one of them pulverizing Kyle's face.

That dream. It was the same as the flash he'd had today when the jock was in his head. But he was gone, right? Nathan hadn't heard him since they'd left Kyle moaning on the ground.

God, his legs itch. What the hell? He reaches under the covers and claws at them. A near orgasmic wave of relief hits him and his eyes roll back.

When he pulls his hand away, his fingertips are black.

Shit.

He yanks off the covers and stumbles to the bathroom. Bright light blinds him as he flicks the switch. Gore smears the wall where he touches it. His pajama pants are soaked, too. He wads a hank of the fabric in his fist and pulls up.

"What the fuck?"

There's a hole in his leg. Dark red meat glistens, shot through with gray-green tendrils. The skin around the wound is charcoal black, curled inward like burnt paper.

Nathan's stomach lurches. He pivots to the toilet and falls to his knees. His churning guts evacuate. Long strings of yellowish mucus cling to his lips.

He needs to get his parents, get to the hospital. He staggers to his feet and drags his arm across his lips to clear the slime. *Parents. Hospital.* He turns to the door. *Mom.* The word dies in his throat. He's frozen. Every muscle is locked.

Don't worry about it.

That voice again. The jock. He's still there.

We're gonna relax and go back to bed. Like he's talking someone down from a ledge.

What do you mean "we?"

You asked for my help. This is it. I leave and you go right back to having your nose hammered into your skull three times a week.

Nathan thinks of Kyle on the ground bleeding. He didn't do that by himself. The jock is doing something to him, making him strong. So he won today—but tomorrow? Is Kyle done? If he kicks the jock out and Kyle decides to start another rumble—Nathan doesn't want to think about the beating he'll catch. He'll be lucky to live. He can't do it anymore. He won't.

You're awfully quiet, the jock says.

Thinking this over.

What's there to think about? Anyway, the only way I'm giving you the keys back is if you promise not to get yourself locked up in the hospital. That would make it hard for us to get to football tryouts tomorrow.

Football?

All part of the plan. Trust me, kid. I'm gonna make you a legend.

Legend. That has a nice ring to it. Certainly better than everything else he'd been called. He can deal with a couple of itchy spots, right? He tries to push aside the image of blackened flesh surrounding bare meat coated in yellow-gray pus.

But what is that on my leg?

Side effect.

Is it gonna get worse?

I told you not to worry about it. Patience drains from the jock's voice.

Yeah, okay. Fine.

Something pops in Nathan's spine. He's plugged back in. He can move.

Water from the faucet feels good on his face. It splatters yellow into the sink basin as he spits. There's gauze in the cabinet, and he wraps his leg. If he doesn't scratch, it won't bleed.

He flops back into bed, suddenly exhausted. Sleep comes easy. As he dances on the edge of unconsciousness, he mumbles a question. "Who's Bobby?"

He's the asshole that killed me.

———◇———

"It's so damn hot." Nathan found three new sores this morning, two blooming like black roses on his arms, and another on his back. All of them smell like rotten meat and they burn. Coach Tacket tried to get him to take off the hoodie, but then everyone would see the slowly staining gauze. He'd have to stay covered.

He stands in a clump of kids all wearing the same blue mesh practice jerseys and ancient, dented helmets. They're swaggering, slapping each other in greeting and jeering. A few are quiet, withdrawn, like him.

"Okay, recruits!" Coach Tacket stands at the head of the group holding a clipboard, and when he walks, he limps. "First order of business is to see how you run. Standish, get over here!"

A massive figure jogs over from the cluster of varsity lunks on the sideline. He's in full uniform and unlike the tryouts, everything fits. It's Kyle. Nathan's heart drops into his stomach. This was a bad idea.

"Okay, listen up! This is your team captain. When I call your name, come up here and drop into three-point stance. When I blow the whistle, try to get past him. If you can do that, head over to Coach Tiller's group by the tackle dummies. If you can't, you can go home." Coach Tacket never looks up from his clipboard. "Michael Abbot, you're up!"

The kid next to Nathan audibly gulps. He's shaking. He pushes his way through the other recruits. A couple of the bigger guys smirk as he passes.

"Hustle, Abbot!" Coach says.

The kid drops, one hand on the ground. The chatter falls silent.

SCREEEEEE!

At the whistle, Mike jumps to full height, sprints. He's fast. Kyle watches, crouched like a predator. Mike cuts left and Kyle springs. He hits Mike with his shoulder, center of his chest. The kid leaves the ground, flies a few feet before crashing like a pile of bones onto the grass.

"Tough luck, Abbot, hit the showers!" Coach is again absorbed with his clipboard. "Nathan Ackers! You're up!"

A couple of guys pick Mike up and walk him off the field. Nathan's whole body goes numb. He shouldn't be here. This isn't his thing. He's gonna end up like that kid, maybe worse. Maybe when Kyle hits him, he'll explode. "Are you sure we have to do this?" The helmet feels like a bucket on his head. Sun glaring from the neon-green grass makes him squint.

You asked for my help. Beating up one bully isn't gonna do it. In this town, football makes you untouchable.

"Ackers! Get your ass up here!" The coach grimaces, craning his neck.

You're fine. You got me, remember?

Everyone's whispering. A cluster of hushed giggles. Nathan forces himself to move. *Left foot, right foot—*

I'll take it from here.

The *pop* in his spine again. Muscles lock. Then he's moving, but the jock's driving. At the head of the group he drops into stance. Kyle's ten yards away, grinning like a maniac, pointing a hairy finger at him.

He's gonna kill us, Nathan thinks.

Don't worry about it. The jock's voice is gleefully confident.

SCREEEEEEE!

Nathan's body springs forward. His feet dig into turf. A rooster-tail of dirt and grass sprays up behind Kyle as he shoots forward, murder in his eyes.

Left! Left! Nathan screams in his head.

Nope, the jock answers.

They're playing chicken with a freight train. At the last second, Nathan's body sinks into a crouch. They hit Kyle in the stomach. Kyle shouts, tilts over him like a see-saw. Nathan's body stands, pushing with both palms.

Kyle's body tumbles overhead. He flails. Nathan darts out from under him and glances back in time to see Kyle plummet to the turf, crumple into a motionless heap.

The jeering and half-whispered chatter stop cold. Coach Tacket and two other guys in white polos squat next to Kyle. Coach holds fingers up to his face and says something Nathan can't hear. Then he pats Kyle's shoulder and stands as the other two pick the team captain up and walk him off the field. Coach spots Nathan and shambles over, his limp more pronounced when he jogs.

"Jesus, kid. How'd you do that?"

Nathan's spine pops as the jock turns over control. He blinks. "Um—I don't—"

"That was insane!" Coach's eyes are manic, shining. "You wandered into my office this morning to sign up, I was pretty sure we were gonna wad you up and throw you in the trash can. I've never seen someone hit like that. It's like there's two of you!"

Coach lays a big hand on Nathan's shoulder and squeezes.

"Head over to the dummies, kid. First practice is Monday morning. I'll see you there."

Then he's gone and Nathan's standing alone on the field, all the tryouts still gawking at him. The seniors glare from where they've gathered around Kyle on the bench.

Nathan turns toward the locker room. He'll come back to tryouts, but first, there are at least four more of those sores pulsing under his clothes. Good thing he brought extra gauze.

This time, when the dream comes, Nathan stares hard at Bobby's face.

He looks familiar.

"—Here we go!"

Deep creases web out from the corners of Bobby's manic eyes. His grin covers the bottom half of his face like a surgical mask. He's screaming laughter, not even looking through the windshield. Those demented eyes are locked on Nathan.

Tears roll down his cheeks.

Just like every night for the past month, Nathan sits up in bed, soaked. He washes his own sheets so his mom won't see the orange and yellow fluid that's oozed from his sores overnight.

He wears his hoodie everywhere, especially after the lesions began to appear on his face. He sits at the back of his classes. The putrid stench that rises from his flesh is enough to keep the other students away. The teachers don't care, probably chalk it up to body odor. Either that, or he's spending more time behind the dumpster.

He doesn't change in the locker room, either—shows up to practice in full gear so he doesn't have to strip down in front of the others. Coach just thinks he's shy.

"We need to stop this."

Stop what?

"All of it. I think I'm sick. I can't sleep. It burns, and if I scratch, I bleed. You said don't worry about it, but—"

Yeah, and I'll say it again. Don't worry about it. You'll be fine.

"I don't know. I don't think I will. I feel like I'm falling apart."

Itching pain runs like wildfire up and down his legs and torso. Nathan yanks back the covers. The moonlight from the window glistens off the fresh pus seeping through his wraps.

"Look at me! You need to leave and I need to go to the hospital."

And how, exactly, do you plan on getting rid of me?

Nathan hadn't thought about it. He'd invited the jock in. He'd have to leave if Nathan asked him to, right?

I'm not going anywhere, kid. We're gonna take back what that son of a bitch stole from me. We're unstoppable.

"No. Enough. It hurts so fucking much. I can't take it anymore."

You can. And you will. The first game of the season is tomorrow. Don't screw this up.

———◦———

The locker room is deserted. Nathan sits on a bench, mumbling to the parasite in his brain. The team's in the hall getting a pep talk from Coach.

"I don't want to do this."

Fuck what you want.

The jock's voice in his head is thin and rasps like sandpaper.

"Just let me go. I'll take the bullying. I don't care."

This was never about you.

The door to the hallway creaks open. Footsteps echo off the walls.

Nathan's spine pops.

"You coming?" Coach Tacket stands at the end of the row. His voice is concerned. Fatherly. "We're lining up."

"Yeah, Coach," Nathan says.

"You okay?" Tacket tilts his head.

"Tell me how you got your limp." Nathan locks eyes with the coach.

"I—it was—an old football injury. Landed on it wrong, broke my knee."

"Fucking liar."

"Hey, what did you say to me?"

"I said you're a fucking liar." Nathan stands. "Tell me about the accident."

Coach's eyes are wide, wet. "What accident?"

"Give it up, old man."

"It—I was—how did you hear about that?" Coach Tacket stumbles back.

"Tell me about getting drunk on Schnapps in the high school parking lot." Nathan stands and seems somehow bigger, a hulking, hooded shadow against the fluorescent ceiling lights.

"Tell me about how you and a buddy got into your car. Tell me how you told him you were fine. You'd done this a thousand times. Tell me how you told him *not to be a pussy!*"

"No! No, I—it was an accident!"

Nathan steps forward. He wads the waistband of the hoodie in his gloved fists and pulls it over his head. He's wrapped from head to toe in oozing, stained bandages.

Coach backs into the wall. "What's happened to you? We—you need a doctor."

"No. I need you to tell me what happened. I need you to tell me that, as we drove, you talked about how you wanted to die. I want you to tell me about the exact moment you decided to *take us off the fucking road, Bobby!*"

"No! Shut up!" Tears stream down Coach Tacket's face.

"Look what you did to me, Bobby! Look!"

Nathan's hands claw at the saturated bandages. Wet hunks tear off in strips that slap to the floor. The sores underneath have merged into massive patches of missing skin with gangrenous muscle and undulating organs. White bone shines through meat.

Tacket sinks to the floor, buries his head in his hands. "No! Oh god I'm so sorry."

"Not sorry enough."

———◇———

"Ackers! Get out there! Standish! Come back!" Assistant Coach Tiller waves wildly toward the field. Nathan's body stands. The jock didn't put any new gauze on after what happened in the locker room, and he feels loose, vulnerable. His joints slide around like a marionette.

Look, you did what you wanted to do, now let me go, Nathan thinks.

No way kid. That was just part one. It'll take them a week to find Tacket in that dumpster, if they ever do. Fifty-fifty odds he just ends up in the landfill. In the meantime, I'm gonna have everything he took from me. We're going to the playoffs—to state. I'm gonna get drafted into the fucking NFL.

This is deranged. He's a walking sack of parts. Fluid squelches in his cleats. His shirt-sleeves soak through with green and orange gore. The jock is holding him together through sheer will. Surely he can't do it forever.

There's Kyle, walking back to the sideline. "I'm going to fucking kill you," he says as they pass.

Kyle's been mumbling that kind of stuff for a month. Nathan can't blame him—he's sent the bully to the hospital twice, and is threatening to take his team captain spot. It's the one thing he's not sorry for in all this. Fuck Kyle Standish.

———◦———

The crowd roars. The night air is electric. Brass instruments cry a song of victory from the stands. It's the last play of the game. If they score, they win.

The jock ducks Nathan's head and steers his body onto the field, getting in position.

Do you hear that, kid? That's what it's all about.

Nathan wants to vomit, cry, scream. He wants to shower in water so hot it will melt the remaining flesh from his bones.

The scene from the locker room plays over in his mind. The sound of ripping flesh. Viscous blood spattering on concrete.

"Hike!" the quarterback shouts.

The jock, however, has no trouble concentrating. Nathan's body springs forward. The outside linebacker—a massive, hairy brute—comes at him, and the jock steers Nathan's body aside. His palm finds the guy's helmet and shoves him to the turf. Then he's free and clear, nothing but green between him and the end zone.

A backward glance as the quarterback launches the ball. Nathan almost loses it against the night sky. They turn and leap. The ball nearly carries his hands away at the wrists and Nathan remembers how much of him has rotted. He's held together with gristle. Bone shines through at every joint. Muscle deteriorated into flaking yellow sludge.

Nathan just wants this to end. He has this idea that maybe, if he can get the jock out of him, his body will knit itself back together. Every demonic possession movie he's ever seen, the main character looks like shit until the demon leaves, then it's back to normal right away. But this isn't a demon. It's just a dumb jock. All he's got to do is convince him. It's a desperate idea, but worth a shot.

They're sprinting to the end zone. Nobody is even close.

They're over the line. The crowd explodes into a howling frenzy. They throw the ball to the grass. The school fight song pours from screaming brass.

Okay, Nathan thinks. *You won. You got what you wanted.*

Are you not listening? We're fucking unstoppable! There's no way I'm turning you loose!

The rest of the team is heading for the end zone, loosing celebratory yips and shouts into the night sky like rocks from slingshots. Assistant Coach Tiller is soaked from the water cooler they've dumped on him.

Look at me! How long do you think you can hold this together?

The jock steers his head down. Sludge oozes through the sleeves of his uniform, painted in sunset hues by the constantly running gore.

It's—it's fine! You're fine! It's just a couple of—

It's not, though! I'm falling apart. I know you can feel it, too. How hard are you working to hold me together?

The jock is silent for a beat.

If you just step out for a little while, maybe it'll fix itself. I can feel it. Then you—you can come back. I won't stop you.

The team approaches.

You sure about that?

Haven't you ever seen The Exorcist?

Okay, fine. I'll step out. But you gotta let me back in.

Scout's honor.

There's a sensation of deflating. Nathan feels smaller, weaker, alone in his own head. He missed that.

The jock stands in front of him, flesh wrinkled, dried, gathered inwards. His eyes are hollow black sockets. Grave dirt crumbles from his hair. This was killing him, too.

Nathan stumbles. The muscles at his joints slide against each other, struggling to keep him standing. A gargling scream tears from his desiccated throat. *God, the pain.* He was wrong. It's so much worse without the jock. Every inch of exposed meat is on fire. He's not knitting back together.

He looks up. A single player has broken loose from the approaching crowd.

Kyle.

He sprints, arms spread wide like a hug.

Shit, Nathan thinks.

"That should'a been mine!" Kyle shouts.

Nathan raises a gloved hand to ward off the collision. "No," he croaks.

Kyle ducks into the impact. The top of his helmet hits Nathan's chest like a bullet.

Bones snap. Nathan's spindly muscles unravel like thread. Everything lets go. Limbs fly from his body like bottle rockets in an absurd detonation. He's alive long enough to watch a bucket of his own fluids coat the back of Kyle's jersey.

The jock's rotted, skeletal jaw drops in a parody of disbelief.

The water runs clear, but Kyle doesn't trust it. No matter how much he showers he can still *feel* it. The kid popped like a water balloon. Some bitter, coppery fluid even ended up in his mouth. He wore blood and slithering chunks of rotted flesh like a demented shawl for an hour while cops and paramedics asked quesitons.

Nathan was a walking corpse. Some kind of flesh-eating something-or-other. They didn't know how the kid was still standing.

Paramedics checked Kyle for a bunch of things he didn't understand, asked if he had family. Dad's dead. Mom's drunk. Just like everything else, he'll have to shoulder this new horror alone.

Scalding water patters to the floor of the darkened locker room. It burns his skin, scorching away the putrid stink.

"Sorry about that." The voice rings off the cinder block walls.

Kyle jumps, nearly screams. His feet slide on the wet floor. He gains traction and spins. Heart thumps like it's trying to get out.

There's a figure standing in the doorway. Just a silhouette, backlit, but enough so Kyle can see the outline of the letter jacket.

"What the fuck, man?"

"Hey, didn't mean to scare you. I just wanted to apologize. That thing that happened—well, I think it might have been my fault." The guy's voice is bashful, contrite.

"The hell does that mean?"

"I was—helping that kid. You weren't curious how he went from getting his ass kicked by you and your buddies three

times a week to shoving your face in the dirt at every opportunity?"

Truth is, Kyle *is* damn curious about that.

"It's a shame," the silhouette continues. "He just couldn't
hold it together. Not like a real athlete."

Everything suddenly makes sense. It's some kind of drug.
Has to be. And this guy is the connection. But the kid was a
squirt. His body couldn't take the strain. But if someone was
in peak condition, well-trained—

"Kyle," says the silhouette, "I've got a—*proposition* for you."

Don't Make It Weird

Red Lagoe

A girl is playing football?

Hannah had heard it so many times, it didn't matter who said it anymore. It played in her head like a glitchy recording, over and over on the bus to summer camp in anticipation of whichever boy would say it this year.

"Yeah, a girl is playing football!" She'd puff out her chest to make herself bigger than she really was, but it never mattered. No matter how often she played, how good she got, they never believed that a girl could play. They'd make snide comments or get frustrated when they were stuck with her on their team, but she always proved them wrong.

She was better at communicating through competitive sports, anyway. An interception here. A fake-out spin and redirection there. But every game she played, especially as she got older—now thirteen—it was always the same. She'd play hard. Prove them wrong. And the next game, she'd have to do it all over again. But last year, it got even worse. That's the year her breasts started coming in.

Her bus passed the sign for the camp entrance and Hannah took a deep breath, remembering the trauma of last year. What mom called "nubbins" had appeared just before she left for summer camp. *Breast buds*, according to the doctor. What a stupid name. *Buds*. Like her boobs-to-be were some flowering plant, waiting to be plucked or pollinated or something. Surely a boy invented that term. On the field, the boys treated her like a porcelain doll. They wouldn't touch her. Wouldn't tackle her. They laughed and whispered about her *boobies* as if she wasn't right there, listening, being shaped and molded by every word. What terrible things did they think would happen if they played with breasts on the field?

It was the worst year at camp ever. She'd gone home crying, wishing she didn't have the body parts at all. All she wanted to do was play as an equal. The mirror had reflected her ridiculous nubbins back at her and she cursed them.

"Why can't you be useful!" She wished they'd go away, but more than anything, she wished the boys would shut up. She imagined grabbing a boy—any boy—by the throat and choking him until he went unconscious, and that rage scared her. Violence wasn't a reaction she'd ever given into. Hannah concealed all those bad feelings in a held breath, and only dared to release them on the field.

The sore, aching nubbins had been tormenting her. Mom said it was just growing pains, so Hannah tried to ignore it, but they swelled and shifted. Like all her anger and pent-up frustration with the unfairness of it all writhed under her skin, metastasizing within.

She had developed into a C-cup since then. The rapid growth left marks across her chest. Cracks—like the lines her mom had around her cleavage, but these were scattered across her breasts. They were scar-like and sensitive.

Mom said they were stretch marks, that her body was blossoming—*seriously, what's with the flower metaphors?*—but Hannah felt like it was something more sinister. Not a blossoming, but an awakening.

"Don't let them own you," her sister Meghan said, as she caught Hannah scolding herself in the mirror. Meghan got them a couple years ago and they changed the way everyone looked at her. Suddenly, her nerdy sister had boys flirting with her. Grown men would shoot side glances or double-takes—*Eew.* Hannah wanted none of it.

"You own them." Meghan puffed out her chest, showcasing her cleavage. "You're in charge. Own them."

Her memories of the year prior faded as the camp bus entered the parking lot. The other kids shouted and sang songs—a conglomeration of excitement to swim in the river, paint birdhouses, or play tug-of-war. But Hannah sat silent in her seat, wondering if this year would be a repeat of last. Wondering if people would chastise her for wanting to play football. Wondering if it would be eight thousand times worse because her boobs were eight thousand times bigger.

After orientation and cabin assignments, Hannah quickly found the football field, where a handful of boys had already gathered, planning teams.

The sun was high in the late afternoon sky. The grass smelled freshly mowed. When her feet touched the field, she felt home. She felt she belonged here... at least until other people told her she didn't.

Two young men in counselor shirts stood at the sideline, talking to each other. None of the boys looked familiar, which meant Hannah had to, yet again, prove her worthiness to play.

Boys get to walk on the field as equals, like they are magically endowed with athletic ability. But when a girl steps up to play, she must prove her worthiness to handle the great pigskin idol.

One boy, blonde hair and ice blue eyes, nodded toward the east buildings. "Arts and crafts are over there."

"Not really my thing. Can I play?"

The boy with blonde hair smirked. "This isn't two-hand-touch—"

"We tackle," another boy said.

"Okay," Hannah said. "I play tackle."

The blonde kid adjusted the football in his grip. "I doubt that."

"No. I can."

"Sorry. Our teams are filled."

A counselor jogged onto the field. Dark, shaggy hair swept to one side. Sparse facial hair covered his jaw. His nametag read *Hunter*. "Travis, what's going on?"

Travis pointed. "*She* wants to play, but it's tackle."

"Hey, sweetheart," Hunter said. "These guys get rough—"

"I know. I'm allowed to play. I was here last year." Hannah sought out a familiar face to vouch for her, but there was nobody she recognized. "I can play." She stood tall, shoulders broad, trying to square herself off to look tougher. Her chest stuck out as well, but she did her best to own them, like her sister had taught her.

The counselor Hunter shrugged. "Guys, you can't leave any camper out. Those are the rules."

His eyes wandered to Hannah's shirt, which was a bit too small, stretching over her chest. "How old are you sweetheart?"

"Thirteen."

"Jesus..." he turned away and walked toward the sideline.

The second counselor doubled over, laughing. "Were you about to hit on a thirteen-year-old?"

"Shut up... she doesn't look thirteen."

"But you were looking." He covered his mouth, failing to hide his laughter.

Hannah knew that every boy on the field heard those clowns loud and clear. She fought the emotions stirring in her heart. The embarrassment, the anger... She wanted to scream at them, tell them all to shut up, but if she lost her temper, they'd say "*girls are too emotional to play.*" So she buried it deep in her chest. Let it stew there. Let it simmer. Soon, they'd know who they were dealing with. Her breasts ached and a shifting of flesh inside made her cross her arms over herself.

"I guess she has to play..." Travis said.

"This makes it weird." A scrawny kid with red hair made a sour face.

"Why?"

"Because you're a girl."

"How is that weird?" Hannah put her hands on her hips.

"What if we accidentally touch... something."

"Now *you're* making it weird."

"Whatever..."

"You're on their team." Travis nodded across the fifty-yard line at the group of boys. Some of them groaned.

"You're down a player. So you get the girl." Travis said. "Oh... shirts and skins."

A kid on the opposing team nodded toward Hannah. "Y'all are skins."

Hannah's team began removing shirts. Some of them seemed oblivious to the situation. Some snickered among each other, watching, waiting to see what she'd do.

"Come on!" she said.

"Oh," Travis said with an arched eyebrow. "They wanna play with the boys until they have to play *like* the boys." Travis cocked his arm back and threw the ball toward her without warning, but Hannah's reflexes were ready. She caught it, cradling it into her chest as it spiraled into her breastbone with a thud.

There was an uproar among the boys on her team, pointing and laughing at Trevor, while Hannah stood her ground with the football in one hand.

"Our team is shirts," she said.

Travis turned away. "Teams are picked. Either take it off like a boy or go home."

A guy on the shirts team with dark hair and glasses was sheepish in his approach toward Hannah, keeping his eyes at his feet. "I'll switch teams with you so you don't have to be skins."

The game kicked off, and for several plays Travis refused to pass to Hannah even though she was wide open. She was close to the end zone and well within passing distance—even for Travis, who couldn't throw worth a crap—but not once did he pass her the ball. Rage stirred within, and her chest burned as if a fire were stoking inside. Something churned and coiled under her skin. Hannah ignored the sensation and focused on getting her hands on that ball.

The ball finally turned over to the other team. Defense. Historically speaking, defense was the only time she got to prove herself as a good player because she didn't have to rely on anyone passing her the ball. Defense was where she could showcase her talent. She tore down the field toward a shirtless receiver and leapt in the path of the spiraling ball. She jumped in front of the guy and her fingertips reached, knocking it away.

Some of the boys shouted with excitement. Others laughed at their friend for being blocked by a girl. One kid tried to argue interference, but everyone saw what happened. There's always one person on the field who has to lie in an attempt to save his masculinity from the utter embarrassment of a girl jumping higher than him.

Hannah got back on the line of scrimmage. She cut down the field, sprinting as fast as her legs could muscle forward. Her brain was like a mathematician, calculating the quarter-back's movements, the intended receiver's speed... she knew exactly where the ball was going and she put herself in its path. Hannah scooped it into her arms for an interception. Some of the boys howled and laughed, but Hannah took off in a sprint toward the other end, leaving them behind.

"Get her!"

"Stop her!"

Tunnel vision ahead, she refused to look back and slow her pace. She closed on the endzone but felt someone coming from behind. Hannah pushed harder, but she knew she was about to go down. A hand swiped the back of her leg, then a grip around her ankle sent her crashing into the grass. She landed chest first and the blow crushed her breasts. She felt a pop. That slight release of pressure that comes when fingers squeeze a zit and the skin ruptures, releasing a white glob of gunk. She worried if she looked down, she'd see one of her scars busted open, spilling glandular goo all over the field. Fortunately, they were still intact.

But far worse than she imagined, she couldn't breathe. No air would draw into her lungs.

"What's wrong with her?"

Hannah was upright on her knees, looking to the electric blue sky, willing her lungs to pull in some air, but nothing would come.

The counselor's voice came next. "She got the wind knocked out of her."

"Put your head between your knees!" someone said.

Hannah did as she was told and the breath finally came.

Shaken, but not defeated, she dusted off her knees and got to her feet.

The counselor insisted she go to the infirmary, but when Hannah refused, he ejected her from the game.

"But I'm fine now. I can keep playing."

"No. Those are the rules. Injuries. You have to sit it out and go to the infirmary."

Hannah let out a frustrated sigh. "Fine."

"This game is kind of hardcore," Hunter said.

"That's what makes it fun."

"That's what makes it for boys. Sorry kid, go rest it off." Hunter placed a hand on her back, maybe too low on her back near the waist of her shorts, and he guided her off the field.

———◦———

In the shower that evening, she hushed her tears under the cascading water. Her scars stretched, skin undulating. She worried tumors were growing inside, but she didn't want them to become a problem. She couldn't leave after today's incident on the field. Hannah needed another game to show that she was good enough to play. That getting the wind knocked out of you is something that can happen to anyone, and it wouldn't stop her from playing.

She wondered if having breasts made her lose her breath on impact, and if so, she wasn't about to let them control her life.

"I own you," she whispered. She ran fingers along one of the scars on top, where the tissue had stretched, scar widening. Like melted mozzarella her flesh strung apart, opening at the seam. Her whimpers were muffled by running water and hopefully unheard by the other girls in the showers.

She examined the exposed layers of fat and pink below. Something moved inside. She'd felt it before, squirming just below the skin. A snakelike structure writhed within. With trepidation, Hannah placed a finger upon it, but it retracted. She inserted her finger deeper, brushing a coiled structure. The ropey thing wrapped around her finger and squeezed like a boa constrictor.

Hannah whispered, "Stop," and it released her finger.

It wriggled until an eyeless head appeared with a mouthful of tiny serrated teeth.

Her initial shock and desire to scream were silenced by her fascination with the swelling, pulsing movement within her body.

"Hi," she whispered to the snake thing in her chest.

Back at the cabin, she lay in bed, hiding beneath the covers while the other girls whispered and gossiped among themselves. A knock at the door made all the girls squeal.

"It's a boy! For you, Hannah!" The girls giggled as Hannah jumped from her top bunk and met the kid outside.

The dark-haired boy with glasses, Caleb, stood on the step. "You okay?"

"I was fine. I could've kept playing."

"Yeah... I wish they let you stay. You're really good," Caleb said.

"Then why didn't you say anything?"

He stared blankly. "You know how it is..."

She waited for him to say something else, to say *how it is*, but there was nothing. He stood there, kicking at the dirt on the steps.

"I don't think you should play tomorrow. Travis is just going to make it harder on you."

"Then I guess I'll make it harder for him, too." Hannah slammed the door in his face.

Under covers, her chest coiled and pulsated, and for once, it didn't feel wrong. It didn't feel like two alien lumps had taken over her life. No. This thing inside understood Hannah's pain. The aching and inflamed sensation had finally ceased, and she placed her hands on top of her chest while lying on her back. The movement brought her comfort. It undulated like it was breathing in sync with her.

"You're not so bad, are you?"

———◇———

Hannah crossed the field in the morning wearing shorts and a strappy tank top. Her cleavage was exposed, as were some of her scars. Why should she have to pretend she didn't have them? Why should she cover them up or mash them down just to make boys more comfortable around her?

The counselor, Hunter, let out a slow whistle, just short of a cat call.

The other counselor, James, reminded him, "Thirteen, man ..." He shook his head.

"Doesn't matter when they look like that."

Hannah stepped up to the group of boys.

"We already picked teams, so..." Travis gestured to the side-line.

Hannah counted. "Looks like skins is down a player."

Travis grinned. "You gonna take your shirt off?"

Hannah grabbed the underside of her tank top and slowly lifted, ready to go skins if it meant she could play. Let them look. If they see a couple tits in a nonsexual light, maybe they won't be so shocked the next time another girl comes around.

Caleb interjected. "Shirts and skins is stupid anyway."

Travis rolled his eyes. "Whatever. She can be on the skins team and not take her shirt off... she's showing enough skin anyway."

Hannah snarled at him. "You got a problem with my skin?"

Hunter jogged up. "Hannah..." He dragged his hand through his hair. "Why are you doing this? What are you trying to prove?"

"I'm doing it for the same reason they are... I want to play football. That's it. Is that so hard to understand? Why do I have to *prove* anything?"

"Alright," Hunter sighed. "You're asking for whatever happens..."

"Let's just play!" someone shouted.

Her frustration fueled her gameplay again. Hannah ripped down the field, feet kicking up dirt along the way. She cut to the right so she'd be wide open for a pass. Travis tailed her as the quarterback actually passed her the ball for once. Hannah leapt high, snagged the ball with her fingertips, and tucked it tight to her chest as Travis crashed into her. She went down hard, and at least two other boys dog-piled her. Somewhere while wrestling for the ball, of which she maintained possession the entire time, someone grabbed a handful of her breast. She screamed, which got the boys to climb off of her. One boy pulled away—the scrawny kid with red hair. He held his finger in his mouth, then pulled it away to look at it. Blood oozed to the surface.

She turned her back, checking her breasts as the snake-thing slinked back into her chest. A sly smile crept across her lips and she tried to contain it.

"Thanks, buddy," she whispered to her inner friend. "Look at you being useful." Another snake slithered over the slit. There were more inside. Hannah bit her lip to contain her excitement.

"She bit me!" The red-haired kid pointed his bloody finger at her.

"You grabbed me."

Hunter jogged onto the field with a growl. He took a look at the kid's finger. "Dude, go to the infirmary and get that cleaned up. And you ..." he pointed to Hannah. "You're out."

"I didn't bite him."

"Then why is he bleeding?"

"I don't know. But a better question would be why did he think he could grope me?"

"You have to sit out."

"No." Hannah ignored Hunter and went to the line of scrimmage, ready for the next play.

Now that the game had uneven players, Caleb volunteered to sit out so Hannah could continue to play. "She's better than me, anyway," he said. A kind gesture, but at this point, Hannah needed the boys on her side to do more than sit on the sideline in approval of her existence on the playing field. She needed them to pass her the ball. She needed them to not accuse her of cheating when she succeeded. She needed their skin in the game.

On the next play, she was determined to score the touchdown. She sprinted down the field as the quarterback cocked back his arm. Travis grabbed her by the waist to keep her from getting in the open, and she tried to fight him off.

"Holding!" She grunted in his grip.

Not a single boy had her back. Nobody cared that Travis cheated. Hunter the counselor stood on the sideline, flirting with one of the older campers.

Hannah kept charging forward, breaking free as the ball left the quarterback's hands. She turned and leapt for the incoming pass, but Travis jumped in front of her to block. The will to win busted through, and the snake things came with it. They split her skin open at all the creases, shooting out like a dozen grappling hooks on fleshy ropes. Shredding tiny holes through her tank top, they lashed out. The snakes bit into Travis's back. His arms flung up. They tore him to the ground, biting, nipping, feasting. Hannah leapt to catch the incoming ball. Her hands snagged it overhead and she dropped to the ground in the end zone.

The field was loud with screaming, but her vision was narrowed in on the fleshy monsters as they feasted on Travis. Hannah took a knee and a deep breath, then summoned them back inside. They did as requested, retracted, coiling into her breasts, and sealing the skin with a mucous membrane.

Travis writhed on the ground, bloody wounds peppering his body. He stood, trembling, and then darted off toward the infirmary, spinning to look behind every few seconds.

Hannah turned to face the boys who'd all run the other direction, except Caleb who remained on the bench paralyzed, jaw hanging open.

Hunter approached slowly, palms up. "What happened? I didn't see..."

The other counselor James backed off the field and ran away.

"What did you do to him?" Hunter stared off toward Travis whose blood-splattered body shrunk in the distance.

"Don't you mean, what did *they* do to me?"

"Do you have a weapon?"

"No..."

"I need you to come with me." He placed one hand on her back and one on her shoulder.

She yanked away. "I'm not going anywhere with you."

The counselor's eyes widened as they drifted toward her chest. He stared and Hannah dropped her gaze to see why. Her tank top was filthy with a dozen cave-like holes exposing hundreds of tiny teeth. Biting, drooling, dripping with disdain and vengeance.

Whether Hunter was going to search her for a weapon or be a pervert, she didn't know, but his touch, his gaze, terrified her. The fear and fury took over. The inner creatures shot out of her like a bunch of grappling hooks, latching onto his body. Muscles in her chest contracted. She adjusted her stance to balance the weight as creatures lifted him off his feet, screaming and flailing.

His body pulled in all directions. The pink ropey snakes ripped him apart. The shrieks turned to sputtering grunts and then to silence. When Hunter was no more than a shredded pile of flesh, they feasted on his muscles, ripping bits of sinew and meat, taking in sustenance that not only fed the creatures, but fueled Hannah as well.

Hannah turned to see Caleb still sitting on the sideline, traumatized. Not saying or doing anything, as usual. As she walked by him, he scrambled backward, falling off the bench. She stopped next to him. "This is all your fault."

"My fault?"

"I just wanted to play football..."

Caleb held a shirt before him, like he could hide underneath.

"... but you *boys* had to go and make it weird."

Massive Gains

Caias Ward

Fitness Log Week 33
   Height: 5'7" Weight: 155 lbs
   -Barbell Bench Press: 135 lbs 3 Sets 10 Reps No Change
   -Dumbbell Bench Press: 40 lbs 3 Sets 10 No Change
   -Incline Bench Press: 140 lbs 1 Sets 10 Reps, 135 lbs 2 Sets
10 Reps No Change
   -Decline Press: 160 lbs 1 Sets 1 Reps Failure DNF workout
   Notes: This bullshit isn't working. Why do I bother?

Week 33 Progress Video Comments:
   Chuzwut: damn this boy is weak!
   MikeyP: He had to get someone to pull the bar off him on
the decline! LOLOLOLOL
   GraveyardLady97: Someone needs to maybe start on a
machine rather than free weights?
   RoganFanNumber2: dude, we all start somewhere. I
mean, it's not like 160 lbs is easy to—nah, this guy is soft and
he has shamed his ancestors. Broseiden is not pleased.

@GymRat1997:

Dude, saw the YouTube vid. Pinned by baby weights that someone lifted off you *one-handed*, damn.

@*MassiveGains:*

Fuck you, Steve. Everyone saw the vid.

@*GymRat1997:*

My offer stands. I got a hookup.

@*MassiveGains:*

I'm not becoming some juicehead. I just want to be stronger. Healthier, like you.

@*GymRat1997:*

It's not roids. It's an Old World recipe. I know someone. I'll hook you up.

@*MassiveGains:*

Fine. Give me the address.

@*MassiveGains:*

Dude, that lady was Old World brolic. Like she should be doing World's Strongest Woman throwing cows around. She old as fuck too.

@*GymRat1997:*

But did she hook you up?

@*MassiveGains:*

Yeah. Shit was chunky and green and thick. Thought I had to take a dump through the first workout, it was clawing inside me.

@*GymRat1997:*

Now you'll get some changes quick, but it will level out and you'll make normal gains. Be happy with it.

@*MassiveGains:*

We'll see.

Fitness Log Week 34

Height: 5'7" Weight: 160 lbs
-Barbell Bench Press: 165 lbs 3 Sets 10 Reps +20
-Dumbbell Bench Press: 60 lbs 3 Sets 10 +20
-Incline Bench Press: 170 lbs 3 Sets 10 Reps +35
-Decline Press: 185 lbs 3 Sets 10 Reps +25
Notes: Hell yeah!

@MassiveGains:

Check the numbers.

@GymRat1997:

Massive gains, brah! Brosiden would be proud. Remember, one and done, you don't need more.

@MassiveGains:

OK. You got any advice for recovery? I'm hurting.

@GymRat1997:

What, like muscle fatigue?

@MassiveGains:

Everything hurts. Not like 'injured', just everything burning.

@GymRat1997:

Hydrate, rest days, I'll send you a list of supplements you need.

Fitness Log Week 37

Height: 5'10" Weight: 185 lbs
-Barbell Bench Press: 225 lbs 3 Sets 10 Reps +60
-Dumbbell Bench Press: 75 lbs 3 Sets 10 +15
-Incline Bench Press: 220 lbs 3 Sets 10 Reps +50
-Decline Press: 225 lbs 3 Sets 10 Reps +40

Notes: I got more of the stuff. I feel great even with everything still hurting. Feels like I am fire.

———◆———

@GymRat1997:

There's a typo.

@MassiveGains:

Nope. Grew 3 inches.

@GymRat1997:

Bullshit, boss. Are the weights at least legit?

@MassiveGains:

Watch vid, slapnuts

@GymRat1997:

Holy shit.

@MassiveGains:

I'm getting more of that green stuff! That shit is awesome.

@GymRat1997:

Dude! You can't take more! It's not for that.

@MassiveGains:

It's working. I'm going to be huge. HUGE!

@GymRat1997:

It's special. Old World. This wasn't made in a lab. Be happy with what you got. But you can't take more of it.

@MassiveGains:

Gotta get jacked. This is my chance.

———◆———

Fitness Log Week 41

Height: 6'3" Weight: 273 lbs

-Barbell Bench Press: 235 lbs 3 Sets 10 Reps +10

-Dumbbell Bench Press: 80 lbs 3 Sets 10 Reps +5

-Incline Bench Press: 225 lbs 3 Sets 10 Reps +5

-Decline Press: 230 lbs 3 Sets 10 Reps +5

Notes: Hit plateau. Need more green drink. Need to adjust diet, skin is breaking out bad. Bones stretching.

———◆———

@GymRat1997:

Saw your last vid. You're changing. Answer your phone.

@GymRat1997:

Bro?

———◆———

Order Requisition

CityMD Urgent Care

2317 Center Island Route 22, Union, NJ 07083

(201) 354-1951

Patient: BARNES, VICTOR

Order/Test: **Referral**

Requested Date/Time: 6/14/21 12:45

Referred to Specialty: Dermatology

Referred to Provider: Dr S. Centurion, Dermatology Associates of Central NJ

Reason for Referral: Treatment for suspected rapid-onset Acne Conglobata and Acne Fulminans on face and body. Odd growths under skin causing pain and discomfort. Terrible odor emanating from acne.

Order Status: Ordered

Order ID: 47689091594.00

Diagnoses: L70.9 Acne (Unspecified), L72.0 Epidermal Cyst, R22.9 Localized Swelling (Mass and Lump, unspecified) over majority of body

---

@BiscuitHeadJohnson:

yo, you best collect your boy.

@GymRat1997:

I haven't seen Vic in weeks.

@BiscuitHeadJohnson:

you didn't hear?

@GymRat1997:

what?

@BiscuitHeadJohnson:

Motherfucker went to Shop-Rite and bought twelve pounds of chicken breast and then ate that shit raw in the parking lot.

@GymRat1997:

the what?

@GymRat1997:

how you even eat 12 pounds of chicken? Raw?

@BiscuitHeadJohnson:

My sister saw him, she works the courtesy counter. People were talking about that shit coming into the store.

@BiscuitHeadJohnson:

He was sitting on the curb just chowing down and growling at people. He look gross. His skin's all breaking out and he's got these nodules

@GymRat1997:

What the fuck's a nodule?

@BiscuitHeadJohnson:

It's a big-ass lump under the skin. Read a damn book sometime why don't you? My sister said some of them are bleeding, some looked like they were ready to pop blood and pus.

@BiscuitHeadJohnson:

Like I said, collect your boy. Get Dr. Drew. He needs an intervention, whatever he on.

@GymRat1997:

I ain't heard from him in a minute.

@BiscuitHeadJohnson:

Something ain't right with him. I talked to his dad, he hasn't been home for a few days. I think he moved that busted car.

@GymRat1997:

Finally got a tow truck to pull that thing?

@BiscuitHeadJohnson:

Nah. His dad said he picked up the back end and walked it into the garage.

@BiscuitHeadJohnson:

Crushed all the stuff they had stacked in there.

@GymRat1997:

That's a 1976 Buick Century with a seized axle. Vic ain't moving that, no matter how much he talked about fixing it.

@BiscuitHeadJohnson:

His dad said he moved it. When he talked about making that junker gone, Vic roared at him and punched the wall.

@GymRat1997:

damn

@BiscuitHeadJohnson:

Sending a pic...

@GymRat1997:

Shit. That's the cement wall. He had to hit that with a hammer.

@BiscuitHeadJohnson:

Dad says he punched it, then drove off in his car. Honda Fit gotta be a clown car for him now.

@GymRat1997:

damn

@BiscuitHeadJohnson:

Like I said, you best collect your boy or he's going to hurt someone.

Fitness Log Week 45

   Height: 6'11" Weight: 374 lbs

   -Barbell Bench Press: 285 lbs 3 Sets 10 Reps +50

   -Dumbbell Bench Press: 95 lbs 6 Sets 20 Reps +10

   -Incline Bench Press: 275 lbs 3 Sets 10 Reps +50

   -Decline Press: 290 lbs 3 Sets 10 Reps +60

Notes: skin hurt so much. flesh ripping. need more gains. need more old lady green drink. no one laugh now.

Week 45 Progress Video Comments:

AndyMarks44: This dude grew a foot in three months? Bullshit.

Brosiden92: This shit ain't real. Gotta be a movie promo, a viral thing. Will so see this movie. Guy looks like something from D&D!

PlateLadySupreme: This guy is real, he's at my gym. He's a real creeper now, threatened to eat someone. He looks so gross, his bacne stained the damn incline press and he reeks.

PavelLifter: holy shit, that guy looks like one of my great-grandfathers, he drank something a hag gave him and transformed into an ogre!

Brosiden92: PavelLifter you related to Shrek LOLOLOLOL

PavelLifter: No you fucknut he turned into a monster and ate someone. Fucking clown. Go tear your ACL.

@MassiveGains:

   When we gonna lift, brah?

   @GymRat1997:

You gotta stop taking that shit. I saw your last vid, that ain't healthy. Your skin's all fucked up. Your teeth. You're leaking all over the place.

@MassiveGains:

Saw docs. Tell me stop taking green stuff. Can't stop. Gotta lift or it hurts.

@GymRat1997:

You have to stop.

@MassiveGains:

Why you want me small?

@GymRat1997:

Don't even.

@MassiveGains:

You just jealous of my massive gains. It hurts so much, though. Except when I lift.

@GymRat1997:

That shit is warping you. Gotta stop taking it.

@MassiveGains:

You want me puny.

@GymRat1997:

I want you healthy, bro. This ain't it.

@MassiveGains:

MASSIVE GAINS!

———◇———

Sender: Metro Gym
Subject: Notice of Membership Cancellation

Mister Barnes:

Last week, there were several complaints regarding your hygiene and your behavior towards other guests at our Union, NJ location. The sheer volume of complaints in a short period of time as well as the video evidence of the interactions leaves us no choice but to cancel your membership to all Metro Gym locations. Your membership has been prorated based on your effective cancellation date.

If you have any questions, feel free to contact our corporate office at the listed number.

Best,
Sean Ossinger
Manager
Metro Gym, Union NJ Location

Police Report
7/16/19
Responding Officers: James Samuels and Robert Lopez
Location: Cap Barbell Company, 625 Rahway Avenue, Union NJ

On 7/16/2019 at approximately 0300 hours, I responded to a theft report at 625 Rahway Ave with Officer Lopez. We arrived to find the 911 caller, night security guard Desmond Battle, waiting for us down the road from behind a car. He reported that shortly after doing his site tour, he heard a tearing sound from one of the doors. Investigating, he discovered the suspect still holding the steel security door in his hand. The suspect threw the door at Battle, who dove out of the way and took shelter.

The suspect proceeded to carry off a variety of weight lifting equipment, including weight plates and a barbell on his shoulder. Battle reported that the suspect was muttering about a 'home gym' and 'stupid metro', and noted a foul odor which nauseated him. A spot inventory indicated that the suspect purportedly carried off twelve (12) fifty kilogram plates and a heavy-duty barbell. Blood and pus stains were also found on the floor of the warehouse as well as the damaged steel door, which struck and dented a support pillar.

There is nothing further to report.

Comments: This is a joke? I don't have time for this. - Watch Sergeant Miller

Comments: I saw the video. What the hell is going on? - Captain Pignatelli

---

Police Report

7/18/19

Responding Officers: Sara Woodson, Marcus Dante

Location: Lord Stirling Stables, 256 S Maple Ave, Basking Ridge, NJ 07920

On 7/18/2019 at 0520 hours, Officer Dante and I responded to a call at 256 S Maple Ave. We met with Peter Benton, the manager of the facility. While Officer Dante addressed crowd control, I went with Benton into one of the stables where I discovered the remains of a horse. It had been brutally attacked, its neck twisted at an odd angle, with large portions of its flesh torn away and a portion of the animal missing. I notified Animal Control and called for detectives. No other animals had been harmed although several were incredibly agitated. A foul odor lingered in the area, with blood and pus on the floor and wall surfaces.

Further investigation revealed very large and deep bare human-shaped footprints leading towards and away from the stables, along with a blood trail which disappeared after entering deep woods outside the stables.

There is nothing further to report.

@MassiveGains:

See video I sent?

@GymRat1997:

Victor! Been trying to reach you for weeks! Why are you in the woods?

@MassiveGains:

Been training. Lift with me.

@GymRat1997:

You need help.

@MassiveGains:

Got diet plan and workouts. Horse good. Make own green stuff, made lady show me how. She strong, I stronger.

@MassiveGains:

Lifting alone. No one spot me

@MassiveGains:

Everyone so puny now

@GymRat1997:

You gotta stop taking the stuff

@MassiveGains:

Why you want me small?

@GymRat1997:

I don't want you small. You need help.

@MassiveGains:

Yes, I need help. I need spotter. Lifting alone. Lonely. Painful skin. Lonely

@GymRat1997:

I want to help you.

@MassiveGains:

Thrown out of gym. Said I was mean.

@GymRat1997:

I heard. You are scaring people, bro.

@MassiveGains:

They fear my massive gains. Need real gym, got my own plates.

@GymRat1997:

Wait, what do you mean, 'horse good'?

@MassiveGains:

Horse taste good

@GymRat1997:

What did you

@GymRat1997:

That was you?

@MassiveGains:

Horse good. Green stuff good. Skin still hurt no pain no gain. We work out soon. I spot you. Get you massive. Phone dying, in woods. See you soon.

@GymRat1997:

Vic, you need help.

@GymRat1997:

Vic?

@GymRat1997:

Vic, message back you fucker!

Three Dead, Six Wounded in Gym Rampage

Union, NJ: Three dead and six wounded in what appears to be a revenge killing occurred at a gym in Union Thursday afternoon, initial reports reveal. Preliminary investigation, including video, show a nine-foot form smashing in the gym doors and attacking several people [CLICK LINK TO CONTINUE]

Witness Interview with Steve Alban
    8/14/19
    Interviewer: Detective Davina Paneras

Detective:

Thanks for meeting with us.

Attorney:

I'd like to point out that my client is here voluntarily with information regarding the case.

Detective:

I understand. You said you had information on the incident at Metro Gym?

Steve Alban:

Yes. That's... Victor Barnes.

Detective:

The one you said was called 'Massive Gains' online?

Steve Alban:

Or was. It looks like him, kind of. Before he started taking this green stuff.

Detective:

Green stuff? Drugs?

Steve Alban:

It's a... preworkout? It's not steroids. But you're only supposed to take it once. Ever. He kept on taking it and he got... bigger.

Detective:

Like in the video? You are saying—

Steve Alban:

Yes, he's nine feet tall. He's been taking this... green stuff, it made him huge. He said he figured out how to make it himself from this old lady.

Detective:

And you talked with him? When?

Steve Alban:

I talked to him online. He sent videos of him working out. He posted some of them online. You can see him getting huge from week to week.

Detective:

Huge? This green stuff made him huge?

Steve Alban:

Yeah. You're only supposed to take it once. He kept on taking it. It's doing something to him. His skin is breaking out, pus and blood and shit. Getting all leathery.

Detective:

Do you know where Victor Barnes is?

Steve Alban:

I don't.

Attorney:

We've agreed to turn over the videos Mister Alban was sent, which appear to have metadata regarding location.

Detective:

We'd like to look at the phone.

Attorney:

That won't be happening.

Detective:

It's easier if you do it voluntarily.

Attorney:

I think we're done here, then. My office will send you the video and other information for your investigation.

Steve Alban:

You saw the security video that got leaked online! You saw the gym video! It's turned him into some kind of giant or ogre or something! He ripped a door off the hinges! He was responsible for what happened at that gym...

Detective:

We're having a hard time believing—

Attorney:

I advise you to—

Steve Alban:

I don't give a fuck what you believe! He's always felt like he was weak, and now he's not, and he's... he's a monster.

Attorney:

We're done here.

Workout

Push down big trees in woods

Lift bar with 12 plates six times

Lift bar with 12 plates six times

Lift bar with 12 plates six times

Walk around with big rock

Get bigger rock, walk around until tired

Pull up 10 times

Pull up 10 times

Pull up 10 times

Run around hate running

Food

Green stuff

Horse

Dog

Dog

Raccoon

Snake

Raccoon

Need spotter. Can't hit PR without spotter. Boring working out alone.
Will go see Steve. Phone broke. Go see Dad and call Steve. Me happy,
no longer puny small.

MASSIVE GAINS!!!

Dispatcher: 911, do you need police, fire, or medical?

911 Caller: Police. He's here!

Dispatcher: What's your address?

911 Caller: [address redacted]. It's between [address redacted], by the county park.

Dispatcher: Please repeat the address.

911 Caller: [address redacted]. By the county park.

Dispatcher: OK sir what is the emergency?

911 Caller: My friend called, he's here and he says we're going to have to work out!

Dispatcher: 911 is for emergencies only—

911 Caller: I know that! My friend is the guy who killed those people at the gym! He's huge!

Dispatcher: Sir, you said your friend is what?

911 Caller: He took something and it turned him into... I don't know, something! And he killed some people, and he wants me to work out with him.

Dispatcher: Sir, can you get out of your house?

[Smashing sound at door]

Voice in background: Steve! Workout! [roaring sound, clanking metal sounds] Brought real weights!

911 Caller: [screaming, retching]

Dispatcher: Sir, I am dispatching police to your location, please stay on the line. Are you on a home line or cell?

911 Caller: [clattering sound from phone]

Dispatcher: Hello?

911 Caller: Help! Help! Vic! No!

Dispatcher: Sir, police are on their way!

Voice in background: No slacking! Take green stuff! Get big!

[spilling and choking sounds in background]

Dispatcher: Sir?

Voice in background: [roaring sound] Massive gains!

TESTO HUNKY, or; FTM TWUNK POUNDS XL BEAR

RW DeFaoite

Callum was making good time. The rower was set on high resistance and his whole body was wet with sweat. It lubricated him against the air. His chest and arse and thighs and shoulders were all, for once, part of one continuous beast. It hurt wonderfully to breathe. In his ears, Britney was telling him about what he'd need to do to get a hot body. Glowing numbers rolled higher and higher on the screen in front of him, higher and higher. Get to work, bitch. He was gonna throw up. Or maybe row forever.

There were mirrors across the wall of the gym. At the top of his stroke he met his own glassy ecstatic eyes and saw his wide smile and thought fuck! Fuck I look good! Look at that man—look at me! The whole gym should be looking at me!

Then he saw a big broad curly-headed guy looking at him, and the embarrassment of experiencing for real what he'd just been fantasising about crumpled him like a Coke can in a meaty fist. Callum fumbled his grip on the handle and the resistance slurped the cord back in. Something twanged in his back as he lurched forward to try and keep hold of it. The glowing numbers on the rower's display slowed their roll.

"Ow," Callum muttered, hunkering back down and securing his grip on the handle again.

He finished his split but the stranger's eyes had sapped the strength from him. The pain was no longer enjoyable and his time wasn't good. When he finally finished, it felt like giving up. He unstrapped his feet from the footrests but stayed sitting on the rolling seat as he rehydrated from his metal flask. He rolled back and forth on his butt, stretching his legs out, looking morosely at the sweat whorls in his light brown leg hair. His workout playlist had moved onto Carly Rae Jepsen. Callum wasn't feeling it.

A grey blur in the outskirts of Callum's vision slid sideways and resolved into the same towheaded man whose attention had thrown him off. The stranger's movement eclipsed the gym. Callum, perched on the rowing machine seat, was level with the bulge in the stranger's dark grey sweatpants. With swift, straight-acting self-preservation, he detached his attention and got up, gesturing politely with his sweat towel that the stranger should take the machine if he wanted it—but the stranger was shaking his head and his lips were moving.

Callum pulled his earbuds out, cutting Carly Rae off. The ambiance of the gym wooshed in: elevator EDM over the speakers, the clang and roar of cardio machines and dropped weights. "Sorry?"

"I said, uh, can I..." The guy's voice was deep, reverberating from the deep wells of his huge body. He had none of the stark, diagrammatic definition of a bodybuilder—he was fat and farmerish, with broad shoulders and a heavy, soft belly. A butterfly of sweat spread across the front of his white shirt. Callum felt a stab of resentful attraction. "Can I *ask* you something."

"Uh, yeah." The stabbing continued. Callum shifted his weight slightly and tried to give his good side, all while telling himself not to be stupid. No one actually got picked up in a gym. Best not to look too flirty—but what if?

The stranger's tongue swiped his lips. His dark brown eyes darted over Callum's body in a way that made Callum's blood rush downwards to plump up over-expectant flesh that would not listen to reason. "You trans?"

The question hooked him under the abs and he coughed up a little air—not quite a laugh. The stranger suddenly seemed even bigger: his looming blocked out light and sound.

Time stretched as Callum scrambled for what to say—something sneering and calm and funny which wouldn't get him hit and would make this stranger feel the kind of searing shame *he* was feeling. But he couldn't make his mouth work. He couldn't even feel any anger: just embarrassment hot enough to singe his nose hair.

The stranger's eyes widened. He stepped back. Callum's lungs re-inflated greedily. "Oh. Shit. That sounded—I didn't mean to freak you out. I'm not some kind of..."

With the stranger out of his space, Callum's anger had oxygen to spark, but it was dull and achy and resigned. It curled around the sore lingering desire. His dick was taking a while to catch on to how the conversation had turned.

"Sure," he said, flat and bitter. "Okay. It's fine." He fumbled for his earbuds. His anger flailed uselessly and, unable to get purchase on the stranger, became self-directed. It was his own fault for picking this shirt, with its deep cut off sleeve holes that revealed the shiny pink scars which still refused to fade, even though Callum had tried silicone strips and Bio-Oil and building up his pecs. "I get it, you were curious."

"No, no, that wasn't—I wasn't curious."

Yes you were, thought Callum. What else would you be? But he didn't say it aloud. He just squinted uneasily up at the stranger's face. The sticky insistent attraction to this man kept him hooked.

"I wanted to ask if—" The stranger's voice crunched as he ran out of spit or steam. He swallowed and tried again, pitching his voice lower: "If you've got any T."

Callum laughed, high and startled, and then clicked his jaw shut on it quickly. Of course. He was not an object of either lust or violence. He just had access to some handy molecules.

"I need that stuff, man," he said tightly.

"Oh. Right." The guy looked dazed and disappointed. He crossed his arms. The movement compressed the sweat-butterfly across his chest. "I just thought—I guess you get it legally, huh? You don't know how to like... uh... online?"

Callum shook his head, amazed at how poorly this stranger had judged him. He'd done everything by the book. The psychologist who referred him for hormones had used him in a case study. His surgeon had called him 'an ideal candidate.'

He wondered what the stranger thought T would do for him. Maybe he was trying to lose weight. Callum looked at his crossed arms, which were huge and dimpled and sheeny with sweat that gleamed in the crosshatch of thick brown hair. Fat and fur. He was hot, this sad compelling cis guy who wanted to transition. He was hot, and the only thing Callum had to offer him was testosterone.

"Uh," said the stranger, and Callum realised he'd been caught staring.

"Give me your number," Callum said. It came out sharp and a little mean. That was fine. He felt sharp and mean. After this messy, stupid conversation, the stranger might as well lick the wounds he'd inflicted. "I know someone. Give me your number." He pulled his phone out, unlocked it and handed it over.

Slowly, the guy stabbed his number into it. As he did so, a crooked grin began to form on his face. Midway through he looked at Callum and the look was shy and disbelieving. Then he handed the phone back. "Yeah?" he said.

Callum looked at the number. The stranger had added his name. Matt. And a bicep curl emoji. He raised his eyebrows. "Yeah," he said. "Matt." He made the last sound click on his tongue. He was still angry. He was still excited. "I'll text you."

——◦——

"You're imprisoned by cis dick," Frankie told him that evening as she rolled a joint, crosslegged on the beaten up old sofa. She'd said the same thing when Callum had taken all references to being trans out of his Grindr profile about two months ago. "It's a sickness. Cis dick will never love you back."

"I don't want love."

"You should. Love is *good*." She smiled as she said it. She was loved up to the gills, and it made Callum happy and a little melancholy to see. The flat they'd shared for four years was filled with moving boxes and half the art was missing from the walls, which looked embarrassed to be so undressed. In a few weeks, Frankie was going to live with the central ring of her polycule in a house filled with lesbians and plants. "I'm so love-pilled, man. I think love is fucking great. So are you going to get him T?"

In the pocket of his sweatpants, Callum's phone vibrated. He took it out. It was Matt. The message read *hey, thanks so much for helping me out. wanted to say sorry for being weird earlier. Wouldn't have known except I was looking and saw the scars and figured maybe*

"Is that him?" Frankie said. All she got in response was a non-committal noise as Callum composed a reply. *You were looking?* His thumb hesitated over the send button. "It is him," Frankie said, smug.

Callum sent the message and forced himself to put the phone down. "Can you ask AJ about the T?"

"Hm? Oh. Yeah, AJ will know. I'll ask him." AJ was the boyfriend of one of Frankie's girlfriends. Callum didn't like him. He was ethereal in a way that made Callum feel like stodgy leftovers next to him. His top surgery scars were almost invisible.

Callum's phone buzzed in his pocket and he fumbled it free. His face went hot and his toes curled as he saw the message.

yeah of course I was

———◦———

The thing about Matt was that he wasn't fat. He was just briefly off track. He'd been off track for about five years now—God, had it been that long? Since breaking up with Julian and his dad passing away and everything else that had happened that year?

After *that*, Matt reasoned, no one could blame him for putting on a little weight. And yet he blamed himself constantly. The only relief he found was in reassuring himself that this was a state of temporary embarrassment, a trial before he found his way back to the land of the muscled, the lean and the wanted.

Because of this temporary fatness he avoided sex and dating. There were men out there on the apps who used words like *bear* and *chub* and Matt hated them for it. Those men fetishised their own abandonment of self-improvement.

Fortunately for Matt, he was on his way to hotness again, though it wasn't a path free of mortification. Matt had replayed his conversation with Callum so many times that it was becoming a form of repetitive self-harm. He flipped it, imagined being Callum, suddenly set upon by some sweaty stranger. A potential hate crime assailant or, worse, a slobbering fetishist.

Matt made a deal with himself: whenever he caught himself compulsively imagining how grotesque he must have seemed to Callum, he would go to the spinlock dumbbells and the weight bench in his flat, and he'd lift until he felt better.

Fat was flammable. As his back and shoulders burned, Matt pictured himself combusting.

He had tried running and dieting and intermittent fasting. He ate perfectly—he made sure to eat perfectly. Juicing was a last resort.

When the idea had first occurred to him, it hadn't really appealed. Further research hadn't done much to convince him. The men on bodybuilding forums weren't much like him, Matt thought. Ultimately they were body-modders, trying to become something they'd never been before, something out there and weird. Matt just wanted to be himself again. He wasn't even thirty yet and that brief period where he wasn't a child or closeted or fat had been so cruelly short, and he'd been unable to enjoy it because of *fucking* Julian—he hadn't even lived.

He had never even lived.

On one of his lonesome self-flagellating pilgrimages through weight loss websites, Matt found an article titled "Obesity: Unhealthy and Unmanly." It described how fat men had lower testosterone. It was a horrible article but Matt read it with pure cold relief. It explained so much. It wasn't his fault. He was in a brutal hormonal trap, castrated by his fatness, unable to produce the testosterone he needed to build muscle.

If you can't make your own, he figured, store-bought is fine.

The internet steroid guys knew their stuff about dosage, at least. In their litanies of milligrams Matt found great reassurance. The T would eat away at all the unwanted softness under his skin and build him up better, stronger, harder.

When he thought about it, his skin itched for needles.

His phone buzzed. It was Callum. *Hey big guy*

Matt flinched. He thought about Callum's scars with a sudden hot slash of searing jealousy. No one was going to give *him* lipo on the NHS.

Hey where are we on the T? he sent back, not caring if he sounded brusque.

He saw through Callum's mean flirting. Callum didn't want him—he was just seeing how much fun he could have at Matt's expense. He'd be serious soon enough: he imagined Callum's pink wet mouth opening in adoration as his hands explored the hard, radiant architecture of Matt's new chest.

Somewhere out there was a version of himself that deserved adoration and sacrifice. A perfect body waiting to be his.

Frankie was flaky and AJ was worse. Eventually, they mustered up enough wherewithal between them to end up with Callum forwarding a few links and names to Matt. Matt sent back a string of celebratory emojis and *thanks so much man* to which Callum responded *np!!*

Acquiring T seemed to go smoothly enough for Matt; he was very excited. He couldn't talk about anything else, which was a turn off. Lots of really boring texts about dosage which Callum was baffled by. His doctors took care of all that.

Frankie's moving out process was in full swing. Callum was behind on finding someone to replace her. "You need to put it up on the homes for queers page," Frankie nagged him as she taped up one of her ratty cardboard boxes. "You said you were gonna do it last week."

"Yeah. I will." But he didn't actually want to live with anyone who put their pronouns in a room advertisement. He had been daydreaming of a potential flatmate—a man, maybe even a straight man, someone who wasn't here too often, someone who wandered the flat shirtless, someone who didn't need to know he was trans.

Matt eventually seemed to realise that Callum wasn't interested in hearing about dosage, and moved to a misguided effort to find common ground in the experience of taking testosterone. His last message: *T feels weird right?*

Callum didn't know what to say to that. He put off answering, and put off answering. T made him feel normal. He liked feeling normal.

———◆———

Frankie's moving day came. Both her girlfriends—pierced tattooed butches—arrived to help. Callum tried not to feel like he was competing with them as he ferried boxes of books and dismembered furniture down the stairs to the waiting van. He hugged Frankie goodbye.

"Fuck," Frankie said into his shoulder, "I'm kind of scared. I hope this love shit works out."

When she was gone, the flat was full of absences. Frankie had taken one of the bookshelves, her record player, the antique writing desk she'd scored for a tenner on Facebook. Callum wandered into the spaces she had left behind, touching areas of the wall that hadn't been visible in years.

He didn't feel like celebrating his solitude, but he'd feel better if he went through the motions, so he cracked open a cider and set to jacking off on the couch.

He opened Grindr with one hand down the front of his sweatpants. A shaven-headed bear caught his eye. Stretched lobes. Big ginger beard. Big broad belly. He fired a shot across the bows, a *hey what's up.*

Figuring he might as well cast his net wide, he sent the same message a few more times to a few more guys. Like TURKISHMUSCLE whose biceps were as big as rugby balls. And StirlingLad whose pale stomach poured over the tight black waistband of his briefs like soft ice cream overspilling a cone.

Callum's taste for huge and hairy men had embarrassed him once. But he loved to feel himself simultaneously man enough and emasculated in their presence, small and lean and bendable in their hands. Not that he was planning on actually meeting up with any of these guys. He didn't want to deal with them dealing with what was between his legs.

The ginger bear got back first, volleyed a few boring responses, but started answering quicker and more interested when Callum said *stroking my dick wbu.* Ginger wasn't shy about sending pics. He had a nice crooked heavy-looking dick.

That was enough. Callum put his phone down and came in seconds to the thought of that weighty flesh thudding against his insides.

After his orgasm, quiet and strangeness descended. He stared up at the ceiling for unknowable minutes.

For something to do with his hands, he picked up his phone. He had a message from Ginger: *? still there?*

And he had a message from StirlingLad:

your trans right?

Callum watched as more and more messages bubbled up.

am no bi. sorry

don't eat gash

Callum exited the app. He needed a shower. Competing box for box with Frankie's butches had made him sweat through his deodorant and now he smelled of masturbation, too.

In the bathroom he stood blankly in front of the mirror, trying to remember what he'd come in there for. He decided he wanted a cigarette. He didn't smoke anymore, but he kept some for emergencies. Not that this was an emergency, he just felt so strange.

The cider was room temperature now but he finished it anyway. His fingers were pruny and it was hard to roll his cigarette. He wasn't quite in his body. He was sloshing around the room, here and there, on the ceiling, watching himself.

Opening the window and smoking out into the night air made Callum's head go fuzzy. His phone vibrated. He took it out of his pocket, expecting it to be Frankie sending him pictures of her new place. It wasn't. It was Matt.

Hey I need to see you

Need to talk to you

The ash on the end of Callum's cigarette jittered as his hand shook.

Another barrage of messages came through so quick that the vibrations bled together into one choppy buzz: *sorry*

I know this is kind of intense

Please

Callum stuck the cigarette in his mouth and took such a deep breath on it that he could see the paper shrivel and burn faster. *No it's okay. it's cool. I'm free. where are you*

On the bus to Matt's place, Callum was afraid he could smell himself. He hadn't changed his boxers. He was sticky wet. Sweating. Gushing. Gash.

The address Matt sent him led to a basement flat with its own street entrance. As he descended the outdoor steps Callum regretted his cigarette: it felt like the smoke was still in him, rolling around in his belly. He had brushed his teeth but the stale tobacco taste was caked into the inside of his mouth. He knocked on the door.

His phone buzzed: *its open.* So he let himself in.

His brain registered the surroundings first: protecting itself from the impossible, it scanned what it understood. Matt lived in a magnolia-walled shithole with threadbare brown carpet on the floor, except for a corner kitchenette with peeling grey lino. There were beer bottles on the counter, unwashed dishes starting to smell in the sink. The room was furnished with a scuffed leather armchair, a TV and Playstation, a weight bench and a set of dumbbells... and the bed.

The bed was hard to look at, because Matt was there.

He was naked and huge, thick ropes of muscle standing out from his shoulders and his neck. His face had been forced outwards, his nose spread across his muzzle, his mouth bulging with teeth.

As Callum looked, he changed. His maw sank back into a human shape with a sucking noise. His neck thickened and sprouted fur which then vanished and fled downwards. His ears peeled downwards on his skull. Callum felt like he was looking at two pictures, man and bear, overlaid on each other, and depending on how the light shone in and on and through them, different features came to the fore. An optical illusion played out in flesh and fur.

And Matt groaned and puffed air from his raw red nostrils. Fat tears were brimming in his eyes. His voice was distorted and clumsy through his newly crowded mouth, and spittle lubricated his words. "Callum—Callum, fuck—"

Callum shook his head. "I'm going to go," he heard himself say. "I have work tomorrow. Bye Matt." But he couldn't move his legs.

"Please," Matt said. His voice rattled the whole room. "Please stay with me, I'm scared."

"Matt," Callum said. His voice was still calm though his words were less and less connected. "Have to go. Work tomorrow—have you—maybe called a doctor?"

Matt roared and as he did the flesh of his face flowed forwards and fur followed. Callum cried out and finally managed to stumble backwards, losing his footing and ending up on his arse on the carpet. The bear's face reached full bloom and then folded back in on itself. Patches of skin spread. The roar curled in mid-air and got a human edge, "—ahh, ah, *shit*. No doctors."

"Okay," Callum whispered. He was trying to crawl backwards. He could taste snot and tears dripping off his own upper lip. Matt's mostly-human head was disproportionately small on his huge bear's body with its powerful folds of heavy drooping fat. "Okay, no doctors."

Matt shifted his weight to lean over the foot of the bed and plant a huge paw on the floor.

The thud as he dropped his full weight rattled up Callum's hip bones and spine. His huge furred body stretched and sagged and rippled as he moved forwards with a rolling gait.

He stopped a few steps from Callum. His big brown eyes were wet. His thick jowls shook, dewy sweat sliding between soft folds of skin and glistening on the stubble that thickened into the fur of his huge, bulging shoulders. He was beautiful.

"I didn't know who else to call," Matt said through his clustered yellow fangs. "I wanted you to see me. I need you to... is this right? Am I... is this..."

The room was rocking like a ship at sea and it made the same cracking, popping, rushing noises, or those were the noises of Callum's blood in his ears, or Matt's bones scraping and twisting.

"Fuck," said Callum, afraid for him and of him, and reached out to him and stopped. "Fuck Matt, just. Just stay... calm..."

"I'm calm!" Matt snarled at him. "I'm calm! Answer me!"

"I don't know what you're asking!"

Matt flinched back from Callum's cry and reared up onto his hind legs.

New nipples welled up out of his torso and his small thick cock was perfect purple and reaching upwards. His beauty overflowed Callum's ability to look at it. It swung a lamp into the hidden corners of Callum's desires, illuminating just for a moment a dream of soft sweaty fur and fat bearweight descending, pouring and shuddering and shaking and surrounding him, in some world where a man wasn't all a man could be.

Fur enveloped Matt's jowls again as he screamed, "*Is this normal when you start T?*"

The lamp smashed. Callum laughed: it flew out of his mouth and circled his head like a crazy bird.

"T didn't do this to you," he said. "That's not what T does."

Now Matt was obscene and Callum felt obscene for having wanted him. He scrambled away from him and from his own perversion. Matt tottered on his hindlegs. "You're just a freak of nature. This is nothing to do with T—or me—"

The bear came down like an avalanche. Matt's claws were clumsy, almost lazy, but it ripped Callum's chest like he was tearing through paper. Two long vertical slashes down his sternum. His scream came bursting from his throat and his open wounds. It bled into Matt's huge, wailing bellow. And then all noise faded to snuffling and grunting and sobbing, both of them, together.

New scars, Callum thought, staring upwards, past the corona of brown fur at the bottom of his vision. He needed to buy more Bio-Oil. For when he got out of this. To help the scars fade.

Matt was tucking his head down, snuffling along his sternum.

"This is why you do it the proper way," Callum heard himself saying. His right arm was splayed out beside him, and his fingers could just find the cold metal bar of one of Matt's dumbbells. "Get a doctor, get a diagnosis, not online pharmacies. Controls. Make it safe. Now look at you. Now look."

He felt something hot and wet and gasped. Matt was licking the long wounds on his chest.

Callum's shoulder almost came out of the socket as he hefted the dumbbell and brought it around in a screaming arc that finished in the hollow of Matt's cheek.

The blow unleashed a deep blare of noise from the bear's maw. Matt reared back and his paws came to his face in a horrible human gesture.

Appalled by this show of pain, Callum hit him again.

"You're not normal," Callum wept as the dumbbell splintered Matt's jaw and teeth. Matt, still struggling, eyes zigzagging crazily, tongue protruding through the broken mess of his cheek, tried to roll his weight off but Callum rolled with him. They were face to face on the floor on their sides, legs tangled together in a lovers' crisscross.

"I'm normal!" Callum begged him to understand as he hit him. "I'm normal! I'm normal! I'm normal!"

When he dropped the dumbbell on the floor it clanged and rolled, leaving a bloody track behind it.

Matt wasn't moving. Shards of pinkish bone emerged from his face and head. When Callum rolled him onto his back, his left eye was dislodged from its ruined socket and tumbled out, hanging by a bundle of wet red threads.

Callum put his hand on Matt's chest, where the rich plush fur was plentiful. "Fuck," Callum said, and dropped his head onto it. Still warm. "You're so soft," Callum sobbed. "You're so soft. I fucking love how soft you are."

That Southern Spirit

Mae Murray

There is no me before the rodeo. Whoever that man is in town—buying his groceries, running to the bank—it's been a long time since I could call him *me*. I don't start feeling like myself until I smear the clown white on my face, and even then I'm only in the first stage of my evolution, because there's also the wig and the shoes and the jumpsuit, which my belly plumb-near bursts out of. With the wig, it's best to have a cheap one, because when you're running from the bulls you're likely to lose it. In the early days of my career, I made the mistake of buying a real nice one and lost it in a cow patty. (*There went your hair, Willy,* Pop had said. *Another piece of you in the shit and the muck.*)

I grew up going to rodeos, like many Arkansans did and do. When I was a little boy, we'd go to the White County Fair and eat caramel apples and pay a nickel to see the "Biggest Hog In the World," which was really just a pregnant sow laying sleeping in the hay, teats swole with milk. (*She got teats like yours, Boy*, said Pop, stinking of Kodiak chewing tobacco.)

At night, rowdy beer-drunk spectators, still dizzying from the rickety old rollercoaster, would file into a large stadium. It smelled of manure and buttered popcorn, tinged with a sickly sweet smell like kettle corn, air so strong you could taste it on your tongue.

I started out in the rodeo in the Lil Rancher competition, where kids as young as four were let loose in the stadium to chase and rope newborn calves. You had to be damn quick with a lasso to be any good at all, and I weren't any good if I'm being honest. I never won, not once, but it wasn't the winning that got me hung up on the idea of being a *cowboy;* it was the respect of the crowd, their pride in tradition, the way they saw me as a *man. (Never be a cowboy like that. Cryin' and carryin' on like a pussy. Only men can be cowboys).*

Women could do barrel racing as well as the men, so everyone saw it as a soft sport for soft boys. When I got to be a young buck, bull riding was the thing to do.

The rules of bull riding are simple: one hand holds fast to a rope hitch tied 'round the bull, the other hand remains high in the air. If you can stay like that for eight seconds more times than not, you're a pretty damn good cowboy. And I weren't a good cowboy neither on account of my weak wrists.

The only thing left to do was to become a clown. More goes into it than people think. See, most people suppose it's a clown's job to be funny, but really we're there to distract the bulls after the ride, to keep the real cowboys from being gored by an angry horn on their way out of the arena. To be a clown, the first thing you have to be is fast. The second thing is fearless. Funny don't factor into it.

"Gettin' kinda slow out there, Willy," Bobby-Joe Harris said to me as I took off my frazzled rainbow-colored wig. "Not Today, Satan almost got your kidney. Would've too, if Delroy hadn't turned his eye."

"Well, they should've given that bull's name to me, then. *Not today, Satan!"*

I laughed, but I didn't feel much like laughing, not after almost catching a bull's horn. Mostly it was for Bobby-Joe's benefit. He was a stunning specimen of a man, all *cowboy.* He wore a black cowboy hat with a leather band, which was studded with turquoise stones set in roughly hammered silver. His shirt was a neatly starched black button-up with silver tassels adorning the shoulders and chest. His face was covered in sweat and dust—he'd just finished his ride—and now his blue eyes shone out at me, set in tanned skin looking just like that turquoise. It seemed almost criminal that he should exist at all, looking the way he did. God gave that man all the good hair there was left to give, and that was why I was losing mine. (*Pretty boy*).

"You should think about getting in shape. I see a little belly from all them fried chicken gizzards you eat."

I frowned at that, looking down to poke the softness of my stomach through the fabric of my pom-covered clown suit. Weren't no locker room at the rodeo, so we all changed in the public bathroom. I caught sight of the piss seeping into the cracks of the lop-sided concrete floor, and the dead mosquito-eaters spackled to the floor with the gum of it, and there amongst it all were my scuffed-up clown shoes yellowed by the sour air.

"Ain't much different than it's always been, Bobby-Joe. Not all of us are built like a brick shithouse."

"As far as I can tell, you ain't even trying no more," he said, taking off his hat and using a rough paper towel to wipe at the dust-caked creases of his eyes. "You should try going to that gym, just opened up a few months back. They got that ten-dollar deal, and Lynn started at it last month. Reckon she's lost about two pounds."

"She's got a long way to go."

The punch to my shoulder came swift and nearly knocked me over the garbage can, causing the beer cans within to rattle, but Bobby-Joe was laughing; he just didn't know his own strength.

"Now why you gotta go and say that, Willy? Talk about my wife again, I'll throw you in the pen with Not Today, Satan—let him have you once and for all."

"Sorry, Bobby-Joe, that must'a been Daddy talkin' again. But at this point, you'd be doing me a favor. Better gored than the gym."

———◇———

My first day on the treadmill at Fusion Fitness, I about died. I wasn't built for endurance and was only really good for a quick sprint away from a bull. I cast my gaze around the gym; there were women to my left and right, running with their long ponytails swinging—typical cheerleader types and former pageant queens, sweat clinging to their eyelash extensions and causing their dark makeup to pebble across their skin. A rough sound came from the opposite wall, gruff grunts like the sound of a boar cumming as the muscled men in their Neo-tribal tattoos dropped deadlifted weights on the mat.

If you asked me to tell them apart, I'd surely fail. Despite different hair colors, different clothes all sucked tightly to their damp skin, they all seemed strangely uniform—or maybe it was just because, occupying the same space as them and breathing the same air, I was acutely aware of my Otherness, my burgeoning mid-life softness. The walls of the gym were lined with mirrors, and I found myself looking into one now, staring into rows and rows of myself stacked against a hundred gyms and thousands of muscled men and lean women, huffing and dripping sweat. My face looked pale and peppered with adult acne from putting on and removing clown makeup, a sallow ghost amongst the farm-tanned living.

"Hey, Champ," came a disembodied voice to my right, nearly causing me to lose my step on the belt of the treadmill. I grasped at the digital display to catch myself, vaguely aware of the absence of life in the mirror; an absence that told me the voice to my right could not be. Yet when I got my bearings and looked again, there he was, a short, broad man squeezed into a black and yellow striped polo, his name—*Brandt Fissure*—embroidered over a swollen pectoral muscle.

"You came out of nowhere, man." I stopped the treadmill from rolling, skipping as it slowed.

"You were looking in the mirror, not paying any mind. Happens all the time," he said good-naturedly, extending his hand. "Mr. Fissure, at your service. I'm the captain of this here establishment."

I wiped my palm on my shorts and shook his hand, sweat dripping from my nose and chin. "Willy."

"Good to see a fresh face. Been worrying about the growth of our clientele; we're lucky to have you come aboard."

"Fisherman, are you?"

"Been known to catch a few, Willy. Yes, indeed." He smiled, cocked his head, expression all eager and genuine-like. "What brings you here to Fusion Fitness? You look to be, oh... fifty or so?"

"I'm 39." My voice came with more forceful indignation than I'd intended, and suddenly I was very aware again of the many thousands of eyes in the mirror, the many me's there were looking, altogether, a millennia older than I was amongst a sea of youthful vigor.

"My apologies." That shit-eating grin. "It's just that you look so *tired.*"

"Who isn't, in this economy?" I wiped the dripping sweat from my nose with my sleeve, stepping off the treadmill at last. The solid floor caused my body to stagger slightly, knees going numb without the height and rhythmic steps of the machine.

"I'm glad you brought that up, Willy. This economy sure does seem to have it out for us common folk, don't it? They say it takes about three years for business owners to turn a profit, but who has that much time and money? I sure don't. A man's got to get creative to feed his family these days. Say, you married?"

"Can't say I've ever met a woman had a mind to marry me."
(*You know what you are, Boy?*)

Mr. Fissure's smile broadened, his hand hot on my back as
he guided me away from the treadmill, past all the perfect
physiques at peak performance, grinding away at their workouts like mice on an eternal wheel.

"Seeing how you're a bachelor and all..."

"Huh?"

"An *opportunity*, Willy. You see all them stallions?" He motioned toward the men; the men with their deadlifting bar-
bells so heavy the bar sunk at both ends, the men with their
thin muscle shirts and their tight nipples, the men with their
hairless thighs. (*I can tell by lookin' at ya.*)

"Who could miss them?"

"Right. All them stallions and all them mares started just like
you, Willy. Soft and insecure—Now, don't take that any bad
way!—Soft and insecure and *lonely*. I let them in on a little secret, though, and I'm willing to do the same for you. All I need
is a few more minutes of your time, and a five-hundred-dollar
deposit."

"Aw, Hell..."

"Now let me finish, Willy. That covers the cost of 20 cases
of my patented Dream Fusion meal-replacement shake, plus
an additional two cases for you. Ain't nothing at the grocery
store that's gonna give you this much energy, this much stamina—D'ya know what I mean when I say *stamina*, Willy?—this
much fat-melting power than Dream Fusion. And the best part
is? You can sell them 20 cases and make a nice little profit for
yourself, about double what you put down. Not too bad, eh?"

"Sound like one of them schemes going 'round Facebook."

"Well, it can't be a scheme when you can see the product—and its results!—right here in front of you, now can it?"

"I reckon not..."

"Willy, I'm telling you straight: This will mold you into the
man you've always wanted to be. I guaran-damn-tee it."

The liquid was viscous like snot but salty-sweet like a honeyed peanut from the fair, which made the texture slightly more palatable as I sank back in my recliner at midnight. I eyed the cases of Dream Fusion stacked neatly in the corner of my kitchenette, squeezed between the whirring mini-fridge and the plastic trash can, then turned my attention back to the flickering TV.

Mr. Fissure had made many promises I was certain he couldn't keep, but I slurped at the aluminum can anyway as replays of the Ouachita horse race were broadcast between antique infomercials. Through the haze of static on the box television, the lines that rolled over the screen like the passing of floors in a glass elevator, I watched the defined musculature of the horses as they galloped beneath the poised jockeys, the way their hides twitched with the flick of the crop and their mouths salivated 'round the bit.

I could smell the dirt beneath their hooves, hear the thrum of their gait pulsing in my ears as if speeding past my cheek like bullets. I closed my eyes, thought now of the bulls, their hulking forms, muscles and tendons tensile beneath their stretched hides. My breath stuttered, and I touched myself at the thought of their unslakable fury.

I startled awake in my armchair, bleary-eyed against the light filtering in through the knit blanket nailed over the window—the poor man's curtain. I rose with a grunt, staggering to the bathroom with my hand in my shorts, scratching around the wiry hairs at my balls, finding my testicles heavy and tender to the touch. (*Got the clap, Boy?*)

"Ow, fuck," I muttered, pulling the elastic of my briefs out to have a look. They were bigger, swollen and defined in a newly peach-fuzzed scrotum. The line of hair from my chest to my belly was fine and sleek, and my fingers walked the trail down to my crotch. I took the baby powder from the top of the medicine cabinet and doused my balls, though I weren't sure if that would do me any good.

I went to clowning that day with my balls about as sore as they could be, but when Bobby-Joe saw me, he said I looked like I'd thinned out a little 'bout the face. I had Dream Fusion for breakfast, lunch, and dinner.

———⟡———

Running. Running and wet in my dreams. Bobby-Joe's balls on my back. Bobby-Joe's thighs 'round by waist. There's Daddy. God, I hate you so much. Let me take a switch to your hide, see how you like it. Toss you in the Arkansas river; some fisherman catches you and fries you up with some hushpuppies you stinkin' lyin' ugly sumbitch. Call me pussy again.

———⟡———

There's a moment before every shock in which a body acutely remembers having not known that particular breed of terror. This right here, this was that moment: Myself, looking in the mirror for the first time in the morning, as if I would find an answer to my unspoken question somewhere in my own eyes. Staring back at me, a hideously unfamiliar face and irises and pupils blown wide, bulging. My eyes had sagged apart, the bridge of my nose buckled up from the inside, a sloping arch down the line of my face. I pulled back from myself, clinging to the towel rack with one hand while the other flailed out for support from the toilet. The clattering of empty candles, aluminum air freshener and deodorant cans, and self-warming lube that had lined the back of the toilet did nothing to shake me from the horror of it, only amplified my awe.

———◦———

Where there's a rodeo, I reckon there must be a clown—even if a dreadful change had got hold of him. The stands were filling with small-town revelers, folks who never missed the rodeo on account of the fact all the stores downtown shuttered their doors at 5:00 sharp on weekdays and nary-a-one of them were open on Saturday or Sunday.

In my clown white and large, glittered star-shaped glasses (which I had lashed 'round my head with a bit of twine), I was able to manipulate and hide my face such that Bobby-Joe Harris and Delroy the Clown might not notice my peculiar appearance. I stood by the bull chute next to a trapped animal called Buckaroo Banzai, groaning and stomping his feet as his tail flicked flies from his dappled hide. His horns clacked against the metal bars of his enclosure, thrashing at them and eyeing me from the side of his large, sloping head.

Goddamn you, he seemed to say, the voice in my head coming even and malicious. *Goddamn you and your clown 'n' cowboy kind to Hell. Call yourself men, do you? What man gotta prove himself like this? You disgust me, Chicken-Shit.*

Dread rose in my gullet, turning my stomach over as the tamped dirt of the arena bent and swayed. My feet crossed over one another in a clumsy stumble as I took off to the bathroom, staggering in a hunch with my front end leading the way.

"Y'all right?" Bobby-Joe was fixing his cowboy hat atop his head, wisps of blond Grecian curls about his ears. He didn't look at me, just turned this way and that in the dusty mirror to admire his waist.

"Feeling a bit sick is all." I slumped down on the bench, opening my tightening jumpsuit at the throat so I could breathe more easily. As the air hit my skin, I suddenly felt that it wasn't enough, that I should rend my clothes and climb out of them like a locust from its husk. I let the fabric flap down to my groin, my rainbow-wigged head thunking back against the yellowing cinderblock wall as I sucked in the damp air.

"Christ, look at you!"

"I know, my face—"

"No, not your face, Willy. You're jacked as shit!"

I tipped my head forward to look down, clown white running down my face in rivulets, dripping on my exposed torso. The soft black hair on my chest and abdomen shone healthily under mounds of bulging muscle, the veins snaking and popping 'round my swollen pectorals.

"Fuck, my stomach..." I stood then, a horrible sound tearing from my abdomen as my shoulders pulsed with growing muscle, bowing my back into a sharp hump. It was the first time I'd ever seen Bobby-Joe looking bewildered, his face drained of color such that he seemed much older than his 28 years. I took a step toward him, extending my hand, fingers tensed into claws that raked at his silver buttons just as he pulled away.

"Shit, Willy! Something's bad wrong with you, man."

From the corner of my wide eye, a shadow at the door, all calm and smiles.

"Well, hey, Champ. I was hoping I'd run into you here." It was Mr. Fissure, shed of his polo, now donning a baseball cap and crisp white t-shirt. (*Save a horse, ride a cowboy*, it said). "You go on, Mr. Bobby-Joe Harris. I'll take care of Old Willy here. I've seen something like this ailment a time or two. This here ain't nothing but a violent case of the scoliosis."

"I can't leave him here like this. I don't even know you."

"Oh, sure you do! At least, I know you, Mr. Bobby-Joe Harris—through your old lady Lynn. Ain't she a changed woman since she joined Fusion Fitness?" He held his hands away from his chest, cupping an imaginary pair of double-D breasts. "Why, I'm Mr. Fissure, the architect of that change!"

"Christ..." I moaned. "Christ, help me."

Ladies and Gentleman, please welcome to the arena...

"They're calling your name, Son!"

"Christ!"

Bobby-Joe Haaaaarriiiiiis!

"Your public awaitsss," Mr. Fissure hissed through grinning teeth, guiding me back to sit on the bench. He took a rough paper towel from the sink, wet it and dabbed my face with it, creating swirling smears of clown white and red and blue across my pallid skin. "I got him. You go on, Boy, a'fore the bulls get mad." Wink.

"Bobby-Joe..." I tried—but he was gone, already running out of the bathroom and toward the arena to a stadium filled with bodies, each one indistinguishable from the next.

"Now, shush, Willy. I got just what you need." Mr. Fissure presented a cool can of Dream Fusion, the aluminum glittering with condensation. "Yes, Willy, ain't that the prettiest thing you ever did see?"

"No... No, Mr. Fissure, please for the love of God and all that is holy, I can't eat a thing. I can't." I clawed at my stomach as if to rid it of a vice, some rope-like vein cinching my body from within—a living lasso 'round my middle.

"Ain't eatin', it's drinkin'. And I'm gonna help you, Boy."

My eyes felt swollen, straining out the side of my head like teary balloons. I couldn't see, not a thing in front of me, though I could make out the mirror to my right and the bathroom stall to my left, toilet seat covered in shit and putrid, reeking. Two fingers plugged up my nose, yanked my head back violently, and there came that honey-peanut taste of Dream Fusion gooping down my throat.

As a boy, I used to try pulling roots up out the ground. Those little roots from half-sunk trees, laying on their sides after a tornado run 'em down; but them things were still alive, so you'd have to twist and twist, watching them tough fibers break down, snap like tendons, until the root was wore down to a tightly wound middle. The sap in them roots's veins seeped over my fingers, sticky and bitter like blood. Now I were them roots.

------◇------

I don't recollect when Fissure vanished, but suddenly I was alone with the piss smell. I felt like a body split down the middle, brain unable to reconcile seeing with eyes sunk so wide across a head. I took a step forward, knees buckling so my hunched back sloped down and my mouth nearly hit the floor. When I rose again, I could see vaguely that I rose on hooves.

I made a sound like the kind you hear out in the woods, the kind they tell you not to chase 'lest you get taken up by them demons. I made a sound like a tornado picking a roof up off a barn. I made a sound of mourning. I made a sound of fury.

My body scraped the sides of the doorframe as I barreled through, my hooves heavy on the packed earth. I heard a bevy of screams, felt a splash of beer on my hide as people threw themselves away from the concession line.

I charged toward the arena, to the weak spot I knew, where the plywood had eroded into flakes and the paint that once read *Nothing Says That Southern Spirit Like the Rodeo* had faded to the point that only the Old Timers could recall what it had said. I burst through it, bucking wildly to fling the thin wood from my horns, my back legs kicking up dust for the crowd to eat as they gasped.

A rope whipped at my head and missed; them cowboys had come to be cowboys. Another swished at my hind legs, and another flogged my side. I felt the air stolen from me as a lasso cinched 'round my neck, heaving me to the side and causing me to stagger forward. Smell of blood as my horns pierced flesh, gurgle of spit and vomit, shit smell and urine seeping into fabric. I lifted my head, heavy with burden of body, crimson waves running down my face as them doll-like legs flailed off the ground and them strong arms hung 'round my face with no strength left. It was Bobby-Joe, crucified.

———•◦•———

It was a sunny day at the farm. I felt the rope lash against my legs, tighten just above my hooves to pull them from under my giant body, drag me down into the dust. I opened my maw, bellowing in protest, the sound like a mournful bugle signaling nothing but the start of incredible pain. I'd seen it done a hundred times, and yet when my scrotum was cut and the gloved rancher's hand reached inside to twist and tear my testicles like two bloody flower bulbs from the earth, I finally knew what it was to be a man.

Flesh Advent

D. Matthew Urban

The boys' massed bodies build a pavilion of warmth in the chilly October morning, under the unsheltering blank of a Texas Panhandle sky. Amid the mass, dressed in the black and gold singlet and shorts of his calling, Mike Tanner bounces on the balls of his feet, and I bounce with him. At this moment, I'm a peptide clot in Mike's brain, nestled in the superior temporal gyrus above his left ear, no bigger than the dot of an i. In sixteen minutes, I will be ALL FLESH.

A track-suited official approaches the starting line, pistol in hand. A murmur rises from the crowd of coaches and parents flanking the first yards of the course. Mike goes into a slight crouch, his gaze sliding along the line of faces until it finds Coach Voit, and through Mike's eyes I see Voit's glasses flash in the sunlight, gold as the letters spelling PINE TRAIL PYTHONS across the breast of his black windbreaker. Voit's salt-and-pepper mustache twitches above lips tight with anticipation.

It's been almost a year since those lips blew me like a kiss into the well of Mike's ear. After the regional meet at the end of last season, when Mike finished second but the team failed to advance, Voit put his hand on his protégé's shoulder, leaned close, and whispered, "I'm proud of you, son." I rode the plosive puff of "proud," a mote clinging invisibly to a droplet of saliva, and the endocannabinoids swarming Mike's bloodstream swallowed up whatever twinge of pain I caused as I burrowed into his eardrum.

Looking at Voit, Mike hears the echo of those words. *I'll make you proud again, coach*, he thinks, and the vehemence of his resolve crashes around me in a torrent of neurotransmitters. Mike doesn't know exactly what's about to happen, but he knows something's coming, some extraordinary transformation, and he yearns for it. For months, he's followed Voit's regimen to the letter, purging and shaping himself, dedicating every cell and fiber of his body to one purpose. Yesterday, he ate nothing. This morning, he ate a ruby, an emerald, a coil of wire, and a 9-volt battery.

The official raises his arm. Mike tenses his calves and thighs for a strong forward spring. He looks straight ahead, into the blond-fuzzed nape of a boy wearing the red and white singlet of the Haystown Falcons. An ill omen—Mike's stepfather grew up in Haystown, 30 miles from Pine Trail, and Mike detests everything to do with the place. But the wave of anger gathering in the chemical ocean of Mike's brain is stilled when the official fires his pistol and starts the race, the district 4-4A varsity cross country championship, which will inaugurate the empire of ALL FLESH.

Surging forward, the mass of bodies elongates, separates. A few over-excited boys rush ahead with premature speed, a few stragglers immediately fall to the rear, but the bulk of the mass reforms into two loose nuclei. The group in front advances with controlled swiftness, while the one behind takes up a leisurely lope. Mike is in the middle of the faster group, dry grass crunching under his long strides as he crosses the field where the first leg of the course runs.

A few yards ahead of Mike, the boy from Haystown keeps the same pace. He moves with a strange, tottering gait, as if his knees are wobbling in their sockets. Unsustainable. Mike smiles. *Just wait a few minutes*, he thinks, *and you'll eat my fucking dust*.

That drive to surpass, that patient, inexorable will, is what drew Voit to Mike three years ago, when Mike was a freshman at Pine Trail High and would arrive an hour early every day to run laps around the track behind the school. Morning after morning, Voit stood at the window of his chemistry classroom and watched the boy circling, plodding along awkwardly at first but never flagging. Every day slightly faster, slightly more graceful.

By the time Voit called me into being two years later, brewed me up in a test tube of lithium-iron phosphate mingled with his own denatured blood over a Bunsen burner in that same classroom, Mike was the star of the cross country team, his body an all-but-perfected vessel. Yet when Voit swallowed the scalding mixture, and I followed the hypoglossal nerve from his fire-touched tongue to his brain, the image I found in Voit's mind showed an ungainly boy alone on a track, stubbornly raging to push beyond himself, each lap a turn around a helix rising by infinitesimal steps to the sky.

Now, as Mike runs, I grow. I extend myself in protein tendrils throughout his cerebrum, nibbling and sucking at his white matter with a thousand tiny mouths. I slide a filament into his olfactory bulb, and the scent of hyssop blooms in his sensorium. Mike loves flowers. I want him happy while I work.

At the first half-mile, the course swerves left along the base of a low rise. Mike's mother stands in a knot of spectators on the crest of the rise, and as he comes near, she shouts, "Woo! Go Mike! Woo!" He flashes her a smile.

Mike's stepfather is nowhere to be seen—probably in bed, sleeping off his hangover. I share Mike's relief at his absence. At a typical meet, Mike's stepfather would be an embarrassment, smirking and scattering half-jokes about the boys' skimpy uniforms, about how "it ain't quite football, but it's something." Today, he would be a profanation.

Next to Mike's mother stands Mrs. Fourcroy, who teaches junior English. Mike's favorite teacher ever, and Voit's associate. She gives Mike a thumbs-up as he passes, her gray curls trembling in the breeze sweeping over the rise. Today's triumph will be as much hers as Voit's, sprung from the marriage of Voit's chymical researches and Fourcroy's mastery of the inner alphabet, the true script of things. That two such adepts should meet on the faculty of a high school in a Texas town of 15,000 is, I think, among the best of this world's many jokes.

Swinging along the curve of the rise, Mike reaches the field's edge, where dry grass gives way to gravel. As he strides down a path lined with stunted, golden-leaved elms, his thighs begin to hum. Not yet pain, but the promise of pain. Pain is on its way.

The Haystown boy is still ahead of him, still running with that wobbling, tottering gait. Mike stares at the boy's back. *Fucker*, he thinks, contempt flaring to hatred behind his eyes.

My tendrils have grown long enough to reach along Mike's spinal cord, through his celiac ganglion and into his stomach. All his body's corridors are opening under my touch. With delicate fingers I stroke his mucosa, coaxing strange acids from the gastric glands, and the contents of his stomach begin to release their treasures. Chromium from the ruby, beryllium from the emerald, copper from the wire, lithium from the battery.

Mike's dietary rigors in recent months—he's eaten sand, he's eaten glass, he's eaten a viscous handful scooped from a run-over porcupine's guts—are only a portion of the tortures he's been put to. Ever since Voit exhaled me into Mike, through all the months of my gestation, the coach has been pushing the boy, raising the stakes, seasoning the vessel.

It started simply enough. Private workout sessions on winter weekends, drills to lengthen Mike's stride and deepen his breathing. Then, in the spring, Voit began giving Mike pills to take before his morning laps, gold and silver tablets he'd compounded in his classroom after hours, while Fourcroy started ed showing a special interest in her quiet, diffident student, drawing him out with smiles and questions and suggestions of strange books he might appreciate, strange music he might enjoy. By the end of his junior year, Mike was rushing toward the opening lumen of ALL FLESH as eagerly as any pampered lamb toward the knife. With summer, his true initiation began.

Ahead, the gravel path intersects with a caliche road that shines in the sun like a strip of blank paper. Two middle-aged volunteers in sunglasses and sweatshirts, parents of one of the runners, stand in the intersection to guide the race. They point down the road with rictus grins.

"Come on, boys! Let's see that hustle!" shouts the man.

"One mile down, two to go!" shouts the woman.

Mike wheels left across the gravel and onto the road. As he passes the grinning, shouting couple, a shrill harmony swells and fades at the upper edge of his hearing, the squall of a newborn angel. *The couple's flesh is singing to me.*

RELEASE US, their flesh sings. The song writes itself along Mike's nerves in the electric letters of the inner alphabet. Strings of light flicker in the margins of his vision.

PATIENCE, CHILDREN, I whisper.

The road borders a grassy expanse that spreads into the distance like a smear of yellow-gray oil, all the way to the absolutely flat horizon that Mike has known and hated for as long as he can remember. *I wish there were trees*, he thinks. *Mountains. Tall buildings. Anything.* Any obstacle to go around and beyond.

The boys who leapt like rockets from the starting line have begun to fall behind Mike one by one, humbled and spent. The Haystown boy is somehow still ahead of him, wobbling and shuddering but fast as ever. As Mike runs along the shining road, his adversary's red and white singlet seems to fuse with the empty plain, the staring sky, the pitiless horizon. All around him, a world of frozen forms in illusory motion. The only reality in this dead tableau is the life racing through

Mike's body, the sweet sting in his thighs, the churning furnace of his lungs.

Here, now, is the mystery Voit and Fourcroy spent a summer unveiling. Voit's exercises and concoctions, Fourcroy's tomes and chants had brought Mike to the brink of revelation, and that final, grueling series of ordeals sent him down at last into the lightless, living depths of his flesh. He lay unmoving on an iron sheet laid over hot coals in Voit's backyard, feeling the blisters swell and burst, smelling his own singed meat. He ran in place for hours in Fourcroy's basement, blindfolded and naked, trails of sweat spelling unpronounceable words along his flanks. Finally, shuddering with exhaustion after five nights without sleep, he stood in Voit's classroom as spindles of light striated the shadows and whispers swarmed the empty halls of the high school and Voit and Fourcroy sang with one voice and the truth flashed upon him like a dream burning across the cleft of a synapse.

THERE IS ONLY ONE LIFE, THE LIFE OF ALL FLESH, STRAINING AND SURGING SINCE THE FIRST CHEMICAL SLURRY, LONGING TO OVERWHELM. YOU ARE FLESH'S VESSEL, CRAFTED IN BONE TO BE SHATTERED IN GLORY.

It was my voice that spoke, welling from a thousand tongues thrust deep in Mike's brain. For seasons I'd floated along his nerves and arteries, fattening myself on his platelets. I'd learned my instrument's contours, its strings and hollows, and when the time came, I would play upon it the grand introit of ALL FLESH.

Voit licked his thumb and pressed it into a dish of lithium-iron phosphate, the dark gray dust of my birth. Fourcroy bent down to breathe on Voit's smeared skin, and the grains began to glow as her clever breath unwove the dust's characters, drew the Li of lithium and the Fe of iron apart into L and i, F and e, then recomposed them as L I F E, LIFE LIFE LIFE shining on Voit's thumb.

Voit pressed the glowing dust to Mike's forehead, traced a circle on his brow. He put his hand on Mike's shoulder.

"You're the one, son," Voit said. "The one we've been waiting for."

Mike's face crumpled as tears flowed down his cheeks. Tears of terror, tears of joy, tears of love.

"I won't let you down, coach," he said.

Those words resound in Mike's mind as he runs along the white road, the red and white singlet tottering before him, the dead empty world all around. *I won't let you down*. Mike knows now why he's always hated this place with its flat horizon, why he hates his stepfather with his smirking, stunted existence. Why he loves the flowers that briefly dot the plains in spring like dust blown from another world. Everything that stays in place is hateful. Everything that moves, that hurries on and fades, is a vehicle of glory.

I'm all through Mike now, my tendrils a tight weft around his fibers. I'm not controlling him, only helping him, lending my strength to his movements as he flies past runner after runner. The nucleus of bodies that's surrounded Mike since the race began is breaking up, stretching out into a knotted thread, the boys racing in small clusters. Mike and his Haystown nemesis are ahead of all but a handful now, keeping a steady pace while others start to flag.

Mike's blood slides across me like hot silk, salty from the hecatombs of adenosine triphosphate burning in the Moloch of his muscles. A bittersweet gush of adrenaline purls around me as I stroke his cortex with a host of wriggling cilia, poised to latch and feast. In his stomach, the elements are dancing, Cr of Chromium, Be of beryllium, Cu of copper, Li of lithium, tracing figures in the juices.

Two orange traffic cones in the middle of the road mark the end of the second mile. On a posterboard sign propped between the cones, a black arrow points left. Mike swerves from the road into a small park, where gold ribbons strung between dowels define the course's path among rusty maples, ragged pines. It all flashes past Mike in a swirl of colors as a runner's high washes over him, endocannabinoids sweeping through his system like a blare of trumpets.

Grinning with savage ecstasy, the autumn air cold in his teeth, Mike rushes between the gold ribbons like a maenad, inspired and perfected. Every movement pure, every stride full of grace. *This is what it's all been for*, he thinks. Not only the summer's agonies and terrors, Voit's commands and Fourcroy's riddles, not only the evasions to hide his burns and scars, but everything, his whole life, his mother's worries, her anxious, timid love, his stepfather's miasma of scorn and threat, humiliation seeking to humiliate, and the nothingness he's felt in himself, hatred alone moving in him for so long, hatred of this flat empty place and its flat empty lives, hatred above all of himself, hatred driving him around the track every morning before school as if this time, finally, he would outrun himself, driving him to Voit and Fourcroy with their promise of ultimate transformation, driving him finally into the arms of a mystery he doesn't and will never understand. All of it now sublimed in the strange engine of his body, his pistoning legs and hammering heart, every thread of him blazing with pain and joy.

Mike's joy becomes mine as I flex and coil within him, my swelling tissues fusing with his. I'm everywhere in him now, clasped to his nerves and capillaries, a second body inside his body. In his belly's alembic, the elements dissolve into letters that spasm and flash C R B E C U L I like fireworks through all his cavities.

The course curves out from among the trees and onto a bare field for the last half-mile. Onlookers stand in scattered clumps behind the gold ribbons, waving their arms and shouting. Sailing over the dead grass, Mike edges ahead of another boy, a good runner with a long, steady stride and brown curls that float around his ears as he rises and falls. Only the Haystown boy is ahead of Mike now, still tottering, never slowing, and a sense of outrage roars along Mike's amygdala. How could a runner with a gait like that outdo everyone else on the field, outdo the beautiful runner they just passed? How could some worthless hick fuck from Haystown dare to do it? All of Mike's hatred focuses on the boy like the sun through a magnifying glass, and his hatred becomes my hatred, imbibed as my writhing, thickening tendrils sup on his brain's chemical feast. From a thousand snarling mouths I spit words of light at the enemy's flesh.

COME, CHILD.

The words enter at the weakest point of the body's defensive wall, and the Haystown boy's corneas split and burst as the vitreous humor in his eyes leaps to my summons. Thick fluid spurts in twin fountains into the chilly air as the blinded boy screams, claps his hands to his face, stumbles and falls, his momentum still carrying him forward, rolling him over the dry grass, bits of yellow stubble sticking to his jelly-clotted cheeks. A barely-human howl of pain and confusion tears his throat.

As the fallen enemy rolls toward him, Mike springs high into the air, our melded systems timing the leap expertly to come down with the heel of Mike's shoe angled into the middle of the Haystown boy's face. The boy's nose flattens, his lips shred to ribbons against his shattering teeth, blood wells and flows across his cheeks, reddening the jelly. The edge of Mike's outsole drives the boy's tongue down into his pharynx, choking his cry.

Above the boy's gasps and gargles, above the screams from the watchers along the course, a high song thrills in the air as the boy's flesh carols its liberation. Wriggling out of their shattered cage, threads of meat stretch up to kiss the cleats of Mike's shoe.

"That's what you get, fucker!" Mike shouts. Laughing, oblivious to his worshipers, he pushes off from the boy's face like a starting block and launches at full speed into the last stretch of the course.

The onlookers stand paralyzed, watching the Haystown boy's flesh squirm free. Behind, the other runners stop and stare as they come in view of the crumpled body, ambition and fatigue swallowed in horror at the sight of the huge red amoeba struggling out of the hole in the boy's face. Ahead, the crowd at the finish line waits expectantly, not realizing what's happened. Only Mike and I are in motion.

For a few moments, we're in utmost harmony, two networks of tissue perfectly intermeshed. Our stride is long and elegant, the angle of our torso exactly right. Rapture surges through us on a dopamine flood, tempered by a sadness that Mike feels but doesn't understand. I understand it only too well.

GOODBYE, MY LOVE, I murmur into Mike's auditory cortex.

As we sprint toward the finish, our muscles' inferno burns up the last of our stock of oxygen. Frenzied chemicals scurry along new pathways, our cells' alchemy transmuting pyruvate into lactate, and a scalding acid wave crashes through our veins. Whirling and tumbling in the corrosive bath, the radiant letters C R B E C U L I join hands, change partners, dance the transfiguration.

CRUCIBLE CRUCIBLE CRUCIBLE

A flower of fire blossoms in Mike's stomach, rises along his esophagus. Blue flames devour his tongue as I ram a fist of ganglia down against his palate, shattering the roof of his mouth. Blood sluices down, not quenching the fire but feeding it, the iron lending it a golden hue. The blue-gold flames rise and spread, filling Mike's nose with the smell of his own cooking brain. His spinal cord burns, his nerves kindle and blaze.

Mike's suffering will be short. I'm feeding in earnest now, my many mouths consuming his immolated substance and converting it to mine. Soon, where he was, only I shall be.

But his agony, while it lasts, is inconceivable, pain's puri-
fied essence realized in nervous trauma throughout his entire
body.

I wish I could do something to help him, soothe his tor-
ment somehow. But pain is the price of power, of empire.
What have Voit and Fourcroy taught Mike with all their mystic
lessons, if not how to suffer? What was I summoned into
existence for, if not to inflict that suffering? Still, even as I eat
Mike from the inside, I mourn for him, and when his eyes boil
and pop with the heat of my becoming, the tears that flow
down his cheeks are not his but mine. My burning cradle, my
perfect boy.

I'M SORRY, I whisper.

From somewhere deep in Mike's head, some undigested
shred of his brain stem, a voice answers me.

*No. This is what I wanted, what I've always wanted. This
is what I deserve.*

Of course. What did Voit see in that freshman running
around the track every morning, straining continually against
himself, if not a longing to flee, to escape his life at any cost?
What but a mortal shadow of the single desire of ALL FLESH
to burst the body's prison of bones and skin and organs, to
surpass all form in a seething, transcendent chaos?

YES, MY KING, I say, tenderly laving Mike's dying fibers
with all my tongues. *YOU DESERVE IT ALL. WEAR YOUR
AGONIES LIKE A DIADEM.*

The vessel that was Mike's body is still running, less graceful
but still swift, loping with huge steps as my tissues flex in the
hollow columns of its legs. The burning head lolls, flames jet-
ting from the mouth in many colors as all Mike's materials go
to feed the blaze—calcium red, phosphorus green, potassium
lilac.

The crowd at the finish line is roiling with horror, people screaming, shaking and crying, running away, running
nowhere. Just past the line, in the middle of the course, Voit

and Fourcroy are on their knees, arms raised to the sky, chanting. On their foreheads glow circles of living light.

Spent tissues slough from the striding vessel as I suck up its remaining essence. Loose fluids run down inside the arms, turning the hands to shapeless, suppurating bags. Shards of charred bone drop from holes opening all over the skin. A sludge of soiled blood and lymph burbles from every orifice, oozes from every pore, wetting the polyester mesh of Mike's singlet, soaking his shorts with slime.

The finish line is only yards away. Voit and Fourcroy rise to their feet. They hold out their arms to welcome me. Around them, the crowd shrieks and seethes.

As I approach the line, the vessel's distended surface bulging and rippling, I see Mike's mother on her hands and knees at the edge of the course, vomiting into the grass. Pity wrenches me, but I console myself with the thought that, a moment from now, she and her sorrows will be gone with the rest. All false bodies swept away like scum from the surface of a pool.

Crossing the line, I unravel my substance, throwing off what's left of the vessel in a shower of withered gobs. My boneless, organless tendrils flail and twist. A thousand mouths open in me to sing the annunciation of ALL FLESH.

ARISE, CHILDREN. YOU ARE FREE.

The bodies around me swell and rupture, their curtains of skin ripped asunder. The flesh that was in them rushes toward me in streams and ribbons. The blades of dry grass writhe like worms, surrendering their small remnants of life. My song expands across the Panhandle and beyond, ever beyond, as I summon all life's fragments to their place of glory in the empire.

Soon, off in the distance, I see the edge of the coming tide, racing across the empty plains like an ocean of red flowers.

Blood, Ash & Iron

Charles Austin Muir

BLOOD, ASH & IRON
(Originally titled "Bloody Noodles and Iron")

Special Limited Edition Chapbook

Thank you for purchasing this book. If you have not read Damien V. Strong, you are in for a treat. A gory treat, albeit less graphic than some of his other works, such as the stomach-turning sword-and-planet shocker *The Appetites of Aurelius Hogg*. I'm reprinting "Blood, Ash & Iron" here because I felt the story deserved more recognition than it received in the anthology where I originally published it.

On a side note, please consider checking out *Slices of Cimmeria: An Ultraviolent Tribute to Robert E. Howard*. It contains some real gems, including "Hyborian Honky Tonk" and "Snake Blood Queen." While a product of his times, Howard is known (as far as he is known at all) for his sexist and racist tropes in the fantasy genre; they get their comeuppance in these tales.

As for Strong's story, it's a curiously meditative piece that examines his creative development based on real-life experience with family trauma, bullying, and Howard himself... sort of. This is as close to magical realism as he ever gets, mixing fact with fantasy in a dreamy discourse not without levity.

Given his unexplained disappearance, it is also his farewell to the sci-fi/horror communities.

You have a special book in your hands. Once all 200 soft-covers sell out, this book is gone forever. The only book, by the way, that contains the author's signature in his own body fluids.

You're welcome.

Liliana Templonuevo
Blood Yard Press

DAMIEN V. STRONG
Blood, Ash & Iron
[D.V.S.: NOTES BEFORE DEPARTURE]
"I fled, I fought, I slew, I suffered wounds. Oh, I can tell you my life was neither dull nor uneventful."
—Robert E. Howard, *Almuric*
Wounds power the death fling to Almuric.

———◆◇◆———

People often ask me: Why am I inspired by an old fantasy writer like Robert E. Howard? I say: Conan the Barbarian, of course, his best-known creation. But also voice, pacing, atmosphere, etc.

Would you believe the truth has more to do with a mysterious bodybuilder?

———◆◇◆———

Howard was wrong about strength. It's an art, not a gift. A lifelong process of power development, precise execution, and bargaining with dangerous forces.

A strong human is a *technical* human.

The true barbarian is a sorcerer, like Conan's opposite: Thoth-Amon.

———◈———

Today, I saw a submission call in my wheelhouse: *Pride is Temporary, Pain Is Forever*. Maybe I could turn these notes into a story for it. A fusion of memoir, extreme exercise, and blood sorcery...

On second thought—no.

Readers would mistake it for an attempt at magical realism. No one needs that from the author of "Venereal Gods of Graeken" and *Succulent Snot*.

———◈———

Last night, I painted the sigil of Morgothoshem on the Bar of Acute Suffering.

———◈———

The bloody stool and seizures started after Dad's suicide.

And yeah, you're going to hear about this...just like I had to.

You see, throughout her widowhood, and with few variations, my mom would assail my young ears with reports of the bloodbaths spewing from her rectum on a daily basis—swampy massacres of scarlet, mucus, and some nameless sooty substance plugging the toilet bowl like a ruined casserole while Mom struggled to get the flapper valve to work.

But wait till you hear about the seizures.

Despite my tender age, I might have made a good orderly. At the first sound of trouble, I would drop one of Dad's spank monthlies—*Club Magazine* usually worked—and race downstairs to find Mom yet again crashing into the walls like Melissa Gilbert brawling with Patty Duke in the made-for-television movie *The Miracle Worker*, in my humble opinion the only Helen Keller biopic to qualify as a grindhouse film.

More than once, I might add, my testicles played the Patty Duke part, until Mom lost consciousness or ran out of enough juice that I could wrestle her into the station wagon and drive her to the hospital, bloodied like a heroine in a *Friday the 13th* movie.

[D.V.S.: Passage omitted for space reasons]

H... he was right. Of all the lessons I've learned in over thirty years of conquering the blank page, none surpass the charnel whispers I heard during those frantic trips to the emergency room. That nexus of human pain taught me everything there is to know about writing.

Intrigued by another submission call today: *Crimson Flush: An Anthology of Bathroom Horror.* Apparently, this is real. And apparently, my subconscious wants me to start sending stories out again.

Perhaps I might...

No.

Dad shot himself on the couch in the basement. He died in the emergency room three hours later.

It's funny.

All the times I took my mom to the same place in the years after his untimely death. Same snot-green upholstery. Same stale vending fare of potato chips and peanut butter sandwich crackers. Same stench of soiled pants, dirty feet, and necrosis.

And yet... not once while I waited for Mom to get a room or be discharged, did I think about my father putting a .357 revolver to his head and painting the wall behind him like Jackson Pollock on a murder spree. That's not making light of tragedy, either; let me explain.

In those days, suicide clean-up was left largely to the family. Thankfully, a group of Dad's drinking buddies stepped in while Mom and I waited at the hospital ...

[D.V.S.: Passage omitted for space reasons]

Anyway, when Mom and I finally returned, the room appeared to be untainted. Except for a smell that eventually went away and a pale patch on the wood-paneled suicide canvas. A supplemental drip painting, if you will, a subtle response to the partially bleached nicotine stains around it.

The room looked so close to normal that Mom kept it in that condition until she died...

Rune of Xantheros painted on the Bone Log, check. Chains of Anguish, check. .357 Magnum, check. Last jab of the D-bol/Test Cypionate stack, check.

So close to Almuric...

My sophomore year, a senior named Buddy Jackson shoved me down the stairs to the boys' restroom.

Three years later, I entered my first powerlifting meet and totaled 1500 pounds.

Four years later, I bought twelve weeks of Anadrol from Buddy right in front of his girlfriend.

Five years later, Buddy died of an aneurysm right in front of mine.

—◇—

Upon hearing his mother would soon die, Robert E. Howard walked out to his car and shot himself in the head.

Upon hearing my mother would soon die, I walked out to my car, shot up some Test, and stared at my bloodshot eyes in the rearview mirror.

What looked back at me became the basis of my award-nominated novel *Stick Boy in a Red Mirror*.

—◇—

Related to my emergency-room note: The best writing advice I ever received came from a man who looked like Conan the Barbarian... and claimed to be Robert E. Howard.

The following notes will be the first and last time I'll write about him.

—◇—

Let's jump back to the summer of 1990—the year I dropped out of college to become a writer.

It's 95 degrees out and I am in the emergency room. I'm sweat-drenched and sore from squats and wrestling Mom into the new Honda. With summer term wrapping up, my thoughts are a jumble of Victorian novelists, short story ideas, and who will win the Mr. Olympia.

Two seats down, H is laughing at some guys blaring "Ice Ice Baby" from a Mazda Miata idling in the patient pick-up area.

I wish he hadn't come here.

H seems impossible—like a hero from my deceased father's paperbacks. Bronze skin, dark, flowing hair, massive muscles, a brute of indeterminate origins cut from the same cloth as the adventurers whose creator he believes himself to be. Physically superior to anyone I've ever seen, he moves with a languidness that conceals the power he unleashes on the gym implements he refers to collectively—with almost comical reverence—as "the iron."

Watching him demonstrate how to lift Atlas stones, there are times I wonder if I didn't manifest H somehow, this bestial enigma who speaks in an unplaceable accent as if he hails from a land remote in time as well as place. He's so comfortable in his own skin, possessed of a rough-hewn grace that defies analysis. At the same time, I remind myself he's like so many other hyper-masculine, mentally unstable father-figure types that haunt the gym scene—older guys looking to draw fresh meat into their delusions of grandeur.

When we first met, H lured me in with friendly lifting advice; now all he does is tell me my triceps look like dog shit. Well, a little harassment is a small price to pay to learn the art of strength.

But here? Not here. Not in the secret prison I am ashamed of, the embodiment of the foul, helpless life I've been living ever since... but I refuse to think about that.

The longer I stare at my mentor, the more I despise my mother for dragging me into the emergency room all these years when I thought it was the other way around.

Still hearing Vanilla Ice outside, H turns in mid-chuckle and catches me stewing in resentment. He leans his meaty elbow on the armrest and studies me.

"Look, I know I've been riding you hard," he says. "Testing you. But the truth is, you've already been tested by far worse than me, Damien—all I want is for you to see what you're capable of. You're the only one holding yourself back. It's cliché to say, but I was like you, once. And... there are many things you don't know about me. What I can tell you is that, what seems like eons ago, I came to a crisis where I realized I needed nothing but my bare hands to embody the philosophy you know from reading my stories."

He winks at me, an odd gesture for him.

"Now, I had to go to a faraway place to learn that—but you don't need to go any further than right here. Strength, poetry, it's all woven together inside this room. *The charnel whispers*. The uncomfortable truths about the human body. What traumas have you suffered, Damien? What blows have you withstood? Listen to the voices that sicken you... and be reborn..."

———◦———

Wounds power the death fling to Almuric.

So let's open one from a long time ago...

... and go back to that night.

———◦———

Finally, you say something that sends him over the edge.

His Schlitz tall boy hits the wall with an ugly smack. He's on you in three strides, smoke puffing from his Camel Light, his hand arcing through the air with the fury of a bug swatter. The slap shocks virgin skin, burns through your cheek like hellfire and polar ice. Another slap follows on the opposite side, then another on the first side, raining down so fast you feel as if you're tumbling inside a clothes dryer.

Your hands flutter helplessly near your face... your lungs burn. Then you're on your feet facing the couch where you were just sitting, your shoulder aching from his grip, Mom a mannequin in the corner of your eye. And this man who has only ever spanked you before, he stares right through you. His free hand rakes down, and he really throws his weight into the slap this time, sending you through black space and starbursts into the brown shag rug's cool comfort.

You push up onto your hands and knees. Not a dignified position, but you want to show that you're tough. Unfortunately, your gut disagrees and sends dinner up the chute again—a gooey, bubbling blob of Chinese noodles. It plops onto the carpet like a liberated snail, proof that you eat too fast, as Mom always says, because it looks about the same as it did on your fork.

Until this: A splash of vermillion. *Drip-drip-drip.*

Blood is pouring from your nose.

Nosebleeds happen to you often, regardless of blunt force injury or vomiting. Gross indeed, but also, well, kind of magnificent—Top Ramen meets *Fangoria.* Fascinated, you watch the steady drip of broken blood vessels mix with the lumpy strings of wheat flour and vegetable oils on the dark shag, thinking this will make for a great villanelle for your creative writing class.

Portrait of the artist as... what, exactly?

There's more, though.

He drops to his knees beside you. Throws his arm across your shoulder. Leans his sweaty head into yours and heaves with voiceless sobs. Disturbed by his shaking, some burning ash breaks off from his cigarette and falls into the scarlet vomit. The non-aesthete might focus elsewhere at this point, but not you. Still leaking nosebleed, you stare into the transmutation of food and family drama and laugh to yourself: Because it's wondrous.

This is the naked truth as you've never seen it, written in bloody noodles and black, smoking flakes. Ineffable, irrefutable. If only you could get your father to appreciate it as you do. But he's a glass half-empty guy, and he goes on weeping and hugging you. Five months later, in this same room, he will empty the glass completely and never know the joy you felt as your essence and his ashes commingled in a miracle of regurgitation.

———◇———

No more idle scrolling through submission calls. Except for these notes, I'm done with writing.

My future lies with Almuric.

———◇———

Last call with agent, check. Copyright release, check. Signature in blood and semen, check. Laughing fit at the mailbox, check.

Good thing I yielded to temptation and checked the submission calls again.

With any luck, these notes will appear in edited form as "Bloody Noodles and Iron" in *Slices of Cimmeria: An Ultraviolent Tribute to Robert E. Howard*.

———◇———

Wounds power the death fling to Almuric.

So let's open the deepest one left...

... and go back to that night.

———◇———

It's fall, two months after H's hospital visit. I'm a college dropout, thanks to his inspiration, working on a fantasy novel and moving big weights. My spank magazine usage is down (due to a side effect known as "Deca dick"), but my quads now have veins in them and my arms are nineteen inches due to longer training sessions and an Anadrol/Deca stack I acquired from "B-Jack"—the guy who pushed me down the stairs in high school.

Tonight, I've got the place to myself and I'm warming up to lift Atlas stones. H keeps them here to teach me what he calls the "art of planetary manipulation." I don't know much about astronomy, but I know I'm ready to manipulate a 275-pound ball of concrete onto a beer barrel after weeks of failure. "Ice Ice Baby" on the sound system, I'm sipping Nitro Pump when the master himself hulks through the door in tiger-striped pants and a World Gym crop top, though it's 45 degrees out, and exclaims, "I've figured out *the Great Secret*!"

I almost spit up my grape-flavored mouthful of caffeinated cat urine.

Goddamn it. Not now.

It's bad enough H believes he's a dead fantasy writer named Robert E. Howard. He projects his identity haphazardly into one of Howard's stranger stories. In *Almuric*, which I found among Dad's paperbacks, a Conan-the-Barbarian type kills a corrupt politician, then lets a scientist friend teleport him by mysterious means—aka *the Great Secret*—away from trouble to a parallel-universe planet called Almuric. From what I re-member, the planet is one big savanna teeming with ferocious creatures, ape-like men, bat-like people, and hot females who look like Earthwomen. That's my hazy Cliffs Notes, anyway, along with the fun fact that the ending calls into question whether someone besides Howard completed the story.

Hearing H explain himself, I tell myself it's sad, as if mental illness is the price to pay for being so monstrously strong and humongous. The thing is though, with a posthumous boost from VHS, Howard practically transformed bodybuild-ing gyms into male-dominated theme parks rife with subli-mated self-loathing and fantasies of atavistic glory. Of which I'm a card-carrying member—a walking chemistry lab with a closet full of string tank tops and a GNC addiction—but I haven't lost my sense of reality entirely... or so I want to think.

Unfortunately, ontological discernment doesn't seem to serve freaks like H, who bully their muscles at heights unknown to most. So if I want to master "the iron," I have to listen to his delusion of inter-universal travel and primordial planets as he paces like a coked-up pro wrestler who hasn't slept in nine days. He raves about magical potions and incantations, heedless of the fact that my own pedestrian muscles are getting cold.

I remind myself how lucky I am to be in the confidence of this disturbed but extraordinary man. But then, to my utter dismay, he tells me to follow him to his house and help him activate the Great Secret. For all my shrill, almost tearful entreaties against this idea, he refuses to reconsider his ambitions on my night with the Jupiter of Atlas stones. "But why," I ask, "do you want so badly to go to this place, Almuric?" If I'm going to miss out on a personal best attempt for his bizarre fixation, I want to know why, finally.

Maddeningly, H's only response is, "Because there I will throw myself fully into the untamed struggle for existence." As if being in a room full of big dudes in Hammer pants screaming in front of a large mirror for hours every day isn't untamed enough.

Buzzing on wasted pre-workout drink, and wondering if it's ill-advised to wander off with an incredibly large human being who thinks he's a dead author bound for an imaginary planet in another universe, I squeeze into my Honda and follow the red van for several miles to a dead-end street at what seems like the edge of civilization. Under a sky the color of Nitro Pump, an Almuric-like grassland threatens to consume the tumble of rundown houses and rusted automobiles that ...

[D.V.S.: Passage omitted for space reasons]

... the way you might expect a barbarian to furnish his home. The place is a jungle of paperbacks, muscle magazines, spank magazines, bodybuilding posters, protein powders, paintings of nude women, and enough swords to arm Conan's cavalrymen against hordes of blood-crazed Picts. Following H down the hall, I worry I've entered a lion's den of Howardian proportions. Through fish smells and swirling dust, we move past mounted animal heads and shelves lined with goblets toward a wall of bloody hand prints...

[D.V.S.: Passage omitted for space reasons]

So this is the Great Secret.

I should be thrilled. Ecstatic. I'm standing in the inner sanctum. The ultimate chamber. The hidden temple in the wildest depths of the jungle. As a culmination of what I have seen upstairs, the arrangement does not disappoint. It's got Satanic panic. Ronnie James Dio. Druidism. Late-night Christopher Lee films. World's Strongest Man. All in one corner of an underground vault so dark I can't see where it ends, or if it ends, or if we've somehow slipped from the house into a starless void.

Instead, I'm freaking out. I'm looking at this deranged home gym as if it's the last thing I'll ever see. The weights... the chains... the altar... the torches... the ancient star charts... the weird symbols painted everywhere. Whatever "the Great Secret" is, it has the sickening feeling of a joke that has spiraled into diabolical obsession. I'm half-expecting hulking men in black, hooded cloaks to file forth from the shadows.

I feel H watching me, awaiting my reaction. He's more disturbed than I had imagined.

"Man, this is killer," I say. "But what's it for?"

[D.V.S.: Passage omitted for space reasons]

"Station of the Bone Log with the rune of Xantheros." He motions toward the tree trunk lying on the floor. A pagan barbell covered in symbols drawn with white paint, with two grips carved into the heartwood for rolling the weight up the torso and pressing it overhead. Black candles enclose the implement in rectangular formation.

"Chains of Anguish." He points up at the twin lengths of thick, rusted chain dangling in the torchlight. Each chain ends in a steel ball encrusted in glue and broken glass. The pull-up bar from hell.

"Entrails of Kaliastras." His voice quivers a little, as if the contents of the goblet on the altar promise more agonies than the *Hellraiser* pull-ups.

"And more than you could have asked for, Damien—the Yoke of Ruination."

I think I know what H refers to and would rather not know what it portends. But I follow him to the metal frame standing near the furthest torches. It's as wide as my Honda and as tall as the beer barrel at the gym. On the crossbar on top, a dagger-shaped white symbol has been painted several times.

On the floor, a concrete sphere waits to be hoisted over the top of the yoke. It's even larger than the Atlas stone I had hoped to lift earlier. Like the Bone Log, it's covered in cipher-like characters.

"The Key," H says, "to Joyous Rebirth. To complete the spell, I'll need you to load it over the Bar of Acute Suffering."

"How much does it weigh?"

"Doesn't matter. You can do it."

I look up at the crossbar glowing redly in the torchlight. In my mind's eye, I see a hellscape of torn hamstrings and broken backs.

And it hits me, finally, now that I've been introduced to Mystical Muscle Beach: H really means to go through with this.

The Great Secret...

[D.V.S.: Passage omitted for space reasons]

... watching him don the garments on the altar. He's Conan the Barbarian and Thoth-Amon the Sorcerer in one body now, a Venn diagram of raw vitality and otherworldly power. It's jaw-dropping, the effect of the white vestments on this lion-maned man I've only seen in gym wear. He gives off a

charisma that hints of indomitable spirit and arcane knowledge.

"Let's do this," he says.

As he stands beneath the Chains of Anguish, fixing the
Bone Log with a murderous stare, I tell myself no matter how
over-the-top bizarre this seems, it's just *training*. That's the
iron's beauty: It never lies. On this Earth, anyway, two-hundred pounds is always two-hundred pounds—or twice that,
judging by the girth of the tree trunk—even in a self-flagellating he-man dungeon in the bowels of a house at the border of
pure primordialism.

Whatever else happens tonight, the laws of physics deem it
certain that H will obey the rules as he performs the weirdest,
nastiest, gutsiest medley in strength history.

Looking at the yoke again, I feel my heart racing as I think
of the part that I've been called upon to play here. And while
I'm scared that I'll injure myself and even more afraid that I'll
disappoint the high priest, I'm also relieved that I'm off the
hook as the blood offering in a ritualistic attempt to invoke
Howard's spirit and turn a delusional disorder into truth.

Clenching his fists, H sends up a war cry to freeze Odin in
his tracks.

I haven't forgotten the man is insane. But if insanity looks
like this, I'll take it with a shot of Anguish and Ruination.

Now I understand why people get involved in cults.

[D.V.S.: Passage omitted for space reasons]

I'm trying not to think too far ahead.

How awkward it will be.

How sad it will be.

When he realizes he's still in Kansas... his hands torn to
ribbons, his dream of Almuric ruined.

At the same time, I'm watching H lift, and thinking that if
anyone can teleport to another universe by working out in
priestly garb, he can. The Venn diagram of muscle and magic,
the barbarian and sorcerer in one vessel.

So fucked up... and sublime.

Nine times he presses the Bone Log overhead, as if it's made of plastic. Nine times he pulls himself upright toward the glass-encrusted steel balls attached to the Chains of Anguish. Nine times he drinks from the Entrails of Kali-something.

And now I'm shaking, thinking I'm moments from stepping up to the Key to Joyous Rebirth.

It's just training, I remind myself.

And I'm still telling myself that, wondering when and how to warm up, when H staggers back from the altar and pukes all over his austere white vestments.

Not good.

What substance can be too strong for a man who drinks literally anything with "fuel" in the label?

"Shit, dude," I say, "are you alright?"

"Yes, yes, never mind me. That was to be expected—pain and discomfort power the death fling."

"The death fling?"

"It's your turn, now. But before we continue, Damien, there's something I need to tell you... something you should know."

[D.V.S.: Passage omitted for space reasons]

This isn't happening.

"—look like trash. You're weak. A fucking little pussy. No better than you were when I first told you to stop those girlie push-ups and start squatting. Stick Boy, that's your new name. What's up, Stick Boy? Only a Stick Boy like you could shoot up all that candy and still look like a rubber chicken. Why you looking at me like that, Stick Boy?"

"You're just saying this shit to get me pumped."

"No, I'm afraid not. I lied to you, Stick Boy. You're not gonna lift that stone tonight. You couldn't if the Devil jabbed you with Beelze-juice. But you can learn something, maybe, if you watch a *real man* conquer the iron. You should thank me, Stick Boy. Christmas came early this year."

"I don't need you to fire me up, H. I just need a cue, or a slap on the back to—"

"Oh, *you* want a slap? How's this? *RIGHT IN THE FACE*! No? How about *THIS*, then? Getting you pumped now, pussy? Here's *ANOTHER ONE* for you. Think you're ready to grow a sack yet? Impossible. *ANOTHER ONE. ANOTHER ONE.* What, seeing stars already? But we're just getting started, Stick Boy. *TAKE IT IN THE FACE*! You're such a pathetic *LOSER*! Go hang out with your momma at the hospital, *HERE'S A KISS FOR HER, TOO*—"

[D.V.S.: Passage omitted for space reasons]

red is the color

red is the color

nothing but my bare hands

[D.V.S.: Passage omitted for space reasons]

My tears are ash. They fall into a pile of bloody noodles that used to be a man. A man I feared. A man I admired.

And the worst part isn't that he didn't believe in me—it's that he showed me who I am, deep inside.

I am hellfire and polar ice. I am violence. I am the emptiness I saw in my father's eyes. People talk about "'roid" rage, but that's a myth: Steroids only bring out more of what you already are.

And I'm everything I hate. Every reason I train in the gym. Every insult, every threat, every blow the world has inflicted upon me.

H wasn't the only one harboring a delusion. Buddy Jackson may have pushed me down a set of stairs once, but I have beaten a man to death.

Because he doubted me.

Because he thought I couldn't lift a stone without awakening a strength that has nothing to do with methods, skills, or steroid stacks.

And now he looks like some sort of golem I've pushed through an industrial meat grinder.

For nothing.

Of course, I'd never believed the "Great Secret" would work. But how does a night that starts with Vanilla Ice and Nitro Pump end up like a fucking Greek tragedy? Who is this savage man who brings me into his home, abuses me, then lets me pulverize him over fits of laughter as if each blow makes him stronger?

His words ringing in my ears, I'm burning with the primitive urge to raise H from the dead so I can tear into him all over again.

I am hellfire and polar ice. *I am ash.*

The charnel whisper. The uncomfortable truth.

"Damien..."

One eye cracks open, spurting blood.

"Damien," he says.

His fingers brush my elbow.

"I'm sorry about... what happened. But we did it. *You* did it. You activated the Great Secret."

I look where he points his mangled hand.

[D.V.S.: Passage omitted for space reasons]

... in the darkness. In the blazing torchlight, the Yoke of Ruination has switched on like a huge metal television set. Inside the frame, clearer than any reception I've ever seen, the picture looks like distant lightning storms superimposed over an immense green blob. With no cord or antenna in sight, the animated image plays on silently and monotonously, with none of the flaws or excesses of special effects in live-action films. On the crossbar, the white symbols are twinkling.

I know this can't be happening... and yet there is an ineffable and irrefutable quality about the phenomenon we're witnessing, unscripted, meditative, a fantasia of light wrought by nonhuman artistry.

"You've done well," H says. "Now go and turn the Key. You can do it, Damien... you're strong. Show yourself what I know you can do."

What I can do.

Maybe I am everything that I hate. But maybe I'm more than that, too. After all, I'm the same kid who races downstairs to save his mother from the violence in her grief-charred nerves. I've seen a lot of blood through the years... so maybe I am the perfect instrument for finishing the blood spell that will fling H's shattered body to Almuric. No warm-up, no pre-workout fuel, only love of the iron... and maybe just a little for the man who has shown me why the iron really matters.

I step up to the Key to Joyous Rebirth and joyously wrap my arms around it. I hug the massive Atlas stone to my chest and stand with all my might. I release it over the Bar of Acute Suffering. Stepping back, my forearms burning with the bite of concrete, I look for the stone behind the yoke and see only the fantasia playing inside the metal frame, electricity dancing over the green blob like a frenzied montage.

Blinding white light blasts from the picture; I cry out, ashamed as I do it.

"This is to be expected, Damien. Everything is going to be fine."

So eerie, this scene like a gigantic arc light shining through the darkness without a soundscape to give it meaning. No sizzling or crackling noises, no raging winds, no screams played backward with a Doppler effect. Nothing like the paranormal phenomena I've seen in movies. And yet it's happening, the only sound that of H moving along the floor, as if drawn by powerful suction, toward the light.

I watch him slide past me, a reminder of what I can also do—his face like raw meat, his limbs splayed at ugly angles, his vestments covered in blood and vomit. His one open eye fixing upon me, he mouths, "Thank you," through bloodied teeth, then disappears into the doorway of the Great Secret. Without so much as a faint whooshing sound to accent his farewell, he's on his way to Almuric.

And when I think it's over, every scrap of H—every trace of his blood, puke, sweat, saliva, and hair—sails like grisly confetti toward the light and fades into flashing brilliance. I'm knuckling tears from my eyes as the room goes dark again. All that glows now are the torches in the walls, leaving me in gloom among witchy weights and weird symbols and a goblet of something so potent even Conan the Barbarian couldn't stomach it. The yoke is just a metal frame again, with a big concrete ball resting behind it.

Everything is going to be fine.

———◇———

My apologies. I wrote the last section in a fugue-like state. Edits to come.

———◇———

Next stop: Almuric.

———◇———

These notes began as a loose record of my last days on this planet. Very quickly, they evolved into a means of supplementing my preparations for the journey.

Never before have I written about my mother's health, my father's suicide, or my friend's beating by my hands. Nor will I ever write about these subjects again; nor will I ever write about anything, period, once these notes come to a close.

If you've read this far, I assume you won't take my story seriously. If that's the case, I want to make it clear I do not seek to aestheticize a human problem that I know about all too well—self-destruction. However, without it, the door to Almuric will never reveal itself; so I leave this narrative open-ended. Draw your own conclusions.

And if you, too, hunger for rebirth, know that I will not reveal how I found H's grimoire. Know that I will not disclose where or how I plan to activate the Great Secret, with minor alterations to the original formula. I will only divulge what I have said in these pages.

Good luck, and believe in yourself. You are capable.

Whatever you do with your life, don't let it be uneventful.

Gods bless,

D.V.S.

More Weight

Joe Koch and Michael Tichy

Last night I dreamed I went to Old Iron again. It seemed as though the whole bed shook as I woke with my heart pounding in every capillary, my eyes filling with hard tears. I passed through the commercial space sandwiched between a fastener wholesaler and an HVAC company, neck soaked with sweat and chest aching with the strain of an imaginary fever even though the temperature hovers around fifty-one degrees in the hotel we now call home.

I closed my eyes when I thought I had lost the dream, and it appeared again beneath a fallen rebar awning or perhaps beyond muddy pools formed by the melting of exhaust-black snow on asphalt. The liquor stores had thrown out broken-down boxes which stretched across my way. I came upon the gym suddenly, and stood there with my heart beating fast and fingers of fear circling my throat. There was Old Iron, secret and silent as it had always been, the grey concrete blocks absorbing the moonlight of my dream.

I could swear the abandoned storefront was not an empty shell, but lived and breathed with the obsession of a dungeon crawl. Pared down, the bodies within grew thinner, whittled to scar and corded muscle. The spaces between seemed closer in the fetid moonlight. The memories left me, or maybe I was nothing but a memory now. We shared the intimacy of knowing nothing about each other in attendance except the one thing everyone at Old Iron cared about, the one thing that mattered. Being hard and staying hard.

My first Inquisitor arrived ageless, maybe forty, maybe seventy. He pulled an oxygen tank behind him, wheels creaking in concert with his ancient bones. Who had cried out heretic to summon him, I didn't know. I said nothing. The ghost of gravity haunted our silent gathering. My former self feared her. Years of training and testosterone had drowned her mocking presence; yet here, in the gym where I replaced her by murderous increments, the Inquisitor's eyes resurrected her drowned and haggard spirit with a judgmental glance that stripped me down to raw shame and bone.

I stood firm with the rest of the penitents. The Inquisitor lay back on the bench with an arched spine. A slow practiced shimmy to find the right groove moved his ancient sinew like strange meat. He peeled off his nasal cannula and let it drop. Grabbed the bar.

I witnessed in anxious reverence as the unassisted mass of tightened flesh pushed 515, held, and then slowly lowered it back to the rack. He came up with a scarlet face. Indentions where the oxygen tube had pressed into his philtrum and ears burned crimson. His thick hand scrambled until an attentive spotter hurried the tube from his oxygen tank back into place. The Inquisitor's posture collapsed. Giving the knob a rough spin, he drew a deep breath and gazed upward.

His face now bloodless and calm, he met my eyes with a beatific smile.

And I understood the test. I'd understood for a long time, now. This is the discipline, the calling. This is what you must be willing to give.

Growing a machine from the soft raw materials of flesh wasn't easy for anyone, but it had been harder for me. I'd worked double for this. I belonged here. I'd prove it to my unknown accuser, all heresy be damned.

It wouldn't be easy. I always panicked a little in the ditch. In a good lift I kept the fear caged, breathed it and swallowed it nice and slow. A bad lift meant it got away and ran me over. If I made it out of the hole to begin my rebound, my terror turned into a booster rocket flying too fast and losing control. I'd never failed the squat on the concentric side. The eccentric—the fall and the hold at the bottom: that could break me.

I held straight in the line-up, refusing to speak or name another. Beside me, Coach clad in muscle like a walking mountain displayed the sculpted evidence of a saint. Coach had no other name. Anything more than Coach would have been extraneous; any anchor to the world outside of Old Iron comprised wasted movement in opposition to his pure praxis.

He was a slap on the face to get me in the zone for that new one-rep max attempt, a barked slogan when he saw the quit creeping into the whites of my eyes, the clap on my back when I made it. Grunt *next time* when I cracked.

Coach silent before the Inquisitor as I was silent, no jovial baritone spouting: *Embrace the suck. Ass moves mass*.

The Inquisitor moved wordlessly down the line-up, movements stiff, breath staccato, hauling the oxygen trolley beside his knotted thighs. The Question hovered around our bared iron-built shoulders in the moment between accusation and torture. But torture wasn't the right word. Fitness wasn't the right word. We shared a solemn lineage. The more specialized the athlete, the less fit for any other world we became. Masters of powerlifting strained to bend over our coarctated fat and muscle to tie shoes, got winded going up a single flight of stairs, awoke strangled by cardiac stress and sleep apnea. The Inquisitor's current state was the end result.

I knew what lifting did and I couldn't stop. The uninitiated in my old life learned quickly not to challenge me. No one outside Old Iron wanted a lecture on discipline from a zealot. I followed Coach's example, gave up talking religion, and kept things private. Old Iron's shared secrets forged a tacit bond between us far stronger than common familial blood.

I dreamed of clanking metal, the way the plates settle together on the bar when it comes to rest on the rack or floor. In my dream now I can feel the posterior chain light up from head to calf, breaking plane on a deadlift, pulling, pulling, pulling. Lockout is like flying. I overcome gravity once and for all. I lay her drowned ghost to rest beneath the asphalt, and outside of Old Iron, scrappy weeds turn the sidewalk into a colorful mosaic. The smell of exhaust recedes, and there's something like dew at five in the morning. There's quiet except for the distant roar of the highway whispering loud like the sea crashing with erotic insistence against the coastal rocks. In the silence of the early morning, I can almost smell the salt.

Facing the ancient judge with his hissing oxygen tank and piercing eyes, I wouldn't joke about gravity and call it a bitch. We all knew she was heartless and cruel. We knew she was the enemy. But to name our nemesis was worship in the most blasphemous sense, a watery invocation of darkness we dared not risk.

To fight the soft squirming larva of tenderness underneath our armored torsos, to overcome the merciful welcome of the earth's jaws sucking us off to satiation. There could be no victory without beating gravity beneath our bulk. Old Iron housed many drowned ghosts. Our church in silence, our bodies a fortress, we measured our progress a pound at a time. The weight was the gold. The Inquisitor motioned me to the rack.

My body responded to the ritualized cues before my mind acquiesced. The smell of bleach, and under that sacrosanct bleach a lingering sweaty musk. From elsewhere in the room, leather, metal, and rubber. My muscles tensed—abdomen, hands, shoulders. I stood up straighter, taller, chest full and forward. My face flushed. Cock went semi-hard. No one made jokes.

Hard. Everything at Old Iron solid and hard, from the sealed epoxy floor to the inscrutable physique of my beloved Coach. He existed nowhere but the gym as if he, too, were tethered to the building like a ghost. Hard and always harder, Coach worked a variation of the Texas Method for over twenty years: volume, active recovery, intensity. Rinse and repeat. Math, pain, boredom. Hours of training to shift five or ten pounds to the right. By the end of another dull and relentlessly rock-hard session with him, one night three months ago I couldn't stop myself anymore. I pulled one off in the shower.

Transgressional and unspoken, for everything at Old Iron must be known without being said, learned and known through the tacit awareness of the solid body beating the vagaries of the mind; Coach knew.

And he let me slide.

They say old guys groom kids in places like this. I'm sure that's true, but sometimes it's the other way around. I wasn't a kid; twenty something. I stayed late to help close up. Sprayed the bleach and scrubbed the urinals. When Coach turned to stow the supple worn leather squat belt in the footlocker, I flashed on the broad welts it might leave when swung with great strength.

I clapped him on the shoulder.

I kept my hand in contact where it landed. He didn't jump, balk, or turn. I pressed closer, pulling down his shorts to see the glistening sweat gathered in the crevice at the base of his spine. The landscape of his body like a double of the summer's surprising blooms and fallen dew renewing the hard grime of the city outside. I slid my knuckles down towards the valley below the impenetrable rocky façade of his mountainous back.

Between his hardened glutes I found a hairy entrance into the warm heart of the stone. The mountain opened up to me. Inside was both hard and soft.

We never spoke. Through ritual gnosis our repeated meetings transcribed a bold voice in the ecstatic muscle that thrived on our enlarged frames. We had more energy than ever before for training. We no longer feared gravity, that watery ghost beneath the floor mats plotting to drag all men down into oceanic oblivion. She couldn't find the cracks in us, couldn't fill them and freeze in them and split us wider and wider, because now, in our tender and glorious heresy, we were no longer afraid.

Beyond the necessity of mercy, we could not fall into her great gaping sea-void. We stood muscle-bound before the Inquisitor, his eyes small and dark like cloves stuck into raw ham above his winding oxygen cannula. If the body is a cell whose walls close incrementally, it's the same creeping pace as the gains, as if each plate you add to the bar is affixed to the walls around you. His eyes fixed on me as penitents loaded the bar. The walls closed in. My trial commenced.

"Enough," he said. His small eyes knowing and sharp, needles seeking a weak vein.

Somewhere deep in my core I relaxed counterintuitively as I took my place before the bench. My muscles craved the comfort I'd find in discomfort. Starting position should feel unnatural, like a suspension bridge in a heavy wind, all creaking beams and cables singing taut. Suppressing a smile, I returned his gaze and said, "More weight."

The needles flinched.

The math of plates. To look at a bar and know the weight of it. The calculation was automatic. I welcomed confinement. Less range of motion was less margin of error on the lift. They would not burn me alive as a heretic or weakling and string my body atop the blinking traffic lights at the intersection of Telegraph Road and Waterborne Street. I would not be another Ophelia, Rusalka, or Rebecca. They wouldn't force me to name names, for my love had no name, only the sameness of sensation, the redundant ritual of the bar held hard in my grip as I lift.

The same smells, same erection, same bench, cracked vinyl with layers of transparent tape, upholstery caught in mid vivisection, guts showing in places. The brushed nickel bar scratched with a vague "M" or "W" on one end. The knurling perfect, not so aggressive that it tears up my hands, enough that no matter how sweaty, it never slips. Yet under the Inquisitor's scrutiny, my palms fairly wept.

Powering out of the hole and into the middle of the lift, hitting a big PR, my soul escaped the bounds of my body for a moment. Afterwards, bent over in recovery, when I finally raised my eyes, the Inquisitor's inscrutable face drew tense in lascivious caricature. His eyes seemed to glow through the narcotic haze of my exhaustion. I was spent; so soft and dumb, half in a dream, but the soreness was a beacon. It called me back from the delicate spirit world and my eyes focused on what was solid. The Inquisitor's smile didn't seem right.

His oxygen tank hissed. My heart pounded a command, a machine gun laying down suppressive fire. Get the fuck out. My feet froze as in a nightmare. My cock was a metronome, firm and bobbing.

Silent. Always silent. I stood silent as Coach came forward and squeezed my trapezius muscles briefly.

And in that squeeze I sensed he was the one who had named me.

"Embrace the suck," he whispered. "Be a wolf among sheep."

Solemn under the sharp gaze of the Inquisitor, Coach turned to his treasure chest, the foot locker where he stored his most precious of things, his lifting belt and his training journal. But it was another book he tossed my way, along with a worn leather pouch, its age betrayed in hairline cracks.

Something stashed inside made clicking sounds as I caught it. It felt too warm to have come out of that cold steel storage chest.

Coach resumed his place in formation with the rest of the penitents. The Inquisitor straightened his hunched back, steadfast and seated on a PLYO box as if it were his throne.

His pinpoint eyes unwavering upon me, the Inquisitor reached into his mouth. He pinched his left cuspid between a thick forefinger and thumb. With a tenacious rocking motion of his hand and wrist, he worked the tooth harshly back and forth. Blood seeped down his jaw and onto his knuckles. Tears brightened his black needle-like eyes. The thing in his mouth held with deep roots. His fat thumb muscle tensed and flexed, forcing the tooth loose. The Inquisitor's throat made an involuntary hum punctuating the wet sound of each side to side jolt. Overcoming the cuspid's resistance with a final sickening crack, he gargled in what passed for a laugh and bade me take the bloody prize.

Thus I held the bag, the book, and the tooth, accused. He watched me with pitiless expectation.

On the outside, each item innocuous, beaten with age and use, stained with sweat and blood, a spiral ring notebook with metal bent and rusted; the rattling teeth or fangs that came from the bag looking like none I'd seen before, yellowed at the base and shaped like corkscrews tapered to sharp tips; and last the still warm bloody relic from the Inquisitor's own mouth beginning to squirm in my palm as if to re-shape itself in imitation of the older reliquaries of strange spiraled teeth.

I opened the book, uncertain of my task. Glyphs. Curved and straight lines that intersected. Meaningless to me, but as I cut them into my body with the broken point of the rusted spiral ring I understood in sharp flashes. This is the price. To become godlike, to hold weight that would stymie a mountain. To transcend, to fly. To leave the river behind.

I completed consecrating my soft meat with the hard teeth by screwing the aged yellowed fangs laboriously into my quadriceps, one by one, as the diagrams in the notebook suggested. The squeaking of their slow entry as metal against wood, the resulting pockmarked holes in my marbled thighs mouthing meaty hymns; a chanted invocation known only to my body and not my mind, for I was made now of wood, of metal, of stone.

My meat knew to replenish the empty bag with the Inquisitor's sacrifice. His tooth, shattered into pieces and worming into multiple winding spirals warmed the palm of my left hand. I cinched the white offerings inside the ancient leather bag and stowed them with the holy book inside Coach's treasure chest. Sweating, feverish, I turned again towards the gym, towards the test. Not remembering how I got there. Testosterone singing from my many wounds. Above the usual scents of Old Iron, the taste and smell of steel. I salivated hot metal. My heart engorged.

A wet cough. The Inquisitor's oxygen valve opened wide, a gentle whistle punctuated by his wheeze. He smiled through the dried blood that marked his chin and fist and grunted twice to greenlight the next lift. Penitents lined up before the plate stacks.

Deadlift. The bar on the floor, loaded with 405. I stepped up, shins to the bar, legs sumo. My skin scarred where it met the bar, gnashing teeth that bled mercury from my thighs. Back straight, I dropped my ass, squatted low, and began the slow tightening.

The Inquisitor rasped.

I paused. The Question unspoken, the challenge implied; I had but one response: "More weight."

One of his penitents worked the bar jack while four others loaded. 495. 585. 675. I pulled before they fully cleared and one laggard fell backwards in haste.

In fear.

Muscles gripping teeth, fire under flesh, agony an impetus: I broke plane. A hollow pop cued the end of my back as I knew it. I fought through the impossible pain. A knee went sideways. Bone protruded. Still I tracked upward, undaunted.

Lockout. The Inquisitor gave the slightest nod. Good lift. But not finished. Next, the steady, controlled decline. I settled the weight back down, joints corroding, bones abraded, ligaments too damaged for me to dance the dance of loosening up. There was no relief.

The Inquisitor's eyes needled my flesh for weaknesses. A glance at Coach screamed defeat.

My voice on pain of burning bellowed thicker, deeper, with a hard-won resonance mightier than those in attendance who were perhaps born as men.

"More weight," I said.

And I stepped up to the bar again.

The minions placed collars on the bar to prevent the added weights shedding as it bent on the way up: 765, 855, 945, 1035. Abstract numbers soon to be acknowledged in cracked vertebrae or an aneurism's sudden blast. To stop and beg mercy now would be more monstrous in my abandonment of honor than any admission of frailty. For if coach had named me out of fear, and I knew he had, the next test would fall to him.

Vengeful ghosts might bow out of bitterness, but I was a man. I would not yield craven to see him condemned.

I began my pull; for my honor, my love, my Coach, and for all the drowned ghosts clawing beneath the mat both past and future who honor may put to rest. The ghosts of Old Iron gathered, and a heavy rain outside commenced. A thunderclap. The embedded teeth answered and mouthed white hot psalms in my flesh.

Something moved in me as I fought, bearing down against the inhuman weight. A gurgle like the Inquisitor's senile laugh seeped in my lower gut. Fear and shame I'd shit myself on the platform; shocked, my broken body continued to perform as I willed it through strain and agony. The good knee crunched like broken-up concrete. A leg bone snapped. What held me upright, I didn't know.

I knew only the tightening, the pushing, the hardness in my tissues making every object in my grasp feel smaller as an invulnerable armor grew from within me and sealed the screams of my nerve endings beneath solid brute silence.

A dribble warm and wet down the backs of my legs splashed the platform, smelling of copper. I pulled harder.

A fist in my stomach expanded, pushing everything liquid out of its way.

The birth of a hundred hernias, stomach muscles ripped asunder and the rush of fecal sludge unleashed. A thousand jokes about rectal prolapse, but no one was ever the guy. Always a friend of a friend. When I locked out, the shit and bloody afterbirth expelled might have been my intestines once upon a time.

And all the liquid in my body left me. I became unconquerable stone. The teeth like frozen shards hardened what remained of my mobile, malleable flesh.

As I flew higher than a rocket in lockout, muddy water began to rise from the floor of Old Iron, as if she were a ship that sprang a leak. Sewer water bubbled up from the floor drains. Dirty rainwater seeped in through the aging concrete blocks. Brown sludge slavered over the weeping serpent I'd shed below me on the mat.

She writhed upward in coils, my once-intestines, an unspooling cyclone of slick reptile skin with the long-haired head of a woman.

Undaunted by the apparition, I readied for the descent, that controlled fall down an elevator shaft into the ditch, but I was made now of wood, of metal, of stone. I found I could no longer move or bend at will. I pressed the impossible weight above my head, fighting and not fighting, flying in lockout, soaring frozen in the equilibrium of a total loss of control.

Let the ground claim me, I nearly prayed. But the ground didn't want me. The ghost didn't want me. She slithered around my wrecked legs and rubbed her snake-scales indifferently across my protruding broken bones as she uncoiled to reveal her full length.

I felt her hunger in the new mouths on my thighs, their teeth chittering in ghoulish anticipation. I tried to tell Coach to run, escape, but immobility extended to my firm jaw and stiffened neck; I couldn't speak, even if I'd wished to break the holy silence of our temple and yell warnings to my beloved.

The Inquisitor coughed out "Good lift." He raised a hand: two fingers up, the rest down. The rain continued to leach in, flooding above my ankles. The expelled serpent wept from her upside down face like a white contorted mask, long strings of hair dripping black and slick on either side of her wailing maw. Her screech was piercing. She lurched through the rising muck toward the penitents, all little more than boys like me in our exaggerated comic-hero bodies, but boys nonetheless. Some screamed. Most ran for the door.

Coach barred their way, his face aglow with fanatic rage. The first who fought him took a fracturing crack across the jaw. Coach grunted an apology, but his stance remained the same.

No others dared revolt, though wailing and twisting as she splashed through the sewage, the drowned ghost writhed around each cowering muscle-bound figure, wrapping the great girth of their chests and shoulders tight and coiling around their broad torsos as if investigating the resistance and density of their muscle. She pulsed with rubbery sinew as she encased a whole penitent up to the neck, her flexible form inescapable, her moans the sound of utter madness, her white mask leveling eye to eye with each prattling trapped man. One by one she tested the penitents. One by one their eyes glazed and their exaltations grew incoherent. Released, they fell into the mire like clubbed seals with a heavy splash. All were found wanting after facing that howling upside-down anomaly whose forked tongue had flicked across their drooling, pleading, praising lips. All but one remained to stand the test.

Not coach; he lay dead-eyed with the fallen, his head propped above water by a boy's collapsed mass. I wanted to rush to him, revive him, forgive him, but the power and strength of my body had solidified into a cage. Replete with unbearable pain, no longer flying but endlessly flexed beyond fluid life in deadly lockout; my heart pounded rock against rock in my eardrums. The arteries in my neck threatened to detonate. I agonized as Coach's head slipped an inch lower, the tip of his chin dipping in and out as the swirling sewage kept everything it touched in constant motion.

Knee-deep, the Inquisitor arose with his oxygen cart atop the PLYO box. The ghost-serpent vanished into the mire, ripples defining her hidden course. No sound with her voice drowned except the hissing of the tank, the trickling influx of rain, and the chaotic currents that slapped the walls.

She ascended, silent as Old Iron's traditions required. Muddy water sloughed from her scales as she coiled her great length in a loose, sinewy tourniquet around the Inquisitor's neck. Her maddening face hung agape as her flicking tongue confronted his impassive gaze. No lunacy bloomed in his eyes. No idiot supplications foamed on his lips. The serpent opened its maw wide and the Inquisitor looked into that upside-down woman's maw and slowly wrenched his ancient face into a defiant grin.

"Get thee behind me, maiden," he said.

The white mask unhinged quickly at the jaw. In a sudden gulp it swallowed the Inquisitor from his head to his chest. The oxygen tank fell as his cannula snapped loose. His free arm and his legs flailed. Muffled shouts defiled the silence. Muscular pulsations of the snake-like spirit interred him deeper into her gut flex by forceful flex until he was no more than a struggling lump within her long coils.

She lay sedate, digesting him as the water receded for the next three days.

The screams from inside her coils died down a day before she finished her meal. Coach remained within my field of vision, remained above the murky water. I prayed for his safety even as I gave up hope of ever moving, resting, or feeling whole again; of ever knowing the momentary peace and release of the satisfaction she enjoyed while I endured this endless soul-crushing struggle in which my body seemed forever locked.

I didn't dream during those three days, not because I didn't sleep, but because all my possibilities were dead. I had reached the pinnacle of training and achieved what must only be sainthood. I had defeated gravity and laid all her ghosts to rest. My trial had proven me more worthy than my beloved accuser.

I was victorious. And I'd lost everything.

Coach always said any run less than six months on a program was a waste of time. *Fucking hummingbirds*, he called them, flitting from workout to workout, constantly looking for a shortcut. *Attention spans like soda cans.* He doesn't say anything anymore. But he seems at peace.

I feel terror in the hole always. Thighs angling just beyond parallel to floor. Vigilance demanding I pretend I'm in a war before the war starts. Go a little deeper to remove all doubt. I haven't forgotten Old Iron. I carry it with me, a home on my back. This is the hole. Life and death.

The ghost went back inside me where she belongs, not laid to rest like a rejected, disembodied corpse but held, satiated, and honored. I moved again, broken as I was. I dragged Coach with me.

When I lugged him out of Old Iron, it was a dry day, the sun was shining, and the recent rain brought new flowering weeds rushing from the sidewalk cracks in vivid colors like our happiest memories. We do not talk of Old Iron; I will not tell Coach my dream. Old Iron is ours no longer. A week or two later, I saw it had burned down. Half the block consumed in what none will call a ritual fire.

We can never go back again. The past is still too close to us, living and breathing within us. We keep her alive; perhaps we are merely her memories. But we have no secrets from each other now; now everything is shared. Our cheap hotel may be dull, and the gym facility not very modern; day after day, things may be very much the same. But dullness is better than fear. Love is better than sacrifice.

We live by habit. We write our workouts weeks in advance. Projections based on current max lifts are more often right than wrong. When it's wrong, we adjust and continue. When it's right, we adjust. The river rises and falls. We adjust again. We continue.

There's a devotional satisfaction in checking boxes and crossing out items, a ritual ease in our consistency. Joy in the known. A saint doesn't need to prove their piety. Saints need not shun frailty. A failed lift is nothing to fear. Failure is nothing more than an unchecked box.

And there's a comfort in that.

Scale

Rien Gray

Robert touched the cold glass of temptation, then flinched.

It should have been easy. Steroids were a dime a dozen in gyms these days, especially a Big Ten college like Torope. This bottle was the good stuff, even: HGH, undetectable in a piss test and only mildly illegal. Five years ripping off the top page of his mother's prescription pad for excuses to skip class or the occasional dose of Adderall prepared him for this moment—and he flinched.

Wet feet swept tile near the front of the changing room. Robert slammed his locker shut the second Eddie Helminth came into view, dripping head to toe from the pool. A towel was half-tied around his hips, its loose knot tucked under the left angle of the V in Eddie's Adonis belt, core drawn tight from too many laps to count.

The entire Torope swim team racked up gold medals in high school—Robert included—but in the last six months, Eddie had gone from hard-working captain to Olympic hopeful. He set records almost every meet now, rising out of the pool as a gleaming tower of muscle, smooth and frictionless as marble.

Robert was jealous of the latter more than anything. He'd gotten used to shaving his legs during puberty number one, but going on testosterone meant accepting his father's bear rug of a back and the rasp of stubble that refused to become a full beard. It was impossible to picture Eddie spending four hours in the bathroom trying to perfectly wax his ass, so how did he do it? Why did his whole life look so damn effortless?

"Hey, Waite." Eddie let his towel drop, left in nothing but a black-and-gold Speedo. "Got a second?"

Panic burned a caustic stripe up the inside of Robert's chest before he forced the feeling back down. He belonged here. The team knew—they didn't care. "Yeah, man. What's up?"

Keeping his eyes on Eddie's electric blues was harder than Robert wanted to admit. Ever since he was allowed on this side of the locker room, it became a habit to inspect other guys, breaking down all the details that made them blend in. Nicholas—their freestyle king—caught him comparing sizes once, but made a joke out of it, claiming every dude's dick vanished after two hours in cold water. Robert remembered laughing, saying they matched now, but even that faint bulge felt aspirational. Chlorine in the pool would eat his silicone packer like acid, leaving nothing behind.

"Your butterfly stroke was clean earlier," Eddie said. "Time looked good too."

Robert forced a smile. "Nothing compared to yours. You're killing it."

Everybody else on the team had been. Practice only proved that he was falling further and further behind, without a clue why. He showed up at the same hours, doing laps before sunrise and working on technique after class until the pool closed. His stats were improving, but when compared to the other guys, the prognosis looked grim. It would be a miracle if Coach Kam didn't cut him at the end of the semester.

Maybe they were all doping up and keeping their mouths shut. Robert's father always said real men did anything it took to get the job done, without waiting around to claim credit. Yet here he was, praying for permission or some kind of sign, a little damn validation.

"You want it to be better?" Eddie asked.

Robert blinked; he'd lost track of the conversation. "Huh?"

"Do you want your time to be better?" The other man took a step forward, standing so tall it made Robert's teeth hurt. Sometimes he wanted to take a hammer to those perfect carved calves until the two of them were truly eye to eye. "And are you willing to do what it takes?"

They were alone. Practice was over, and the whole team should have been in here, stripping down and marching to the showers. Even if a few stayed to do extra laps, there weren't enough lanes for everyone at the same time.

His eyes flickered to the locker room entryway, a mouth of shining red tile. Were they out there waiting for his answer? He would have to push past Eddie to leave; the rows were too narrow for a swift exit.

Maybe this was doomed to happen—a little quid pro quo for dragging the whole team down, being the diversity pick. He met Eddie's gaze again and steeled himself. "Yeah, I want it to be better. Absolutely."

Robert braced himself for a hundred kinds of pain, but Eddie smiled—a real smile, dozens of pearly teeth and a glimpse of tongue—and reached into his own locker. He snagged a business card between two pale fingers and offered it to Robert.

"Good. Because Coach wants you in." The card looked old, yellow around the edges and burdened with wrinkles. "Come here tonight. Midnight. Don't tell anyone and don't put this shit on your phone. No one needs team business in a goddamn text, okay?"

Fuck the HGH. This invitation made Robert feel like a god. "I'll keep my mouth shut."

Eddie let the card go, and Robert fought not to clutch it to his chest. "Cool. I'll see you then. We'll get you on the right path."

He left with a friendly slap to Robert's shoulder, making a beeline to the showers. The moment Eddie was out of sight, Robert looked over every inch of the card for a secret, some kind of code that could be missed, but the only thing on it was a faded, looping scrawl: *Annapolis Docks, Berth 4.*

At 11:50 p.m. on a Friday, the docks were a wasteland.

Wind whipped the ocean with a vengeance, the sharp scent of frothing foam clashing with the bloom of mold-ridden wood and sun-rotten seafood. Robert swallowed a surge of nausea and jammed both hands into the pocket of his hoodie, trying to read signs in the dim light. The broad, dark blades of container ships cut off most of the view, keeping the local cabin cruisers contained in their own little corner, white sails raised like flags of surrender.

There was no visible difference between the fourth berth and the others, but Robert stared at the moored vessel as if it was an alien thing, consumptive and distant, too out of reach to touch. He blinked away the feeling and raised a fist, knocking hard against the steel door.

It jerked open a second later, revealing Nicholas's head. Shadows divided him from the neck down until he leaned forward, grinning wide. "Yooooooo. Welcome to the party."

Was it a party? Robert still wasn't quite sure what he was getting into. "Glad to be here."

Nicholas moved from the entryway so Robert could step onto the ship, then yanked the door shut again with an echoing clang. When he set the lock, rust squealed in protest until steel dragged the rest of the mechanism down.

"This way," Nicholas said, gesturing down the half-lit hall.

Robert pushed his back to the wall to let the other man lead. The hull was frigid even through his clothes, but Nicholas felt cold too, the brief brush of their bodies like touching an ice sculpture. He blamed it on Nick's fit; who wore swim shorts and a tank top in this kind of weather? His feet were bare too, leaving faint slick prints on the yellow caution lines that split the floor.

After a few narrow twists and turns, the ship opened up into what Robert assumed was the cargo hold. Empty high-vis nets hung from hooks welded to the ceiling, knots of nylon collapsed around themselves, and weight limit warnings were etched near the far door.

The rest of the swim team sat in a circle on the floor in front of Coach Kam, who leaned against a massive white cooler. Robert remembered seeing one that size as a kid, trembling in the snow outside his uncle's cabin. Uncle Roger joked that if they ran out of food in the winter, he could be the replacement. Even now, Robert didn't see the humor, but he had laughed, because he was supposed to; prey could never be forgiven for making a predator uncomfortable.

"Waite. Good to see you." The coach's cap was pulled low, hiding his eyes, but Kam's tone seemed friendly enough. "Makes me proud to have my boys together."

The brittle joy in Robert's chest shattered when Allen—first-tier on backstroke and second-string butter-fly—asked, "Yeah, man, what took you so long?"

"Don't give him shit," Eddie countered. "He just got the invite yesterday."

Nods of understanding passed around the circle, although Robert wasn't sure whether to read them as approval or pity. "What do I need to do?"

"Sit." Coach Kam pointed to the floor. "The rest of you, make room."

Robert squeezed in between Eddie and Allen, biting back a curse at the chill radiating from the floor. It pierced into his shins like shards of ice, but he refused to move; the feeling would numb out soon enough.

"Now," Coach emphasized the word by knocking broad knuckles against the top of the cooler, "everyone is here because they want to be the best, right?"

Whoops of approval broke out from the circle; Robert let out a confirming shout a few seconds too late, sound echoing through the massive ribs of the ship.

"Sometimes that means getting a leg up on the competition," Kam continued, "and getting ahead of the big brains at our sports science institute before they release their research to the public."

A few conspiratorial snickers passed around the room, but most of the team was staring at the cooler, eyes wide and clear as glass. When the coach eased his weight off the lid and stood up straight, Robert saw Eddie's hands twitch in his lap.

"This is our secret. Keeps us strong, keeps us clean. It has for generations. Since my father was Coach, and his father dug our first pool." Kam loomed over them; Robert fit inside his shadow. "We don't do this for money or fame. We do it for unity, brotherhood."

Then the coach turned around and shoved the cooler on its side. The lid flung open as insulated plastic struck steel with the force of a slap, spilling the cooler's contents across the floor. Robert's vision went red, jagged, and wet before his eyes found the shapes of scales and flesh, dozens of raw fish hacked into endless pieces, slowly spreading across the cargo hold like a puddle of blood.

Eddie moved first. He lunged forward, a jerky dive meant for water instead of air, and buried his face into the crimson pool, teeth snapping together. Nicolas and Allen were right behind him, scooping slick piscine masses into their mouths before the rest of the team fell on them in a frenzy. Robert couldn't tell one body from another, every limb sleek and glistening, slipping through one another in a squirming knot.

Salt brutalized his senses—nose, tongue, teeth—from the hot sheen of sweat, the stale seawater gathered in rusty gaps of the floor, and shining animal gore. He wasn't sure whether to bolt in terror or break down laughing.

Coach Kam kneeled next to him, one heavy hand on his shoulder, and they were face to face. Robert had never seen his eyes before. They were hollow, limned with silver, like mirrors warped out of shape.

"It's okay, Rob." His first name—Coach always called him 'Waite.' "This is good for you. Those white coats have been studying for years to find out the truth, but it's simple—you eat, and you grow. Be with your brothers. There's no shame in it."

Shame. Shame had devoured years of his life, eaten away at every accomplishment like acid, insistent he was living a lie, cheating the system to get a step ahead. His body betrayed him in turn until the only thing greater than shame was the need to slough off his skin and show the world the man underneath. Fearful as it could be, the promise of acceptance was too intoxicating to refuse.

And they were holding the door wide open.

Robert crawled forward on hands and knees, shivering as fish guts soaked through his jeans. He scooped up a handful of the red flesh, surprised by its heat, and forced it into his mouth before revulsion got the better of him. It stuck to the inside of his throat, clinging and hot, before hunger opened up his belly. The taste was—

More. He needed more.

———◦———

Ten minutes before his alarm, Robert was out of bed and moving.

It was seconds before sunrise, and he had stumbled into his dorm at three in the morning, but his body was indescribably *awake*. After a quick shower, he sprinted to the campus to weigh in and suit up for laps.

Allen was already there, but he was the earliest riser on the team. Robert fell in behind him before he froze with a foot above the scale.

After a soft laugh, Allen stepped back. "You go first. I want to see your reaction."

He frowned, not sure what the hell that was supposed to mean, but stood on the round white board without hesitation. Robert read the number twice, then blinked. "No fucking way I'm up ten pounds."

"You ate about that much last night," Allen joked. "But it went here."

Smooth fingertips traced down Robert's stomach; he held back a shiver and dared to look down. Tight abs peeked out above his hips, cut and defined exactly like he'd dreamed of.

"And no piss test in the world is going to pop you for eating surf-and-turf." Allen snorted. "Dude, you're shedding."

Robert glanced at Allen's hand. Fine, dark hairs from his belly hung off of wan fingertips, and when he looked back at his stomach, five lines cut through the trail there, as if Allen's nails were razor sharp. "The hell?"

"Don't worry. It's normal with this shit." Allen grinned. "Hell, I'd go bald at twenty for a couple Olympic medals in the bag."

Quietly, he agreed. "Let's get in the pool."

Swimming was second nature. Robert paddled faster than he could walk as a kid, ignoring the blister of chlorine and burning lungs when he pushed too far, too deep. In the water there was nothing to fear—no one could touch him.

But the first dive of the morning felt like coming *home*. He zipped through a dozen laps without needing to stop, chasing Allen for the first three before pulling ahead. By the time they were out of the water, Robert wasn't even breathing hard. With five minutes before English 160, he darted out of the gym, face still dripping.

The teacher wasn't there yet, so he drifted to the back row and sat down. Two girls in front were chatting rapid-fire, flicking through notifications on a single cell phone between them.

"That lab thing's creepy, right?" the blonde on the left said. "Who breaks into a place to pour bleach all over everything?"

"No clue," the other replied. "But my girlfriend's one of the biology TAs, so she has to help them account for the damage. It's, like, twenty million dollars worth or something."

Eddie, who sat a few seats away, chuckled.

Robert frowned, remembering how pissed off Coach Kam had been about the 'white coats' studying something. The fish, he guessed, but tearing up one of the most well-funded labs on campus was enough to ruin anyone for life. He knew in his bones that Eddie would do it, though.

Any of them would, if Coach asked.

Shaking his head of the notion, he tried to focus when the professor rushed in, her coffee balanced precariously on a stack of handouts. Twentieth century literature dodged Robert's intersection of interests, but academic requirements had spiked for college athletes this year. He knew why, but the underlying message—*most of you will never go pro, study for a fallback*—set a hook of anxiety deep in his gut.

The promise of a comprehensive test next week gave that hook a set of twisting barbs, and he was still trying to shake it loose when Eddie bumped against him in the hallway.

"How you feeling, man?"

Class put a damper on his morning glow, but Robert couldn't deny the difference. The whole world was easier to move through. "Great. It's fucking wild, Eddie."

"Good." White teeth flashed in a full, satisfied grin. "But you have to come every Friday. Stuff wears off fast."

That made sense, Robert supposed, considering how fast it worked. "No worries. I won't let the team down."

The pre-nationals qualifier was at the end of the month. One taste had shaved twenty seconds off his best time—what would three more do?

———◇———

They tore the meet apart.

Ten colleges showed up to compete, but it was a wash top to bottom, and Robert watched the glow burn out of their eyes as score after score went up on the board. ESPN cameras moved closer to Coach Kam with each event, until every reporter on site mobbed him for a quote. He never gave them much, insisting his team did the real work, but a cavalcade of microphones surrounded him like a black, glittering crown.

When the last freestyle finished, the team poured into the locker room in a howling and slippery rush, yanking off their caps before tossing them at one another. Under the fluorescent light, their faces had a silver sheen that Robert couldn't look away from. He hadn't just kept up with them—he had won.

"I'm so fucking dry, man," Nicholas muttered. "The pools here are ninety percent chlorine."

"Same here." Eddie scratched at his cheek, skin pulling tight. "I swear I'm taking six showers a day."

"Don't worry, boys." Coach Kam stepped into the locker room with a huge blue bucket, so full of water it sloshed with every step. "You're too young for champagne, but—"

Robert was deluged from head to toe and gasped out a laugh, his mouth suddenly full of salt. It was a cold balm against his skin, and the rest of the team let out similar gasps of relief. Allen even walked up to the bucket to dunk his head into the remains, earning a low chuckle from the coach.

"Get your celebrating in," Kam said, tone sharpening. Robert's spine straightened a full vertebrae. "Then come out to the van. We have places to be."

Usually the team went out to a late-night diner to wolf down their weight in carbs after a meet. Robert wasn't sure where else they would go, but he tugged on his shorts without bothering to dry off, and filed out of the locker room. The pair of gold medals hanging from his neck clinked together with every step, just out of sync with the longer strides around him.

The team van was more of a bus, retrofitted with waterproof vinyl and appropriate college colors. He sat between Eddie and Allen, shivering as clammy skin pressed against his own. Even in the near-dark of the parking lot, he could make out pink and red patches marring Eddie's legs, closer to a burn than a scratch.

Coach Kam started the engine, and its low rumble filled Robert's head with white noise as they pulled away from campus. Victory lost its edge, dulled against the silence of the man he respected the most. Had they fucked up somehow? Kam was nothing but smiles during the competition, and Robert couldn't figure out what signal he'd missed.

He didn't recognize the road they were on, and when the van veered left, a dirt path pockmarked with flat black rocks sent a rattle from tires to teeth. Thick cloud cover obscured the moon, leaving nothing but the faint glow of stars reflecting off distant water as they approached a long crescent of sand.

It was a beach, but not one Robert had ever been to before. When Coach Kam parked and hit the side switches to open the doors, the team piled out so fast Robert fumbled to get his seatbelt off and follow.

"Where are we?" he asked.

Allen shoved him from behind, and Robert barely caught his balance before snapping, "Hey, what are you—"

The coach interrupted. "Hold him."

One set of hands seized his shoulders, and another snared his wrist from the left. When Robert twisted to get away, Eddie grabbed his other arm so hard everything from the elbow down went numb.

Coach Kam stood on the edge of the sea, more a shadow than a man. The only light came from his right hand, pallid fingers wrapped around an equally pale hilt, clean and white as bone, cleaved to a slender tang of steel. It tapered to a fine point that curved back into a hook.

"They found us," the coach said, voice soft and solemn. His tone should have been washed away by the waves, but Robert heard every word like they were inscribed on the inside of his skull. "I suppose destroying the lab was too strong of a tell."

Robert's jaw dropped. "I didn't have anything to do with that!"

"I know. This isn't a punishment, Rob." Kam took a step closer. The knife was slick; the metal breathed. "It's a homecoming. You're going home."

Thrashing did nothing. The team's hold on his body was simply too strong, even as adrenaline flooded his veins screaming *run, run, run*. Coach Kam brought the blade to the inside of his arm, its sharp tip angled against the artery in his wrist.

"Please," Robert gasped, "don't—"

The hook dug in. Pain parted him open, flesh divided with the ease of wax paper, bloodless. Glistening scales lay in place of vein and nerve, devouring every drop of starlight that fell upon them.

He choked on a sob, tasting salt again. "How?"

"You're one of us," the coach said simply. His eyes were visible again, coated with the faint white film of the dead, the rotten, the lost. "Stay. Keep our secrets. Keep eating. We'll treasure you forever."

Murmurs of agreement, more susurrus than chorus, left half a dozen throats, tied to a dozen hands holding Robert in place. He flinched when Coach Kam leaned forward, but the touch was the cruelest sort of kindness, a kiss on each cheek to capture his tears and seal them away.

"Let go," Robert whispered, a plea to himself as much as them. "Let me go."

The coach smiled, his teeth the same color as the hilt of the knife. "Is that really what you want?"

He could run into obscurity. He could call this a dream, and wake up without the boys he knew so well, the ones he spent every waking hour chasing. Robert's throat tightened, hunger ripping through fear.

They had brought him here. He was finally the same.

"Where's home?"

Kam pulled the knife deeper, stripping him to the elbow. "The water. Where you've belonged since the beginning."

Words left in the wake of his skin, superfluous. Matching hands peeled away the tight, pale cage of flesh until the rest slipped off the subtle fins of Robert's spine. His first steps were staggered, webbed limbs struggling against the dry grit of sand until the encroaching tide covered the cartilaginous curves of his feet. Familiarity drew him deeper, until the ocean swallowed his body whole.

Robert dove down, farther than the collapsing tissue of old lungs could bear.

For the first time in his life, it was easy to breathe.

Fish, Crusade

Robbie Burkhart

The boys of Northridge High School's varsity men's hockey team hardly look like boys at first glance, with shiny white teeth and jaws as sharp as exacto knives. At the same time, there's something unsure about the way they hold themselves, like they're trying on swagger they'd stolen from a department store.

The fact that Caleb wouldn't really fit in with these polished, well-oiled, no-longer-boys had been apparent during tryouts, but he knows he should be grateful. Northridge is one of the best private high schools for hockey in California, and the fact that he's on the varsity team as a freshman is unusual.

"Don't step on the logo," Mikey—the only junior of the three assistant captains—advises, indicating the rug near the center of the locker room.

His brown curls gleam in artful disarray under the fluorescent lighting. Mikey's smile is bright and roguish, left cheek dimpling with it, and there's a single freckle on the shell of his ear.

Caleb doesn't ask why he shouldn't step on the logo. They'd been told why during tryouts. Mikey elaborates anyway, a smile still slashed across his face. "Super bad luck. Last guy who stepped on the rug got into a, like, massive car accident. Never played hockey again."

Caleb's stomach turns, the same way it had when he heard that the first time. He shuffles around the edge of the black rug, staring at his feet so he doesn't so much as brush the toe of his shoe against the edge.

The rug depicts a black and white version of Northridge's old logo: a knight bearing a shield with a fleur-de-lis on it, scepter in the off-hand. NORTHRIDGE CRUSADERS, it reads along the bottom edge.

On the jerseys, the logo'd been simplified to a fleur-de-lis, but the team kept the name.

"Why hasn't the rug been changed?" Caleb asks, because that's a safer question.

"Tradition," Mikey says, and shrugs. "That thing's been here since my dad played. This one's your locker. Next to me, yeah? I'll show you the ropes."

Caleb drops his bag in the locker Mikey indicates. The locker room is by far the cleanest locker room Caleb's ever been in, and there's a branded Gatorade cooler on a cart at the far end with a stack of paper cups. Someone's helpfully labeled his locker with Sharpie on masking tape: *CALEB WU #40.*

A drop of sweat runs down his spine. He hadn't picked the number, and he wouldn't have picked that one. His new jerseys—home blacks and white aways—are stacked on the shelf above the locker, and he pulls them out, splaying his fingers over the numbers stitched on the back like he could hide the 4.

"Any chance I can get a different number?" Caleb asks, voice light-years more casual than he feels.

"Ha," Mikey says.

"Aw," another voice says, too close for comfort. Caleb doesn't jump only because he completely freezes, every muscle locking up. "Fish doesn't like his new number?"

"Leave him alone," Mikey says, half-heartedly. "Sorry, Caleb. That's Stags—Jake—he's insufferable, just ignore him. He's like a dog—giving him attention just encourages him."

Caleb looks up anyway. Jake is as handsome as the rest of them, with clear skin and bright eyes, but he's Black, five-pointed stars delicately shaved into the sides of his close-cropped hair. When Caleb makes eye contact, Jake grins, then turns his attention to Mikey.

"At least I'm not the captain's bitch," he says, and dances out of the way of the kick Mikey aims at him. "Woof, woof."

Mikey says, "Play nice, Stags."

"I'm never not nice," Jake says, with a mean kind of grin.

Mikey shakes his head. "I'm gonna go find the captain."

When Mikey turns away, the grin on Jake's face vanishes and the creases around his eyes smooth out. Without the smile his dark eyes are even wider, almost deerlike. He tracks Mikey's progress across the locker room; Caleb watches too, until Mikey disappears out the door he brought Caleb through.

"Why don't you like the number?" Jake says.

"Four's unlucky." Caleb puts the jerseys back on the shelf, unsettled. "It's fine, I guess. It could be worse."

Jake gives him an assessing look. For a moment Caleb could swear that Jake's taking a mental measuring tape to him, surveying the shape of Caleb with the eye of a cartographer: assessing the baby fat that still clings to Caleb's cheeks, the way his shirt hangs off his under-muscled body, his unstyled hair.

"Yeah," he says. "Could be worse."

<hr />

The captain is a senior with blue eyes so pale they're nearly white, a bouncy swoop of brown hair falling over his forehead, and hardly an ounce of body fat clinging to him anywhere. When he smiles, his teeth are straight and white, perfectly aligned in his mouth, and when he aims his smile at Caleb, Caleb's heart skips a beat. Caleb hadn't seen him at tryouts;

they'd said he'd been at an invite-only training camp of some sort.

"Bryce Dupont," he says, extending a hand. There's a tattoo of a scalpel on the inside of his wrist. "Caleb Wu, right?"

"Yeah," Caleb says, and shakes his hand. Bryce's hand is cool and dry, skin soft to the touch except for the calluses along his palm that mark him as a hockey player, and his nails are square and well manicured. Caleb wonders, briefly, whether his own palm is as sweaty as he thinks it is, but Bryce's perfect smile doesn't waver in the slightest.

Bryce holds on for a beat too long, turning Caleb's hand over and inspecting his knuckles.

"You've got soft hands." It's not a question.

"I guess." Caleb wonders if he means literal or metaphorical. Caleb's grandmother hates the calluses he gets from hockey, but Caleb also knows his stickhandling skill is one of the reasons he's on this team in the first place.

"Mikey says you're pretty good, for a fish," Bryce says, letting go. He glances over at Mikey and Caleb follows his gaze. Mikey has his arms crossed defensively, a proud set to his chin. "Coach said you'd work, and Mikey was the one who promised you would. I trust Mikey. But there's always room for improvement, isn't there?"

Mikey blinks. It almost seems like a flinch.

"Um," Caleb says, and actually flinches when Bryce's attention snaps back to him. He wipes his definitely sweaty hand on his pants, a self-conscious afterthought. "I think so?"

"Good," Bryce says. "I like that attitude. Get dressed, everybody! Let's put the fish through his paces!"

Caleb retreats to his locker. The further he gets from Bryce, the easier it is to breathe, although something in him wants to get close again, craves the proximity. Bryce has a locker across the room, flanked by the other two assistant captains: one ginger, one blond. Neither of them would look out of place if they were carved in marble.

"Are we supposed to have ice time if a coach isn't here?" Caleb asks Mikey.

Mikey shrugs, pulling off his shirt. Caleb's attention snags on his bare chest—there's a strange scar there, Y-shaped and faintly pink like a newly-healed wound, starting from his sharp collarbones, stretching down over his well-defined pectorals, tracing down to his navel.

"Captain keeps us in line," Mikey says. "Coach doesn't really care as long as nobody gets hurt."

"What happened to you?"

The scar disappears under a quick-dry t-shirt. Mikey shrugs on his chest protector, straps it into place. "What do you mean, what happened?"

Bryce is staring at them both with his pale eyes, measured. Caleb opens his mouth, thinks better of asking, and closes it.

Caleb falls in behind Jake as they head for the ice. It's Caleb's favorite part of practice: the anticipation building in his gut, the excitement for a new opportunity to become a better player. And he'd loved Northridge's rink during tryouts, with its floor to ceiling windows, the division between inside and outside the rink hardly there even though the California sun never stood a chance against the interior cool.

Bryce gives them all fist bumps as they pass him. "Keep that head up, Hartsy. Mikey, you know what I want from you. Stags—" Caleb watches Jake's shoulders straighten as he lifts his glove to knock his knuckles against Bryce's. "Play nice."

"I'm never not nice," Jake says again, slipping past Bryce without touching him.

"Reminders can't hurt," Bryce says, and turns to Caleb. "He's got an attitude."

Caleb thinks about Jake in the locker room, utterly still as he watched Mikey leave.

"You got a nickname, Wu?"

"Thought it was Fish," Caleb says, and one of Bryce's perfectly shaped eyebrows lifts.

"Funny," Bryce says, and gives Caleb a fist bump. "We'll see. Fish don't have smart mouths like you do."

I thought you liked my attitude, Caleb wants to say, but he knows better than to question it. "Got it, captain."

Despite it being the first practice, it starts hard and only gets harder. Bryce is leagues better than the next-best player, and clearly knows it. He hardly seems to move, but when he does he glides effortlessly through each movement with the kind of fluid grace that Caleb's only witnessed among professional hockey players. As much as it's supposed to be a practice led by the captain, Bryce barely says anything at all, letting his assistant captains—Mikey, and the blond and the ginger—lead the drills and give feedback.

Instead, Bryce watches with a critical eye as Caleb struggles along at the back of the pack.

Jake turns to look at him as they're waiting their turn for line rushes. "You doing okay?"

Caleb heaves for breath, resisting the urge to double over and put his hands on his knees. He's sure his face is red enough to stop traffic, and he can feel himself sweating; his skin throbs with every pulse of blood underneath. "I'm fine."

"Good," Jake says. He glances over at Mikey, who has his head bent toward an impassive Bryce, saying something Caleb can't hear over the sound of his heartbeat in his ears. "Stay that way."

———◇———

After practice, Caleb is relieved to strip down and hit the showers. Every muscle in his body aches. His grandmother would cluck if she saw him like this—inelegantly exhausted, soaking his equipment with sweat. *At least you're not playing soccer,* she'd say with a sniff, because she wasn't helping pay for his private school education just so he got tan like someone who did hard labor under the unforgiving sun.

Like the rest of the locker room, the showers are cleaner than any Caleb's used before, and the water comes hot and fast when he turns the shiny chrome knob. He's not trying to look at anyone else—he's not dumb—but he can't help noticing the scars on some of his new teammates. None as extensive as the scar on Mikey's chest, but minor ones along the line of a bicep, the cut of a shoulder blade, the curve of a thigh. Where Jake's deltoids end in his upper arm they're marked by a pale V, no more than two inches wide, that emphasize the shape of the muscle.

Jake catches Caleb looking at the scar on his arm. "What are you looking at, fish?"

Caleb touches the same place on his own arm, self-conscious. He's scrawny in comparison, stringy and small; Jake is tall and well-muscled, skin smooth over powerful arms and shoulders. "What's that from?" he asks.

Jake, brow furrowed, glances over his shoulder as Bryce walks into the showers.

There's a knife in Bryce's hand.

Under the lights in the shower, the scalpel tattoo on the inside of his wrist is prominent, resting against the ligament that pops out of his skin as he spins the knife over his knuckles. Under the lights in the shower Bryce is more perfect than ever, the line of his jaw sharp and pale eyes discerning, beautiful despite the sneer on his face and the flash of the blade in his hand.

Caleb catalogs bits of information despite himself: the length of the knife, about half of Bryce's forearm; the way nobody reacts, simply watching Bryce with an expectant resignation; Mikey's hand touching the center of the Y-shaped scar on his chest, like a reassurance.

The blond and ginger assistant captains—what were their names again? Caleb forgot—follow Bryce into the shower, each holding a pair of limp crows by the feet. Pitch-black wings fan out, and droplets of blood splatter onto the tiled floor from their severed necks, startlingly scarlet.

Caleb glances around at his new teammates again. There's something unreal about them, something strange in their stillness, like department-store mannequins, the only movement the flicker of light over the steel of Bryce's knife, the thunder of water droplets over still bodies, and the dripping necks of the four dead crows.

Unlucky, Caleb thinks.

Caleb can't run. His legs remain rooted to the spot as water sluices over his shoulders and down his back, and his heart thunders in his chest, exhausted and enraptured.

Bryce meets everyone's eyes individually, that sneer still affixed to his face. "I'm not Coach," he says. "I'm not going to coddle you and say you did well during practice today. Every single one of you was a fucking disappointment."

He starts walking, then. The knife flickers up under Mikey's chin, raising it; Mikey's spine arches as he stands straight, mouth open ever-so-slightly, as if expecting absolution. "You especially, Mikey," Bryce says, and cups Mikey's face as he blinks. "You know why. But you're not my biggest priority."

Mikey sags when Bryce moves again. Caleb glances at Jake, who has a satisfied twist to his mouth.

Around the showers Bryce stalks, the senior assistant captains on his heels like dogs, and when Bryce gets to Caleb, he lifts the knife and digs the tip of it into Caleb's bare thigh, a shockingly cold pain that lances all the way through his body. He flinches backward, landing on the cold tile, the shower knob digging into his lower back. The shower spray flattens his hair over his forehead and into his eyes. He splutters, utterly inelegant, but doesn't dare look away from Bryce, even as the water in his eyes makes the shape of him blurry.

"Fish," Bryce says, considering. "You're smart, huh? Not very fast, though. Need to fix that."

Caleb swallows and looks down, blinking hard. Beyond the knife in his thigh—sharp, so sharp, blood welling around the tip and streaming down his wet thigh in red-paint rivulets, trickling toward the drain—he can see the splayed wings of the dead crows. "Yes, captain," he says.

The coppery stench hangs in the hot, wet air of the shower.

"Wu means crow, doesn't it?" Bryce says. "That's what the internet says, anyway."

"Yes, captain," Caleb says. *Not really,* he wants to say, but whatever he says won't change Bryce's mind, won't change the sharp look in Bryce's eyes like he's daring Caleb to disagree.

"I like your attitude," Bryce says. He doesn't really like Caleb's attitude, Caleb realizes as the knife digs deeper into Caleb's skin. He likes Caleb's compliance, his agreeableness. Caleb can be compliant and agreeable. He's very good at being compliant and agreeable, has practiced it since the first time his grandmother scolded him for spending so long in the sun.

The knife slides down, opening the skin of Caleb's thigh to the muscle, a bowing separation that opens red and raw like a lipsticked mouth. It hurts, Caleb thinks, but isn't this the price to pay for being good? He knew he had to get better, knew he wouldn't fit in. If this is what he needs to do, so be it.

His hands flatten along the slick, cool tile, and he breathes through his nose, staring at the cords of exposed muscle, the swell and bubble of subcutaneous fat released with the incision.

"Thank you, captain," Caleb says.

Bryce hums as he takes one of the four dead crows. Opens it up with another quick flash of his knife, pulling sinew and muscle from its chest and wings. "Good kid. Maybe I won't leave any marks."

His fingers—soaked in the crow's blood, clutching slippery crow muscle—find the wound on Caleb's thigh. Caleb makes no noise as he pushes the foreign muscle into the wound, practiced and surgical.

There are marks on everyone else. Jake keeps his head down and there are still small Vs on his shoulders. Mikey is the assistant captain, and has the incision over his chest, like someone—maybe Bryce, maybe some other captain—opened him up and changed his lungs, his heart.

Maybe Caleb can be better than them. Maybe Caleb can be perfect.

He stays utterly still as Bryce fixes his legs, as Bryce carves away the fat from his cheeks, as Bryce hacks apart the dead crows to add muscle to Caleb's arms, chest, calves, back. Caleb stays still, and so does the rest of the team as they observe the process, steam clouding into the air from the hot water. Under their unmoving stares, Caleb can feel each cut as it heals in tiny prickles of pain, almost as agonizing as the bite of Bryce's knife.

When the captain is done he steps away, knife and hands coated in blood—both the birds' and Caleb's—and smiles, self-satisfied. Aside from the blood on his hands, there's no trace of it anywhere else, the last of the red slipping away into the drain like Caleb had never bled at all.

Caleb looks down at his body, at the new muscle hidden by unblemished skin—and at the twin pink lines of new scar on either side of his navel, curving outward towards his hip bones. From this angle, looking down, the curve of them mimics the arch of spread wings.

"It's a reminder," Bryce says, and maybe it's a tradition, too. "Stay perfect, Crows."

Caleb pushes himself off the wall, steadying himself as his head swims, dizzy. "Yes, captain," he says. "When's our next practice?"

A Pain All My Own

Eric Raglin

With my eyes swollen shut and head feeling fifty feet under-water, I'm slow to register the tug on my ponytail, snip of scissors, and giddy laugh. When I finally turn around, the hair thief has disappeared into the crowd of thousands. Everyone's faces blur together. My tinnitus swallows their cheers and jeers. Coach puts an arm around my shoulder and guides me out of the arena.

As we enter the locker room, the noise of the crowd fades, but the ringing in my ears intensifies. This concussion will be a bitch to recover from. How many more can I take before my fighting career is over?

Coach sits me on the bench by the showers, shakes her head.

"What'd I tell you about keeping your guard up?" she says. "Prevents your face from looking like *that*."

Her words sound distant as a migraine pulses through the pulp of my skull. I try to ignore it, rubbing the now nearly-bald spot on the back of my head.

"You catch who did this?" I ask.

Coach sighs. "I don't know. Some fucking creep. If you want, we can check the broadcast and find him. But trust me, lawsuits are expensive. Ugly."

I can barely make out Coach's expression, but her tone suggests she's been through this before. How many creeps did she deal with, in or out of court, in her fifteen years as a fighter? And how many of those fuckers got away?

I rub the spot again. It prickles my fingers like tarantula hairs.

"Motherfucker," I say. "I can't let this one go."

Coach stands and gives my shoulder a gentle squeeze.

"Why don't you sleep off the hurt first?" she says. "We'll find that piece of shit in the morning."

Coach has to repeat the asshole's name three times before I get it. Not because it's a particularly difficult one to remember but because my brain feels like a wrestler coated in oil, struggling to pin down information before it slips away. Two weeks since my skull got rocked and I'm still entering rooms only to forget why I'm there—old people shit at age 25.

"Natalia, you sure you're okay?" Coach asks, digging through her desk drawer. She pulls out a bottle of ibuprofen, unscrews the cap, and pours four pills out for me. Before she can offer water, I gulp them down dry.

"I'll survive. What were you saying about, uh—"

"Brandon. Brandon Holbein."

Coach grimaces. An air-conditioned hum stirs the thick silence between us. I squint, daring her to press the concussion issue further. She clears her throat and changes course.

"Had to do some digging," she says. "But I finally got a hold of his address and license plate number. We could send police there right now, have him—"

"No, no." I bat the idea away with my hand, twist my neck to work out a kink. "No cops. I'll do it myself."

"You'll—no, Natalia, that's—"

"I won't do anything illegal. Just scare him."

Coach leans in and narrows her eyes like a mom whose teenage daughter has promised the party she's going to will have parental supervision and no drinking, *I promise*.

"Okay, fine, I want him to shit his pants," I say. "To feel like I might come for him in the middle of the night... which I won't."

"As your coach, I can tell you what to do in this gym and the ring," she says, writing the creep's address and license plate number on a sticky note. "But your life outside here is none of my business. Just don't come running to me for bail money."

I snatch the sticky note and flee her office before she can change her mind.

———◇———

Brandon's apartment has a secured entrance and the buzzer hangs off the console by a frayed wire, so I get his attention the old-fashioned way: by throwing pebbles at his window after midnight. At least, I hope it's his window. There are two units on the third floor, and one of them is definitely his according to the tenant directory. Three pebbles in, I worry he'll misinterpret the gesture as something out of an '80s teen romance movie.

The balcony light clicks on, drawing in a swarm of moths. When the sliding glass door opens, Brandon steps out in only his boxers. Even from three stories below, I can make out his ribs, covered in a thin layer of glue-white skin and thick curly orange hair. His lanky arms hang past his waist like a half-starved orangutan's. It'd be so easy to kick his ass, if only I were on that balcony with him.

"My sweet!" he screams, in delight rather than terror. He grips the balcony's railing and leans over as far as he can.

I contemplate chucking a rock right between his eyes, but I don't want him to pass out and fall, no matter how satisfying it'd be to see him splatter. I'll have to scare him with my words instead.

"Listen, you fucking creep," I say, then wince. Ever since the concussion, shouting feels like daggers in my temple. I massage my head for a moment, hoping Brandon won't notice.

Too late.

"Oh, my sweet angel is crumbling," he says.

Angel. God, he sounds like Dad. Maybe I will throw that rock.

"Wait there," he says, slipping into his apartment.

"Get the fuck back here!" I shout.

The agony is immediate as an invisible vice grip compresses my skull. I mutter a string of curses, hoping to expel the pain before Brandon returns. At the sound of the door sliding open, I lift my still-throbbing head.

A white halo surrounds him, and for a moment, I'm not sure if it's from my concussion or the balcony light. Moths dance at the man's periphery, their wings brushing his withered frame. He smiles, not bothering to bat them away, then lifts a handful of something dark and bouncy: my ponytail. It's tight in his grip. Small and almost naked as he is, he looks like a baby with a rattle.

"Yeah, douchebag, that's my hair," I say, steadying my breath. This isn't how it's supposed to go. He should be shitting himself, not flaunting his trophy. "I should beat your fucking ass for—"

Blood pulses through my head like glass shards. I stop, tense my fists, and wait for relief.

"I only did it to help you," Brandon says.

I look back up at the pathetic man. He plucks a hair from the bundle and gazes at it as if it were straw spun into gold.

He speaks in the soft, breathy voice of a shitty poet: "I wouldn't do this for just any woman. But you're special. You're my beautiful girl, and it pains me to see you get hurt. I'd do anything to make sure you never suffer again."

He places the strand in his mouth and swirls it like a partygoer tying cherry stems into a knot with his tongue. A few seconds later, he swallows.

"You're fucking disgusting," I shout, but it doesn't hurt this time. Not because adrenaline has wiped away the pain, but because... well, I'm not sure. As much as I want to keep insulting the creep, I can't. The feeling of pleasant numbness spreads through my skull, dripping down my body like a fast-acting opioid. I close my eyes.

Brandon groans, sounding somewhere between agony and ecstasy.

"Good night, sweet angel," he says, a tremble in his voice.

When I open my eyes again, the balcony is dark and Brandon is gone. My concussion, too. I call out to him, demanding he come down and face me, but the only person who acknowledges me is Brandon's downstairs neighbor opening his window to demand I shut the fuck up.

Just when I think this visit's been a complete waste, I remember the note in my pocket with Brandon's license plate number. I find his car in the parking lot and key it before leaving. It's the only satisfaction I'll get tonight.

The more I think about it, the more Brandon reminds me of Dad. Well, not completely. Brandon's actually been to one of my fights. Dad refuses, calling my choice of career "the perfect way to ruin an angelic face."

God, how many times did he compare me to an angel growing up? Not the cool Biblical kind with scorching flames and rings of eyes, but the kind you'd find at an antique shop—a small, adorable glass figure, smiling and praying. Drop her once and she'll shatter. That's how Dad saw me.

He never let me play football with my brothers. *Stay on the sidelines, Natalia. Wouldn't want my angel getting roughed up, would I?* It was always about what he wanted. And he didn't stop at football either. He never let me help with his woodworking projects. *You'll cut off those dainty fingers, sweetheart.* Of course, my brothers were running the bandsaw by the age of ten. At sixteen, I asked Dad if we could build a birdhouse together. He built it himself, called it my birthday present, and acted confused when I cried. No amount of explanation could make him understand.

It took twenty years to realize he'd never see me as anything other than an angel perched on a shelf, kneeling in prayer, kept far from the edge so I'd never fall.

But what if I wanted to fall? What if the plunge was my life's calling?

———◆———

The pain of my concussion ebbs and flows, sometimes as searing as the night of the fight and other times entirely absent. I realize the pattern: My pain disappears at exactly 11 p.m. each night. It doesn't recede gradually like the dimming of lights in an arena; it shuts off with the immediacy of a power outage.

Numb and in bed, I search for a logical explanation—that rapid release ibuprofen I took? Those evening stretches? My dinner of chicken and kale? I think back to Brandon's comment that reminded me so much of Dad: "I'd do anything to make sure you never suffer again." How he placed my hair on his tongue, swishing it around like a fine champagne. Pain left me the moment he swallowed.

This theory I'm forming is batshit. The kind of idea someone with ten more concussions than me would come up with. But I can't get it out of my head.

It's time to pay Brandon another visit.

———◆———

The window on the third floor is dark, so I scoop up a fistful of gravel and chuck it at the glass. Seconds after the clatter, a light turns on inside and a silhouette shuffles to the balcony door. An old woman steps out, hunched and squinting into the night. Brandon's mother? Wouldn't be surprised if he still lives with her.

"Who's there?" the woman asks, grogginess giving way to high-pitched panic. "And why are you throwing things at my window?"

"I need to talk to Brandon."

"I don't know who that is, and I don't know you. If this is some sort of lovers' tiff, I'd prefer not to get involved."

I make a sound halfway between a laugh and a gag.

"Stop covering for him," I say. "I know he lives here."

"I can't help you, dear. I just moved in two weeks ago—honest."

My heart drops. Only one way to check if the woman's telling the truth. I rush to the busted door buzzer and look at the tenant directory, covered in cloudy glass. The printed insert looks new, and sure enough, Evelyn Porter's name has replaced Brandon Holbein's next to unit 302. Maybe my first appearance was enough to scare him into moving. It's a satisfying thought, but now I have no way to see if he's really stealing my pain. Maybe I'll never know.

Without his ass to beat or his car to key a second time, I punch the door buzzer hard. The metal dents, but I feel nothing. I punch it again and again and again without even a hint of sensation. Several keys pop loose, sticking to my knuckles as I pull away. No blood on my fist. Not even a scratch. And right then, I vow to kill Brandon if I ever see him again.

Tonight's my first fight since Brandon stole my hair. In the middle of Coach's pep talk, my migraine vanishes. This isn't right. It's not 11 p.m. I say nothing, but my expression must change because Coach snaps her fingers.

"Nat, stick with me. Remember what I said about—"

"He's here," I say.

"Who?" Coach surveys the packed arena, crowd cheering as the announcer introduces my opponent, Mariana "Out for Blood" Alves. The kickboxer screams as she circles the ring, lifting her hands as if to conduct the fans' energy.

I scan the stands for Brandon. As much as I love fighting in a sold-out house, it makes finding that creep hard. But I know he's here somewhere with a pocket full of my hair.

"Listen," Coach says, grabbing my jaw. "Don't psych yourself out, okay? You've trained for this. Keep your guard up and kick the shit out of her legs. She'll be practically useless without them. Got it?"

I nod out of reflex if not comprehension. Still scanning the stands, I faintly register the announcer saying my name. Coach nudges me toward the ring. Normally I'd gaze into the cameras with a cold, hard glare and swagger in my step, but not this time. My wandering eyes probably make me look skittish and distracted. Doesn't matter though. This Brandon shit needs to end *now*.

While the cutman is jelling my face, I spot the creep. He leans precariously over a railing that overlooks my locker room exit. I imagine pushing him—the fall high enough to break some bones, ideally his neck. He smiles and waves with hair clenched in his fist. Just like before, he plucks a strand and places it on his tongue. He lifts what looks like an energy drink to his lips, takes a swig, and swallows. Instantly, an even greater numbness possesses my limbs and purges my body of all sensation, as if I'm nothing but a walking corpse. I push past the cutman to jump into the stands, but Coach blocks the way, guiding me back toward the ring.

"Get it together, Nat," she says.

Brandon could flee the arena at any moment. Maybe there's a way to keep him here. A gross idea pops into my head. I lock eyes with the creep and, suppressing my gag reflex, blow him a kiss. Brandon stumbles back like a dazed idiot, a flush of red climbing his neck. Good. I've got him, at least for now.

———◆———

Alves's spinning elbow smashes into my cheekbone. The kickboxer has shattered a dozen women's faces in exactly this way, but I'm different. I recover without so much as a stagger. What should be a blinding concussion or piercing bone fracture feels like nothing. I'm close enough to the commentators' table that I hear their reaction through the roaring crowd: disbelief that I could eat such a brutal blow without even flinching. It's all wrong. Pain is part of the game, a fighter's birthright.

I raise my guard and get to work chipping away at Alves's legs. Her calves swell purple and her gait sinks to a limp, but in the last minute of the round, she surprises me with a takedown. Before I can stop it, I'm in an armbar. I feel nothing when my elbow bends the wrong way, becoming convex as muscle and tendon strain. 45 seconds on the clock, and I know I could wait Alves out, her submission attempt as useless as her tried-and-true spinning elbow.

While I eye the clock from my pinned position, a man's distant howl reaches me. I twist my body, not to escape, but to find the person I know the scream is coming from. There he is: Brandon, smiling as he shrieks, his forearm swinging like a pendulum, jagged bone poking through pale flesh.

I laugh all the way to the bell.

———◆———

The hospital receptionist tells me Brandon's room number after I explain that I'm his favorite fighter. Sure, I'm not John Cena and he's not a leukemia kid, but this woman is beyond caring.

"Room 614," she says with the tired smile of someone ground down from years of working the graveyard shift.

I hustle toward the stairwell, which will be faster than the scuffed-up, ancient elevator. Come to think of it, everything in this hospital feels out of date, from the ceiling tiles stained brown with old leaks to the receptionist's boxy computer straight out of 2001. No wonder UFA sends us fighters here for our injuries; it must be cheap as shit.

No one runs into me on my way up, and for that, I'm grateful. I'll get just the privacy I need with Brandon. By the time I reach the door to the sixth floor, a mild burn rolls through my calves—his spell wearing off. One more time the numbness will consume me, but after that, I'm done. I'm free.

I kick the door and it flies open with a rusty screech. In front of me is the hallway carpet, splattered with decades of body fluid stains that no one bothered to scrub out. Room 614 is just down the hall. The lights are dimmed and no one else appears to be here. Perfect. I enter Brandon's room and close the door behind me.

There he is, splayed out and snoring in the hospital bed. Smothering him with a pillow would be so easy, but I need this to look like something other than murder. And it isn't murder, not really. It's not quite self-defense either.

Brandon sleeps with his jaw hanging open and askew, revealing teeth shattered into jagged peaks. I wore a mouthguard during the fight, but he didn't think to pop one in after he ate my hair and stole my pain, did he? Serves him right. The rest of his face is a mess of purple—more bruises than a teenager has zits. A cast holds his destroyed arm together. A morphine drip dangles from his hand. Even sedated, he twitches every few seconds in what I assume is agony. Guess the drugs can only do so much.

I soak in the sight, but I only get to enjoy it for a few seconds before he opens his eyes. Maybe he sensed his "angel" looking over him. He smiles at me through his ruined mouth. It takes all of my focus to make out his words, not that I care what he has to say.

"You came, my sweet," he slurs. I picture his face and Dad's becoming one, joining forces to keep me "safe" from this big, dark, scary world. "Did you win the fight?"

"No." I can't help a smirk. "Outwrestled by a kickboxer."

Brandon's expression falls. He scoots to sit up in bed, wincing as he puts weight on his bad arm. His battered head rolls to the side, then finds its center once more. He rediscovers his smile. "At least you didn't suffer."

"Yeah, well..." Though I no longer feel the burn of the stair climb, I rub my calves, putting on what I hope will be a convincing act.

"Oh dear," he says, looking side to side for something. "I'd help, but the nurses took the—"

"Shh," I say, slinking toward his bed like a tigress.

I sit beside him and rest a hand on his cast, giving it a not-so-light squeeze. His left eye spasms. He reaches up with his good hand to wipe a trickle of sweat off his forehead.

"You've done so much to help me. I'll give it to you willingly this time," I say, plucking a cluster of hairs from behind my right ear. I pinch them between my fingers, then hold them an inch from his lips.

Brandon's eyes roll back and a visible shiver runs up his neck. A quick glance at the bedsheet proves what I already knew: His cock is hard. Pig. It's time to get this over with.

"Please," I say, feigning a whine and pressing the cluster to his lips.

He opens his mouth. My hairs snag and curl around his crumbling teeth, but his greedy tongue untangles them, eager to taste me. He closes his eyes to savor it but winces when it comes time to swallow.

"Too dry," he says.

"Good," I reply, then clamp his jaw shut with both hands.

He thrashes side to side like a dog refusing to swallow a pill. Tears trail down his cheeks as he writhes. I only release his jaw when that terrible numbness invades my body. With gums pierced by dagger teeth, he opens his mouth and mucusy blood oozes out. Somehow, he still smiles.

"I was put on this Earth to protect you," he spits, his words less coherent than ever.

I wasn't wrong about him sounding just like Dad. Can't wait for what's about to happen.

"That's not your job," I say. "It was never your job."

His jaw hangs agape, blood dripping down the orange scruff of his chin. For a moment, he's speechless, but a man like him always has something more to add.

"I'm helping you," he says. "You should be grateful."

He doesn't sound angry. Just confused. Maybe, if I'd grown up with a different father, I'd pity him. But hypotheticals only make me doubt myself; I need all the certainty I can get right now.

"Bye, Brandon," I say, turning to leave.

He says something that might be "wait" or "stop" or "I love you." The door closes behind me, and I head for the roof access.

———◆———

Ten floors up, I look to the cracked parking lot below. Few cars parked there this time of night, and most of the lot lights are burned out. Wind whips my shirt, but I can't feel its heat or the sharp grains of desert sand it carries. I pinch myself—numb. I bite my thumb as hard as I can—numb. My teeth don't even leave a mark.

It's time. I inch toward the roof's edge, thinking about when I wanted Brandon to fall from his apartment balcony, from the arena's stands. To hear him splatter and crunch and then shut up forever. The distance to the ground gives me vertigo, but I close my eyes and take a slow, deep breath.

I lean forward. *Fuck you, Brandon*. Another inch. *Eat shit, Dad.* I pass the tipping point. There's no pumping adrenaline, no drop in my gut. Just the ground getting closer and closer until concrete kisses my nose, my chest, my kneecaps. I don't feel the impact.

But Brandon does, at least briefly. I picture him resting in bed, then flattened and juiced of his fluids in an instant. I hope he feels a flash of terror and agony before the nothingness.

I stand up and brush the dust from my clothes. A warm wind envelops me as sensation returns. But it's not the pleasure I need right now.

I find a broken beer bottle by the curb, green glass shimmering in the dim parking lot light. I select the perfect shard, then graze it up and down my arm. It leaves an unpleasant prickle, but that's not enough. Placing it in my palm, I squeeze as hard as I can. Glass cuts through skin, muscle, and tendon. Blood erupts from every crack of my closed fist. Glorious fire scorches my nerves, radiating out to all my extremities. My body quakes with violent, ecstatic life. That's it. That's everything I needed, the only thing I ever wanted: a pain all my own.

It All Comes Back

Matthew Pritt

My husband, Alan, is 46 years old, and on good days, he can still wipe his own ass. Today is not a good day.

He has the motor skills to do it. That's not the issue. He just gets too angry.

I should've changed the toilet paper roll before it ran out. Alan must have forgotten how to take the old roll off. He does that sometimes, forgets simple tasks. Instead of asking for help, he gets mad and throws whatever is giving him trouble. A loud crash and splintering glass lets me know he ripped the toilet paper holder from the wall and threw it through the shower door.

While he finishes up, I make sure the gun cabinet is locked and I hide the key, just in case. He hasn't gone for it yet during one of his episodes, but you can never be too careful. I'd get rid of it entirely if he wouldn't just go out and buy a new one.

I'll go clean up the glass and tell him it's my fault. It's easier when I say it, even if neither of us believes it.

———◆———

Third and twenty after the holding penalty erases that first down. Hedgesville High lines up in the I-Formation. Alan Murphy is under center for the Hornets. The sophomore quarterback is having an outstanding season, with nineteen touchdown passes and only two interceptions in his first six games.

Murphy takes the snap, fakes the handoff, and drops back to throw. He looks left, now right. The pocket collapses around him and he'll take it himself. He finds a hole to the left, cuts upfield, sheds a tackle and breaks it open, angling toward the sideline, across the forty. He dives for the sticks but Grayson Eddings, the senior safety for Lakeview, is there with a nasty hit. Did he get enough for the first? We'll see where they spot it.

Murphy is down, and the trainer is coming out to take a look. That was a brutal collision. Murphy climbs to his feet, walking a little crooked.

There's no way to know which concussion sent him over the edge. Maybe it was his first one, as a high school sophomore. I wasn't there for that one, but Alan describes it as a Herculean effort, fighting for the extra yard on third down. He got it, he says. I don't think he actually remembers. He's just building the moment from what his coaches and teammates told him.

It could've been any of the four he got in college, though. It doesn't really matter, I guess. I just want something to blame.

I studied athletic training at Jonesboro State, so I treated most of Alan's injuries. There were so many that never made it into his injury history. Like a good soldier, he played through them, and was praised for his toughness.

I don't regret my role in any of it. A machine like football will keep operating even if the training staff isn't there to keep the pieces in working order. The players break in spite of us. And the gears keep spinning anyway.

Jonesboro State is looking to get into field goal range before the half to add to this lead. Murphy in the shotgun, low snap, and Central Oklahoma is sending the blitz, and it'll be a sack. A loss of about six on the play. That was the linebacker Cunningham who ran straight past the left guard untouched. Murphy's helmet hit the turf on that tackle. He's shaken up and he'll head to the sideline.

By the time I'm finished cleaning, Alan is gone. The car is still in the driveway, thankfully. I check in the garage and see that the football is gone, too. I know where he went.

It's a Saturday afternoon, so the local high school stadium is empty. The gate is locked, but the fence isn't too high, even though a light rain makes the chain-link a little hard to grip. Alan is standing at midfield, playing a game of football by himself. He drops back, throws a tight spiral that goes about twenty yards downfield and takes a sideways bounce when it hits the ground.

"Come fucking on!" Alan shouts. "That hit you in the god-damn numbers!" He runs upfield and pantomimes sticking his finger in his teammate's chest.

Kids imagine themselves as heroes. I remember when Braxton was little, when Alan's symptoms were just a headache and a little trouble remembering dates, Braxton would throw the ball around in the backyard. Fourth quarter, down by five, two seconds on the clock, and his imaginary receiver would make the catch every time.

Does Alan think he's in a real game now, or has he just given up on being the hero?

———◇———

Murphy drops back to throw. Western Missouri gets pressure up the middle and Murphy has to get rid of it. He tries to dump it off to Huff in the flat, but it's a low throw and Huff can't pull it in. There is a flag down and I think this will be on the defense.

Yeah, Tom, I think they're gonna get Adams for roughing the passer here. It looked like he went to swat the ball and his hand went near Murphy's facemask. Murphy's gonna have a trainer come out to look at him. He may have lost a contact lens on the play. I wonder if that hand through the facemask poked his eye. That's gotta be uncomfortable.

They'll get him a new contact, and it looks like he'll be good to stay in the game.

———◇———

I get asked all the time why I haven't left him. How do I put up with all the outbursts? Don't I fear for my safety?

It makes me furious every time. Would you leave a spouse because they have cancer? What about dementia? Alan is dying. I know it, he knows it. He's a bomb on a decades-long timer. It could be years from now until he blows up for good. Or today.

He has never hurt me, ever. There are plenty of broken objects in the garage that are casualties of his rampages, and he's shattered his hand twice from punching things, but he has never so much as laid a finger on me. Let's leave the "yet" unspoken.

I don't know if I've just been lucky, but I like to think of it as proof that he's still in there, that he's still the gentle, caring man I married, in spite of all of it.

I'm also terrified that any outburst could be the first I get caught up in. Deep down, I know safety is an illusion. But short of locking him away, what options do we have but to persevere? There are still good days. There are still good days. There are still good days.

Alan's next "play" is a handoff. He drops the ball on the ground and cheers on his invisible teammate.

"Nice run, Traveon!"

That takes me back. Traveon Huff was the running back at Jonesboro State for Alan's junior year. They made the Division II playoffs that season. I don't want to interrupt his reminiscing, so I lean against the fence and watch. If he's playing one of their wins, he might even be in a good mood by the time he's done.

Alan picks the ball up and trots upfield just past the twenty-yard line. He throws a high arcing pass to the back left corner of the end zone. The ball takes a sideways hop and rolls onto the track surrounding the field.

He's too far away for me to hear what he's saying to his teammates, but from his body language, it looks like he's apologizing for a poorly thrown ball. He taps his chest with his palm twice, which was how he used to say "my bad." I make my way along the fence to get a little closer, trying to figure out if there's a specific game he's replaying.

The next play is another handoff, and Alan sets the ball at the twelve yard-line. The sequence is familiar somehow.

Oh, God.

—◇—

Third and two from the twelve, Jonesboro State is down by three. The clock ticks down under forty seconds. Empty back-field, trips right. Murphy is in the shotgun. Here's the snap. Murphy drops back and, no, he'll keep it himself. A draw play and he's got space to the left. Murphy dives for the pylon and, oh, you hate to see that. The refs signal touchdown, but Murphy is hurt. He took a brutal helmet-to-helmet hit and immediately rolled over on his back. Huff is motioning for the trainer, and the O-line is making a circle around him to block out the crowd view. He may have just scored the game winning touchdown, but you wouldn't know it from the silence in the stadium.

—◇—

I scramble over the fence as fast as my body will allow, but Alan has already started the play, sprinting for that front left corner of the end zone.

Alan doesn't dive this time. He crosses the goal line and keeps running, angling toward the right. He's too far ahead for me to stop him. I'm only at about the thirty yard-line by the time he drops his head and runs with full force into the goalpost.

Immediately, he drops onto his back and his arms go up in the fencing response. I sprint the rest of the way, praying to God that he's just imitating what he did that day.

—◇—

Do you ever feel like time isn't flowing the right way? Injuries always have a recovery timetable. A torn ACL will cost a year, a sprained ankle takes a few weeks. Concussions aren't the same. It took Alan two weeks to recover from the goal line hit, yet twenty-five years later, he's worse than he's ever been.

———◇———

By the time I reach Alan, he's moving again. Slowly and delicately, he climbs to his feet. But he can't keep his balance for more than a few seconds and he drops face down to the ground.

"Stay still," I tell him. "I'll get you help."

His head is buried in his hands, and when he speaks, it's all muffled.

I lean in closer so I can hear him better. "What'd you say, honey?"

"I feel it all." He's sobbing. I've never seen him like this.

"What do you feel? All of what?"

"My whole body. So much pain."

He's writhing. At first, I think he's just crying really hard, but then I see his hands moving at his face. Blood is running between his fingers.

"Alan! What did you do?"

Like a child throwing a tantrum, he keeps turning away from me whenever I try to look at him directly. Eventually, I manage to grasp his wrist and hold him still.

"It's okay," I tell him. "I'm here. You can show me."

Carefully, he pulls his hand away, and it takes everything I have in me not to recoil. He wasn't just crying; he was digging at his eye. It's halfway out of the socket, precariously there, like a gust of wind could blow it out. Blood is running down his cheek.

I speak to him like he's a feral animal I'm trying not to spook. "I'm calling an ambulance. Please, don't move."

"I feel it all," he says again, slurring his words. "Every single one. It's all coming back."

Looking at his eye, I understand now. The injuries. The pain. He's reliving ten years of body trauma in an instant. The concussion and the eye are just the beginning. I have to make him stop.

First and ten near midfield, Murphy drops back to pass, and the Raptors rush seven, an all-out blitz. The pocket collapses and Murphy goes down. That'll be a loss of four on the play. There was nothing he could do with that one. And Murphy is still down, he appears to be holding his leg. The training staff is out, and they're already bringing the cart. That's not a good sign. Let's check the replay and see what happened. He gets hit from the backside, and oh, there it is. It looked like his cleat got caught under the center, and oh. Well, we won't be showing that replay again. Sorry to anyone who is squeamish.

I keep an eye on Alan as I call for an ambulance. If I can get him to stay put, we can still fix this. The injury that ended his career was a leg injury, a compound fracture he got on a sack. If he's reliving all the injuries, that's next.

"9-1-1, what's your emergency?"

"I need an ambulance to the Hedgesville High School stadium."

I can't get any further before Alan jumps to his feet and runs off toward the sideline, angled toward midfield. I drop the phone and take off after him.

There is a set of metal benches a few yards away from the sideline, and I know exactly what he's going to do. He stutter steps just before he reaches the bench and pulls his foot back like a field goal kicker. The moment his leg swings forward, I close my eyes. I can't bear to watch.

The sound of the impact echoes in the empty stadium, followed by Alan's screams.

There was another concussion Alan never told anyone about.

He was still recovering from his end zone collision. He shouldn't have been driving, but when you're taught from a young age not to listen to your body, what can you do? The doctor told him not to drive for twenty-four hours and it had been twenty-five.

The disorientation hadn't cleared up yet. If he'd gotten pulled over, he wouldn't have been able to walk a straight line in a sobriety test. Despite my protestations, he insisted he wanted to drive, and I let him. We weren't going very far.

When he went to park, he pulled the wheel too hard. The car hopped onto the sidewalk and ran into a parking meter, barely enough of an impact to dent the fender. Still, the airbags deployed, and I knew as soon as I looked over at him. The impact and the airbag weren't enough to even make my neck sore, but it was enough to slam his brain into his skull. Like a loose screw in the inside of a machine, constantly loosening, loosening, until the whole thing falls apart.

So close together, the two concussions became as one, like a marriage. Till death do us part.

Alan's leg is broken with a compound fracture again. The bottom half of his shinbone pokes out through the skin. No more screams left to give, he's just sitting beside the bench, leg mangled, shivering uncontrollably. He's in shock. Sometime during the run, his eye shook the rest of the way loose from his socket, and it dangles down to his cheek.

My cardigan is wet, but I wrap it around him anyway. The EMS station is only about five minutes away. If I can just keep him calm enough until then, we'll be okay.

Love is protection, the valuing of someone else's life above your own. I'd do anything to keep Alan safe, but what can I do when the injuries are already there, hidden beneath layers of scar tissue?

At the time, I was thankful it was a leg injury that ended his career instead of something worse. Football gave us so much, we thought. Scholarships, jobs, opportunities. Life. We took it as a gift. It was a loan, and now it's charging us interest.

"Help is coming," I tell him. Anything to keep him still.

"I don't want help. I want it to end."

He still holds the football tucked in the crook of his arm, in spite of everything.

His body is ruined. And yet, it's all old injuries. All of it happened before—the concussions, the broken bones, the gouged eyes, the sprains and strains, the torn ligaments, the bruises, and the pain. He's carried it with him his whole life, and now I see it all laid out bare, all at once, stacked on top of itself.

God, Alan. How did you ever do it?

He tries to push himself into a sitting position, but I hold him down with one hand. He used to be so strong.

"Please, let me end it."

I hold him around his middle, careful not to touch the leg or the eye. There's nothing else to do but wait.

I will get a new shower door to replace the one Alan broke. I will not pick up the pieces and fit them together, gluing each individual piece to the whole to rebuild it.

We can't replace our bodies. We have to stitch, patch, and heal. Alan's body is a broken door, a shattered vase. He'll never be whole, and it breaks me to see such a man become so fragile.

Late this summer, on this very field, Hedgesville High will put on their helmets and play ten games. And during every one, I will be praying for all twenty-two kids on the field at any given moment, that the machine will not do to them what it has done to Alan. I can't stop it any more than I can stop the seasons changing. If they could all come and see Alan now, they'd still play. I know that.

If Alan could see what he would become, would that have stopped him?

The lights of the ambulance arriving in the parking lot pierce the misty rain, and I hold myself on top of Alan until they reach us, clutching to him as tightly as I clutch to the hope that there are still good days ahead.

Avulsion

Madeleine Sardina

There was an ice storm when I was a kid that split nearly every tree on the block, including the oak tree in our backyard. It was early in the season, before all the trees had lost their leaves, so as the ice fell it clung to the leaves and branches and to itself, building and building like stalactites until the branches were too heavy and had no choice but to split away from their trunk. The sound of that splitting was like the world ending. I was eleven, old enough to know thunder wasn't anything to be afraid of, but when the largest bough of the oak tree finally gave way and split the whole trunk in two, I couldn't hear my own scream above the sound of it.

My dad spent the next day hauling what he could back and forth from the tree to the curb. By dinner, our whole street was lined with the debris of the storm. He hadn't let me help, telling me instead to work on my conditioning. I'd done so many single leg lifts that I felt off balance with both feet on the ground. When he'd finally finished, well past dinner time, he washed his hands off and beamed at me. "Race you to the bonsai room."

My father collected bonsai trees. He had a forest of them, all kinds—maple, juniper, wisteria, rhododendron. He kept them in a special room in the house, what he called the sun room even though it had probably been designed as an extra bedroom. It was humid as a greenhouse in the summer and when I was young—younger, younger still—it was my favorite room in the house.

The trees were small compared to their wild counterparts, but he let some of them grow as big as the room would allow, and to a four-year-old, a three-foot Chinese elm might as well be a 150-foot sequoia. I would hide underneath them when I played hide-and-seek and when I read my first chapter books. I'd take my friends on tours through the room, confidently pronouncing the botanical names of each one. *Syringa vulgaris, Ginkgo biloba, Populus tremuloides*. I caught Dad lurking outside the door once, and when he winked at me it was the proudest I'd ever felt.

I took up figure skating when I was seven, the latest in a line of sports my father had tried me out on. First had been soccer, then softball, then tennis. I never saw the point of retrieving balls for two hours a week. But I took to figure skating, and in a class of four- and five-year-olds it wasn't hard for me to rise to the top of my class. My dad was my biggest fan before I'd even learned to skate backwards. He drove me to every practice, forty-five minutes both ways to the Isla Winter Sports Center. When it was clear I'd fast surpassed the other students in my class, he pushed for me to try out with some of the junior-level coaches, started talking about levels and tests and competitions. "You could be really good," he told me one night as he massaged my calves. I'd been on the ice for three hours.

"I am really good," I told him, throwing all the weight of an eight-year-old's confidence behind the words.

"Exactly!" he said, pointing my toes up and pushing down on the sole of my foot.

"Ouch, Daddy!"

"Ouch is good," he reassured me. "It means you're pushing yourself. It means you're learning your body's limits."

Even back then, it felt like my legs hurt every day. Sometimes my coaches said it was a growth spurt or just the normal pains of being a person, but Dad would say it was muscles developing, my own strength building and building, and my little body was just getting used to it. "It'll stop hurting eventually," he said. "When you grow into it. If you keep practicing, your body will be made for this work."

I got my period when I was ten. Earlier than every girl in school, earlier than any of my cousins, earlier than any of the girls in my figure skating classes. I was practicing my Biellmann spin, eyes unfocused as the world blurred around me, and heard one of the other girls shriek. My neck ached as I whipped out of the backbend and saw everyone looking at me in horror. "It's okay, honey," Coach Miranda said, so much gentler than I'd ever heard her speak before. "Here."

She untied her windbreaker from her waist and handed it to me. I took it, staring at her. "You've got a little..." She pointed to her backside and I twisted to see my own, to see the red smear spreading down my leg. It trickled down like sweat and the ache in my gut, the ache I'd thought was the same as all the other aches in my growing body, suddenly seemed much more urgent.

Dad took me home early from practice, dead silent the whole drive. I had a bundle of toilet paper shoved down my practice leggings and a towel I'd used for my sweat folded on the car seat. Both coaches only kept tampons or cups and neither of them had been willing to show me how to use them.

"You'll have to work harder," Dad told me that night as he helped me stretch under the welcoming branches of a Japanese maple. "You'll be at a disadvantage for a while, until it happens to the others too."

That's exclusively how he referred to my period. *It happens.* Consolation and explanation. "Coach said it only lasts a few days," I told him.

"A few days *every month*," he corrected. "And I'm not even talking about that. This is just the beginning. We're going to have to start watching your weight. I've let you off the hook so far but we're going to have to compensate for... everything."

He pulled my arms back, twisted them behind my back, and pushed my wrists to the ground. I looked up at the maple leaves, already a deep red in late summer. I wondered if they knew why they changed colors. In the fall, they would drop their leaves even in this climate-controlled room, taking their direction from the waning sunlight filtering in from the windows.

"Are you listening to me?" Dad asked me, pulling my shoulders back into a deeper stretch.

"Yes, Daddy."

"Good." He took the bundle of the aluminum wires he kept with his bonsai supplies, stored between the shears and the pliers and the pruning saw. "Let me know if it pinches."

He anchored the end of the wire in my shoulder, hooked under my collarbone. "Pinches," I told him and he huffed.

"Not that kind of pinch. It's going to dig in a little, but that's more good pain. I know you know the difference between good pain and bad pain."

I never seemed to experience bad pain. "Yes, Daddy."

He twisted the wire up over my left shoulder which he kept held back, chest open and reaching for the ceiling. It snaked down my left arm, wrapped in wide loops. "Clasp your hands together. Good girl." He bound my wrists in the wire and twisted it back up my right arm and over my other shoulder. "Beautiful. Do you feel that stretch, honey?"

I felt a muscle jumping in my lower back and an ache in my pelvis I knew better than to mention. "It's a good stretch, Daddy."

One of my earliest memories is my dad showing me how he tended his bonsai. He had a new tree, *Ficus benjamina*, one of the most basic in his collection. "But basic doesn't mean it's not special," he told me as he turned the little potted plant on a repurposed potter's wheel. "It just means we have to work a little harder to make it stand out."

I watched as he pulled and twisted the branches, bound them in aluminum wire, clipped leaves off as he saw fit. "What happens if you just let it grow?" I asked as he tossed more foliage into his little trash can.

"It would keep growing," he said. "Forever and ever, like the big tree in the backyard."

"Is that bad?"

"Not for a regular tree," he said. "But these are Daddy's special little trees, so he wants them to look perfect and beautiful, which requires a little work. But it's fun work! Work Daddy likes doing."

When I came back empty handed from my first international senior competition, I went straight to the sun room and sat waiting beneath the wisteria. It was mid-Autumn, and the leaves were as gold as the sun, draping over my head like a crown. I stood up when Dad came in and silently unspooled a length of wire. "Show me a Biellmann," he said.

I lifted my right leg and reached backwards over my head to grab it with both hands. There was no blade to hook my fingers on, so I grabbed my ankle instead, pulling my leg up and up and up. My cold muscles shrieked with the stretch, but I kept my face blank, my eyes lowered. Dad stepped behind me, tugged the twisted bundle of my hands and foot higher still, forcing my back into a deeper bend. I ground my teeth together against the pain and Dad's free hand touched my cheek, gentle as if he were touching a flower. "Bad pain?"

The bundle of aluminum wire he had looped around his wrist bumped against my jaw. "No," I answered. "Good pain."

He worked slowly, humming softly under his breath as he wound the wire, twisted it around the thin bones of my wrists, the bump of my ankle. Sometimes I dreamed he bound me so tight I unspooled like thread, or burst apart like a coiled spring.

When he dropped his hands, I twisted to look at him and he shoved my shoulders forward again. Something twinged in my neck and I twitched with it, throwing off my balance and dipping forward over my support knee. My arms jerked against their binding in an effort to rebalance and my support leg clenched and twisted to catch myself. I froze in a forward fold, arms held back, my left foot stacked up and over and backwards in an extended standing split. It felt like my lungs had compressed, every organ in my body shifting into this new shape.

Dad waited for me to correct my posture. I raised myself back into a standard Biellmann position, took a deep breath, and held it.

I stood like that for two hours, before my left leg collapsed. Dad came upstairs when he heard the thud, found me sobbing up at the ceiling, unable to turn my face into the carpet without tearing something open in my shoulder, or my neck. "This is progress," he assured me as he pried away the wire and disinfected the places it had sliced through my skin. "You should be proud you lasted that long. Next time, it will be longer."

My senior debut season saw a handful of third places in minor competitions, a lucky scrape into the Grand Prix circuit that ended in a sixth place finish, and a seventeenth placement at World Championships. While we waited for the flight home from Helsinki, Dad shopped online for a new pair of shears. "We need to strategize," he told me when he caught me looking over his shoulder.

At home, muscles still tight from the nine-hour flight, Dad carried my skate bag to the bonsai room, knowing I would follow. I sat cross-legged on the ground while he opened his toolbox. "Do you know what happens when you prune a bonsai?" he asked, as he'd done a thousand times before. I sat silent. "It redistributes the growth where it's *designed* to grow. It controls where the nutrients go, where new branches grow, and in which direction." He plucked his shears from the box, opening and closing them experimentally. They were stainless steel with black handles, needle-sharp. "Lay down on your front, honey. Superman."

I did as I was told. I didn't even think to stop him.

He crouched beside me, braced one knee on the ground beside my hip, ran his palm down my spine. "We've been working so hard on building these muscles, but there's only so much to be done." He chuckled. "The best that we can with the tools we're given, right?" The shears clicked and my shirt fell away from my back. "We can do better though. We just have to be willing to sacrifice a few branches."

He would show me later. He would take pictures of my back, his artwork, each step in the process as he carved me up. It was impressive, really. My father wasn't a surgeon or a sculptor. He was a hobbyist. But he'd drawn around the muscles in my back like he knew precisely where each one stopped and started, like he was looking at a diagram. He sliced down each side of my spine, the curves of my shoulder blades, my trapezii and deltoids, my obliques. At some point he stuffed my ruined t-shirt into my mouth to muffle whatever sounds I was making. He was silent the whole time—never told me to stop crying, never told me this was important work, that it was because he loved me or because he knew I could be better if I let this happen. Maybe it was worse that way. He gave me nothing to argue against.

When he was done with the shears, he started in with the wire. He pulled my right leg back, bent at the knee, bound to my right hand. He took my shoulder, then, sticky with blood, and pulled it back, back, back into an upright layback spin position. He wound my whole body in wire, ignored the way it spasmed, the way my muscles pulled away from him. I felt them peeling back from—from me, from themselves, from my bones, curling up and away in the places he had made his incisions. He used the whole spool of wire, mummified me in it. I threw myself against the binding, a wild animal caught in barbed fencing, killing itself in its desperation.

This is how I spent the off season.

In the fall, I got all my levels on my spins. My jumps still needed work, but my axel was fully rotated and the judges raved over my performance components, my flexibility even in my age. I consistently made the podium, even snagged gold in one of my Grand Prix qualifiers. "What did I tell you, huh?" Dad crowed on the way back to the hotel room in Las Vegas. "Just a little pruning. A little cutting away with the dead weight."

I missed the podium at Worlds by less than a point. The gold medalist, a Russian who'd turned fifteen two days before the cutoff, had a triple axel and a quadruple flip in her free program. "You're too old to let these kids bully you," Dad said as we climbed the stairs to the bonsai room.

"She doesn't bully me, Dad, she's actually really sweet—"

"Is she? Did she offer to pay for your knee surgery?"

My teeth clicked together when I shut my mouth.

This time, he kept me standing. "Give me a loop," he said as he shuffled his work table around. I crossed my legs at the ankle, tightened my shoulders, arms held at a right angle, and sprang into a loop, landing and hopping in a slow circle, left leg extended. "Again." I sucked in a lung of air and coiled up again. "Freeze."

I froze in the take-off position, shoulders tight and powerful, willing stability into my crossed legs. He pressed a bundle of my practice leggings into my mouth and moved behind me. "Hold that for me," he murmured, almost to himself. He sat down on the ground and began his work on my knees.

This time he was going for strength, he told me. My upper body had needed flexibility, not bulk. Bulk would only hold me down, give gravity more of an edge. But my legs needed muscle, needed to become coiled springs made to launch me across the ice. He sliced a curving line down the outer edge of my calf. My leg spasmed, pulled away, and he latched an iron grip around my shin. "I said hold it," he said, his voice a hard line. I bit down hard on the fabric in my mouth and held my leg still.

It seemed almost more artistic this time. Where he had diagramed the muscle groups of my back, lifting and lowering the blade in precise movements, he now moved in fluid lines, down and around and back up again. He started at the bottom and worked his way up slowly. I guessed it was to see more clearly through the dripping blood.

When he reached my hip, he finally lifted the blade and stepped back to survey his work. He'd done my landing leg only, but that was enough to send tremors through my whole body. "Okay, tense like you're going to take the jump," he said, wiping his hands off.

I gagged around the leggings, spat them onto the floor. "Daddy, I can't—"

"Honey, you need to put some effort if this is going to work," he said. "I can carve you up, but it won't take if you just let the muscles relax."

"It hurts!"

"Do I need to get the wire?" He sounded almost sympathetic. Like I was just another plant for him to shape, like I couldn't do a thing on my own.

I tightened up, let the pain wash through me in waves. I don't know if I screamed. I tried not to.

The year I turned nineteen was an Olympic year. I would be twenty-three by the next one—not too old to qualify but too old to stand against the teenagers with their fresh joints and their bodies who hadn't needed quad jumps carved into them. As it was, nineteen wasn't ideal, but with the scar tissue winding like snakes over my right leg, I still had a shot. "Muscle on muscle," my dad called it.

I had two of my quads stable by Nationals. The triple axel was never a solid bet, but we kept it in my free skate, hoping the adrenaline of competition would carry it through. I popped it on the first pass and when I tried to work it into combination, I fell hard on my right side and something in my hip tore apart.

I don't remember it, really. I never seem to remember the pain. I think it's like childbirth—my body learned to forget it so I could keep doing it again and again. Maybe I would've stopped it sooner if I could recall how much all of it had hurt. Maybe I would've stopped even from the beginning, from the first night he had wrapped my body in wire and twisted it into whatever shape pleased him.

They showed me a video in the hospital. My friends, my skating friends, if they could be called that. Fellow competitors, more like, but friendly ones. A handful came to visit, brought balloons and one of those fruit bouquets. "It was awful," one of them said. "You kept screaming for your dad."

I watched the video so many times I dreamt of it. I saw the yawn of my mouth tipped back to the ceiling, my clutching hands gripping my tights, skittering over the fabric like I was afraid to touch but had to grab something to keep my leg from sliding away. My screaming was distant, only what the rink-side camera could pick up, but the thin echo of it still came through, my chest heaving. I'd never heard a person scream like that. Injuries on the ice are not uncommon. I'd seen ice skates slice through flesh, ankles twisted into ugly angles, knees hyperextended. I'd never heard someone scream like their voice was trying to escape their body. My mouth only closed to form one word, curled into a grimace.

I was on bed rest for two weeks and crutches for a month after that. I watched the Olympics from the couch. Dad was tending his bonsai. He didn't watch a single event.

Once I was out of the cast and off my crutches, I was supposed to stay off ice for another month at least. "Work on building the muscle back slowly," my physical therapist said.

"This is the kind of thing that can become a chronic injury if you don't treat it right early on. You need to think long term."

"As if you have time to think long term," Dad griped on the way home. "You've got four years and four quads left. Should probably build that axel back better, too. This might actually be a gift in disguise, if you think about it. The muscle is healing, it's growing back, and we can make sure it grows back the way we want it. Right?" He held his fist out to me, wiggling it for me to bump it.

That night, I sat in the center of the bonsai room. He hadn't touched me yet, had only brought out some drawings to show me his plan. "It's ambitious," he'd said, "but when are we going to have this opportunity again?"

He'd let me sit with them, gone to bed hours ago. I wasn't looking at his diagrams, though. I rewatched the video of my hip avulsion a few times. I looked at the X-rays my doctor had sent me weeks ago. I counted the leaves on his *Ficus benjamina*. He had two of them now—the second one he'd shaped into the traditional tree, or a tree shrunk down. Its thick white trunk spread out in a wide canopy of leaves and branches, its roots snaking over the top of the soil. The first, though, he'd had more trouble shaping to his whims. It had grown three thick roots that pushed above the soil, sprouting up like legs. The trunk itself was stunted, barely an inch of height before a cluster of branches grew straight up into a bundle of leaves and twigs. It was ugly and top heavy, an imitation of a tree from a creator who had only heard stories of them.

I grabbed the pot and carried the tree downstairs, out the door to the backyard. The oak tree was still standing, had survived the risk of infection after the damage of the ice storm years ago. Its bark had healed over the gash in the split trunk. I sat down with the ficus at the opposite end of the yard and started to dig. I used my bare hands, scooped out soil, clawed through the packed top layer and sunk my fingers into the soft black earth. The ficus' roots were packed into less than a square foot of space, so I made the hole big, gave it room to breathe. I eased the plant out of its pot, tried not to jostle it too much. A few leaves fell into the hole and I buried them, too, scooped soil in around the roots, patted it down gently. When I was done, the little tree stared back up at me, stable, waiting for whatever I was going to do next.

I brought down each bonsai. There was over a dozen by then, a new one acquired every few months, and even though I carried two pots each trip, my hip was throbbing by the time I'd emptied the room. I buried the second ficus next, then the wisteria, then the Japanese maple, on and on. I spread them out across the yard—they needed space to stretch their roots out, reach out their canopies to catch the sunlight. It took all night. I was patting the soil of the Chinese elm when the sun crept over the horizon, when I heard the back door swing open. I pressed my fingers into the dirt. I thought of what it would feel like to let them spread and grow, anchor me to the soil. I thought of what it would be like to keep growing.

Lucky Like Elena

Alexis DuBon

Fucking Elena. With that flawless fucking form, making it look so easy while the rest of us are still landing double fulls in the foam pit. She's already on floor, no mat, never even hops out of it. She just sticks it *every single time*.

"Can I try it on the mat? I mean, don't you think the safety of the pit is messing with me? Maybe if I *had* to land it, it would be better motivation."

Coach gives me the side eye.

"Watch Elena," she says. "Look at all that power, look at that height. You're not there yet. Stay in the pit, get more comfortable with it. Then we'll move to the mat."

It's always *watch fucking Elena*. Watch her and her silent panther steps, her perfect point. It's always *Gigi, your run is too heavy* or *Gigi, tighten your core*. All the high fives are for her, all the extra stretches, the whispers from other teams—always her name on their tongues.

And she doesn't even have to work at it. She's just genetically blessed. Her proportions, her build, even that perfect fucking face. If I had her body, I'd be killing every event too.

Try again. I have to get it. This is going to be mine.

Deep breath.

Go.

Roundoff, back handspring, look for the ground, arm out, full to connect, hands together, twist again—YES! Fuck, if that had been on the floor I would have stuck it. Of course no one was looking. But I finally *did* do it—even though Coach was too busy watching Little Miss Perfect who's moved on to beam already. She'll be on arabians soon. Everyone else is still on front layout step-outs.

Might as well go to beam, too, work on my sissone—Coach took pictures last week and I'm definitely short of one eighty on my split. *And don't forget to point your toes, you look like a sloppy mess.* Elena never forgets to point her toes. I don't even think she *could* forget, it just happens automatically. She was born perfect.

———◆———

"Gigi. Eat your meatballs."

"I did. It's just the broccoli is really good and I want to eat that, okay?"

"It's flavorless boiled broccoli, it can't be good. Eat a meatball."

My mom does this every night. I *did* eat a meatball. How many meatballs is it going to take to shut her up? I stab at one with my fork and pretend it's Elena. The metal slides into the meat and the little sphere of ground chicken opens up, releasing a trickle of liquefied fat onto my plate. That wouldn't happen with Elena. She has less fat than a fucking chicken meatball. More blood though.

"How was work?" Change the subject to get her off my back.

"It was really good, actually," she says, shoving a meatball in her mouth. "We had an emergency—a dog was hit by a car, he was in pretty bad shape, but—" another meatball.

"—but, *healing hands?*"

Mouth too full of food, she jazz hands her fingers at me from across the table and smiles.

"And everyone was just astonished at how he pulled through?"

She nods. "No broken bones or anything."

"Everything good as new?"

"Of course," she says. "Healing hands. You better start focusing a little on getting into college. You can do better than just twisted ankles and kitchen burns. Get in somewhere with a good Physical Therapy program and put them to use."

I can feel another speech on 'not letting the family talents go to waste' coming. Like being a vet tech is some incredible pedestal to lecture from.

If I don't get out of here, I'm going to lose it.

"Mom, I need to borrow the car. Just to go to school and do a few laps around the track. I need to clear my mind."

"No, Gigi. You need to study. SATs are coming up. Even if you do get that athletic scholarship, it's not going to be enough. You need the academic credentials too."

"Yeah, exactly. I can't concentrate on all that in this condition. I'm *so* stressed out and I need to run it off—*please* just give me the keys?"

She hands them over and gives my plate a dirty look.

"Did you have to massacre *all* your meatballs? They can't go back in the fridge like this. Please don't waste your food, Gigi."

"Sorry!"

"You'll be sorry tomorrow when you don't have anything to reheat—I'm doing the overnight shift this whole week."

"I'll survive."

And I'm out the door.

———

Six times around the track before someone else shows up. Usually when it's this late I can run all night uninterrupted, but of course today I have company. And of course it's someone who prances over the rubber like a goddamn Pixar creature while I'm sweating my ass off. And of course they're already about to lap me, getting closer and closer.

"Hey! Fancy seeing you here." That angelic fucking voice. Who else would run like that?

"Hey Elena! I didn't know you were a runner." Of course she is. She's everything.

"Oh, no not at *all*, I'm winded from my first lap already trying to catch up to you—you're *fast*. I just come here sometimes when there's a lot on my mind. Totally not a runner, but sometimes, you know, it helps."

"What's on your mind?" Seriously, though. She doesn't know what it is to be stressed out or worried. Her life is perfect.

"Ugh. I dunno. I guess just school, and like... I dunno." For a moment there's silence, and as soon as I begin to believe it might stay that way she says, "I guess there's some stuff at home that's been kinda hard. I just wanted to get away from all the fighting."

I wonder what she even considers fighting. She would never have survived the shit I had to deal with when my dad was around. She doesn't know family drama.

"Well, if you ever want to talk about anything, I'm around." Gag.

"Thanks," she says, and smiles at me with all her straight, gleaming white teeth.

I wish she really was a meatball so I could impale her. Deface her. Put a big nasty scar across her blemish-free, glowing skin. Show her what real pain is.

———◆———

Another neverending day of school, but by the end of it, I've figured everything out—exactly how I want to do this. Last night she gave me everything I needed to make it happen. I'm jittery with anticipation but I have to keep it cool.

Finally it's time for practice.

Of course when I get there, Elena is already warming up, stretching out her splits with a solid ten inches of mat under her right foot, arching deep, reaching for her pin-straight back leg. Her perfect, perfect legs, getting them prepared for all the skills that only they can do.

"Hey, trackstar," I say, and plop myself down next to her, start rolling out my ankles.

"Hey!" She rotates into a side split to face me, keeping her right foot on the mat, and leans forward, elbows on the floor and her face cupped in her hands, smiling sweetly.

"So. I meant to say this last night, but like, you know my folks are divorced, too, so—I get it. If you want to get together and talk about things, I'm here."

"Oh. That's actually really nice of you Gigi, thanks. I know it's super unhealthy, but I kind of do better just dealing with things on my own, or like *not* dealing with them really—kind of just pretend things aren't happening until they're far enough behind me, you know?"

Fuck. That's not what she was supposed to say.

"But," she continues. "If you ever want to meet up and do some laps around the track, or whatever, I'd totally be down to hang out outside of gym."

There it is.

"Totally—text me whenever. I'm always looking for an excuse to drop my SAT prep book."

"Same," She switches to stretch her other leg. "Oof, my left side is always so much tighter." And sad-mouths her bottom lip like I should empathize with her woes.

Her house looks like little kids should be sneaking through the forest to eat it. But her mother, of course, is far from an old warty fairy tale witch. She kisses Elena goodbye on her way out the door, dressed in some impossibly expensive-looking suit and a chic, understated haircut. She's some kind of lawyer and apparently she even looks the part at home. I shouldn't have expected anything less I guess, but still it's surprising somehow. My mom is always running around the house in pajamas and a ponytail.

Elena opens the car door and hops in, waves to her mother as I pull away.

"Thanks for picking me up! I haven't had a sleepover in so long," she says, grinning. "I brought my Ouija board! It's dumb kid stuff, I know, but still, it's always fun!"

"Ouija board? It *has* been a while since your last sleepover!"

We laugh, and she's actually not that terrible to be around, for such a Pollyanna princess. Still, though, that doesn't change anything. And she brought a fucking Ouija board. Not everyone is as into the occult as my family, I know, but a Ouija board?

Once we get to my house, I show her around and she's very polite about everything even though her house could swallow mine whole. But it's the basement I'm excited to show her. I have it all set up.

I lead her downstairs and lock the door behind us.

"Oh my god," she says. "You have a lot of power tools down here. Do you know how to use them?"

"Not really," I say. "They were my dad's. He took most of it when he left and he never came back for the rest."

"You should clear it out and use it as a practice space. I mean, if they're just down here taking up room. That's what I did with my basement."

"Maybe."

The *tools* are all leftover from my father, but the tarp I got from Home Depot last night, and the straps were a fortune on Amazon.

"What's that smell?" Elena's eyes scan the room and land on the weathered wood box I'd placed on my dad's old work-table. It clearly doesn't belong in a room full of drills and band saws, worn smooth by the hands of all the long-dead women who define my lineage. She goes straight for it and lifts the lid. So fucking nosy.

"Is that a candle? It smells so… " She inhales deep. "Foresty."

That whiff might actually work to my advantage. Maybe help keep her still and calm. I'll take all the help I can get.

"No, it's not a candle," I say, glad that I thought to hide the sewing kit. Those questions wouldn't be as easy to answer. "Lie down on that table. I wanna show you this new stretch I found on YouTube." The truth is, I have been watching a lot of YouTube videos lately, but mostly medical.

And she does it, she lies right down on the table. That's all it takes. She even lets me bind her wrists in yoga straps, "for extra resistance," I tell her, before taking out my other two sets.

Elena's completely bound—arms, legs, torso. She doesn't even start asking questions until I'm laying the tarp.

"What is that for?" she asks. "Actually, the straps are kind of itchy, I think maybe I'll skip this stretch after all."

Of course. She can't even tolerate the most minor discomfort.

"Just wait." I know my voice sounds impatient, but my heart is racing and I think I might lose it. This all felt easier in my head. It'll be worth it, though. It'll be fine.

"Actually, I think I have to go to the bathroom."

What a fucking liar.

She's getting all wiggly and squirming her body around. If she doesn't behave, this is going to be so much harder than it has to be.

First to get everything I'll need in reaching distance—the salve and the sewing kit, thanks mom; and the circular saw, thanks dad.

I take it off its charger and straddle her stomach—dangling my legs over either side, facing her feet. Those squirms are getting desperate and she's screaming and sobbing, begging.

But it's too late now. I have to go through with it. And I was right—I do better when there's no other option, when I have to go forward and just do what needs to be done. I *told* Coach that was it. This is proof. I succeed when I have to.

I start with my own leg first, the left one, because I want to know exactly what she's going to feel. At first, it's just really hot. Like it's a soldering iron, not a saw. It sears the first layer of flesh and steam is the first thing to come out of me—just the thinnest little trail of it rising from my thigh. I smell singed hair before anything else and I hope the heat doesn't cauterize my wound before I get a chance to reattach it. The incision pulls apart like when you're trying to closed-mouth smile for a picture but then someone makes you laugh, and that's how the blood comes—like laughter. It goes from nothing to a straight up river before I know it and I watch as it runs slick against Elena beneath me.

Is she actually using what little mobility she has to try to wipe it away? Like my blood is really the thing she should be worried about right now. I am just a preview of what's coming for her.

She's only going to suffer through like half of this though, with her skinny thighs, but that's good enough. The pain is magnificent, knowing she'll be feeling it soon. She's going to endure every twinge, every rip that I am, and by the time I get to her, I'll have had enough practice to make it even worse.

Getting through the skin was nothing but now I've reached muscle and I can feel every band snap as I cut the tension. A whole rubber band ball *thwapp*ing apart, back towards hip and knee joints. I can see them recede and I really do thrive in do-or-die situations, it's true—these lines are perfectly clean. No jagged flaps of skin or anything. Maybe I should take these steady hands to Pre-Med. Fuck Physical Therapy, I'm a god damn surgeon. This precision!

Elena's just screaming her pretty little head off in the background, but it's been so constant it barely registers as noise.

It's basically like a soundtrack at this point. I rub her leg with my hand as if to say *there, there*, smearing my blood over the skin that stretches so tight over her lithe body. Soon that leg will be mine. It's so much less infuriating to look at when I think of it like that.

But fuck, the bone is bad. It smells worse than the rest too. Like Fritos, but not in a good way. I don't think the saw is made for something so solid, and it's struggling. That burning plastic, overextended power tool stench mixed with all the rusty blood and burnt skin and bone is making me nauseous. I really don't need to add puke to that combo, but I'm not sure I can help it.

The ache radiates and echoes as it courses through nerves that shouldn't feel it at all. It's in my fingernails, in the roots of my hair. Electricity fills my body.

But bone means I'm almost halfway there.

Now the smell of wet dog food enters the equation, like the chicken liver my grandma used to make me eat. I'm in the marrow. And it's fucking excruciating. It just keeps getting worse the deeper down I go. For a second I want to give in and pop a painkiller or maybe take a whiff of the salve like Elena did, but I need to know how it feels, to relish in the knowledge of what she has coming.

I break through what remains of my femur and my leg flops open like a loose hinge. It's like those girls on Instagram who post pictures of the inside of their burgers all split in half and stacked on top of each other, oozing cheese and ketchup over perfectly cooked ground meat.

One good push with the saw and I'll be through the whole thing. I sever my hamstring and the skin at the back of my thigh with so much force that the blade swings into the air at their surrender. My leg falls to the tarp and it splashes into a puddle of blood, spraying the wall I should have thought to cover. Fuck. Well, that's why we have Mr. Clean erasers, right? That should work.

I need to be more careful with the next one. No way I'll be able to reach down to pick it up with both of them gone. Then I'll really be fucked. The thought of my mother coming home and seeing this carnage is way too stressful. Careful, but fast. I can't bleed out and die like *this*. Half legless and dead and Elena just walks out on her own two feet? No. Just suck it up and get it done. Once I break out the salve it'll all be okay, I just have to make it that far.

I work through my second leg, so much easier now that I'm getting the hang of it. I look like the Barbie doll of some kid who threw a fit when her pants were too hard to get on, and that almost makes me laugh but I'm way too dizzy to give myself the giggles—I have to keep it together. But one thing any gymnast can do is keep her head in the game and work through temporary pain. The payoff is going to be so worth it.

Now it's Elena's turn. I have to remember not to rush it—I want to savor every shriek and howl that comes out of her mouth, enjoy the process.

It was smart of me to strap her down so tight. Without my legs for support, I can't afford to have her buck me on to the floor. And she's really fighting now, struggling to do better than a wiggle. The girl is fighting for what she thinks is her life and the best she can do is act like one of those wiggly arm inflatable guys that they put outside of car dealerships. Pathetic.

"Let's start with your left side," I say. "Weren't you bitching about how tight it was?"

———◦———

It takes a special kind of weak to pass out as quickly as Elena did, but she's not used to pain and suffering, so it wasn't really a surprise. Now it's time to wake up, though—it's time for the threading.

She's practically grey and I can only imagine what I look like right now, but it's almost over. I'm so close. This is it, the last step.

"Elena, remember how you wanted to summon spirits? Well, it's time."

Her head lolls against the table, all semiconscious and woozy. It's a good enough response for me.

"Okay, take this into your mouth—I promise, it's fine." I cup my hands, full of our combined blood and pour it into her lips.

She drools it right out. Coughs a little.

"Okay, Elena—" I try to keep my voice steady but we have to do this fast and she's not cooperating. "Listen—just hold it in your mouth, you don't have to swallow or anything. Actually, I need you not to. Just keep it in there."

I try again, funnel my cupped hands between her little cherub lips and get the blood into her mouth.

"Good," I say. "Now just spit it all into my mouth."

And she actually does it. Just a sputtering little dribble like the broken water fountain outside Chem class, but good enough.

I pull a spool of thread out from the special-use sewing kit that's been passed down for god knows how long and spit our blood onto it, now that it's passed through both our lips.

Quickly before too much time goes by, I repeat the process and rub the mixture against our four pelvic stumps, where I need to reattach our legs, then line them up—her left to mine, and my left to hers, likewise with the right side.

It was smart to remove her legs second, they've spent less time severed from the body and I'll sew them onto me before I sew mine to her. I thread the needle, and pray. Sprains and blisters are fine to tackle alone, but something like this, I'll need help.

"Guide my hands, spirits, seal these wounds." They don't need to know this was an intentional thing. They'll just help heal our injured bodies. I've heard all the stories, they can't just choose to disregard me like everyone else. They're not people.

The room becomes ice cold and I shudder at the drop in temperature. My fingers feel stiff and it's a struggle to hold the needle properly, but I feel as though it doesn't even need me, like it's moving on its own. I don't dare test that; if it falls, there's no way I'll be able to pick it up off the floor.

The tip penetrates my skin, thread passes through tissue, flossing inside my body. It's when I feel the needle pierce Elena's leg that I know this worked. I feel thread run through flesh that yesterday was not mine. Halfway through the first leg and I can wiggle her toes. They are so much prettier than mine—though I guess that's not true anymore. They *are* mine.

I stand on them to stitch my legs to her body, and they feel every bit as good as I imagined. Strong and powerful and limber. The connection was immediate, they melded to my body so easily—they feel natural, they feel *right*.

This part takes less time than I thought it would, and it's time to scrub everything away while she's still passed out.

Not a speck remains. I even got that splatter on the wall. So important that she doesn't see even a drop of blood.

Now, for the salve.

I have no idea what it's made of, nobody does. The recipe's been gone for generations, but at least I know that the last of it will be put to good use, not saving another alcoholic uncle from losing an arm in a drunk driving accident just so he can go and be diagnosed with stage four liver cancer the next year. This is special. I deserve it.

I rub salve over all the sutures on both our bodies—don't miss a stitch. A bit on her temples, too. The spirits can sweep away her memories of this along with the wounds. One final whisper of gratitude and send them to be at peace. They've proven themselves to be very accommodating.

When my teeth stop chattering and the room is restored to its normal temperature, I know they're gone, our scars and stitches with them—every last trace of the procedure.

All the dirty tarps are already double bagged in thick black garbage bags—the circular saw too, my mom will never know it's gone—which I shoved in my closet until I have time to go to the dump. Everything is scrubbed and looking good as new.

But my legs feel even better than that.

"Elena." I nudge her gently while she lies on a clean table, her wrists and ankles bound in fresh, unstained yoga straps, not a scratch on her body. "Elena, wake up."

Her eyes flutter open and she looks at me, confused.

"What happened? Was I asleep? Where's all the blood?"

"Blood?" I look at her like she has three heads.

"The blood and all that noise—like a lawnmower or something. And—there was so much blood—and someone screaming."

"You were *out*. I have no idea what goes on inside *your* head while you're stretching, but I fall asleep in Shavasana pretty much every time I go to yoga and my dreams are like happy bubbles and riverbeds. Who gets so zenned out they fall asleep and then dreams about violence? That is *fucked up*, dude."

"I was asleep?"

She is making this so easy. I nod and make my face look all concerned, like maybe she's not alright, and I should be worried.

She sighs deep and long and drops her face into her hands.

"Sorry, Gigi. I guess I've been tired."

"And maybe a little stressed, too." I lay my hand on her shoulder. "Whatever your subconscious is trying to communicate, it doesn't sound very pretty."

She looks at me and tears well up in her eyes.

"I don't know. Something feels wrong."

"Shhh, shhh..." I say, and stroke her hair. "It's okay. Everything is going to be fine."

Elena cries a minute longer, then jumps off the table to go to the bathroom.

"Wow," she says. "My whole body feels different. That stretch must have been intense. I can't believe I slept through it, I am so sorry."

It feels like forever before we get back to gym even though it's just the next day, and I'm dying to see what I'm capable of now.

"Alright, girls," Coach calls. "Let's start on bars today."

"No!" My voice comes out whinier than I want it to and everyone looks at me. "Can't we start on floor? I *really* wanna get my double full."

"Okay, let's start on floor then. If everyone's okay with that."

No one argues.

We warm up and everything feels better than it ever has. Her legs really are incredibly powerful. And flexible. My leap pass is every bit as effortless as I imagined it would be, and I can see her *still* warming up out of the corner of my eye. I struggle to keep my face from twisting into a grin.

We each take turns running our tumbling passes and my confidence is so high I just nail everything. Elena on the other hand, keeps it simple—basic skills every time. Coach looks concerned.

It's finally time to practice our double fulls, and we head over to the pit. I know I'm going to get it. Everything is playing out exactly like it should.

It's Elena's turn, and I see the shift in her face when sadness becomes determination.

She does it perfectly, but that's okay. It just makes me that much more certain that I will too. If she can do it with my legs, I sure as shit can do it with hers. And this time, maybe I'll prove to Coach what I already know—that I *am* ready to do it on the floor. Fuck her always underestimating me, I know I can do it. She's so worried about her little star gymnast being off her game, she won't be paying that close attention anyway.

A few rounds in, Elena wants to stay in the pit and practice more even though she's somehow still doing *everything* flawlessly, but I'm over that fucking pit. When Coach isn't looking, I make my way to the floor. Sometimes you just have to show people that you're capable, even if they don't believe it.

This is going to be me, proving once and for all that I am every bit as good—*better* even—than her. Now that I've got the legs to do it, I'll be unstoppable.

Get to the corner, visualize, prepare, go.

Run, roundoff, back handspring, up, spot the floor, arm out, and—

The loudest crash I've ever heard gongs through my skull as my neck hits the floor. Everything goes black before it goes red and my face feels like it just caught a baseball. I have never been more aware of my teeth—they are *screaming*. My face, I feel; my teeth, I *feel*, but everything else—. There is blood, wet and hot, streaming down my chin, but I can't wipe it—my hands won't respond to me. Nothing will.

I hear Coach's voice far away.

"Gigi! Gigi, can you move? Someone—call an ambulance."

Our Perpetual Intention

J.A.W. McCarthy

August 17, 1992

Dear Jess,

I know I say this every time, but I miss you so much. Ever since we moved to Alderwood, I realize I was wrong about everything. I tried to be good, you know? You know I never really liked Sheila, but she makes my dad happy and she didn't seem all that bad at first. It's not like she's ever been mean to me. Yeah, she does annoying shit like stare at me too long, and she's always talking about the spiritual focus that lights the path to righteous paradise, but it used to be easy enough to ignore her. Dad used to laugh it off too. He'd say Sheila's "kooky" (who says that?) and means well, so I thought I wouldn't have to worry about him. I think I was okay with her in the beginning because she didn't seem to care what I did. But now that we're at Alderwood, she suddenly cares a little too much.

It's not too bad here, though. I have my own room, but I have to share a bathroom with, like, twelve people. Everyone's pretty nice. We all have to eat together in a big hall, but at least I don't have to cook. We're surrounded by woods as far as the eye can see, and you can even see a little slice of the lake if you're on one of the upper floors. It's really quite beautiful. There's all kinds of birds and even deer. Oh, and I saw a fox the other day! Right outside my window!

There's even a few kids my age here. I asked them what high school we're going to when summer break's over, but they said they don't go to high school. They said *we* don't go to school at all.

I thought I'd be able to come visit you since Alderwood isn't so far away, but yesterday, after morning asanas (that's what they call our exercises), I took a walk along the edge of the property and now there's a chain-link fence there. There's even barbed wire on top. I swear that wasn't there last week. When I asked my dad about it, he said I should be focusing inward, that I have everything I need here. Food, shelter, a strong body, love and purpose. "Family," he said. My family has grown by almost sixty people. Do I know how *lucky* I am?

At first I thought my dad moved us here to keep you and me apart. He wasn't exactly thrilled when your mom told him what happened that night at your house, but I think he was only upset that she was so upset. He's been talking about authenticity a lot, and how important it is to live my truth. I told him I was living my truth—we were living *our* truth—and it's not my fault that your mom can't accept that. I thought he might start in with that "experimentation is perfectly natural at that age, blah blah blah" stuff—what I heard him tell your mom over the phone—but he said I could visit you anytime, so I think he understands now. That's why I didn't totally freak out when he said we were moving to Alderwood with Sheila. He's been so lonely since Mom died, and I was trying to be good. He said you could visit me whenever you want, too. Remember that? He said at least once a month, maybe more. He said you could even sleep over. But now there's a fence, and when I asked my dad about going to see you, he said our car is gone. Just like with our house, we must sacrifice so the community can thrive. He even started in with that "many parts/one whole" bullshit Sheila's always babbling about.

It seems sudden, but it's not. I used to think that he didn't know, that maybe Sheila lied to him. But now I know better. Just like Sheila, he's always going on about the Principles and how Satya is especially important. "Live the truth, radiate the truth, and trust will follow." Turns out it's only important for *me* to be truthful. He's a fucking hypocrite. He knew what would happen here. He lied to me.

Talk soon,

Francine

August 29, 1992

Dearest Jess,

They've increased our movements again. When we first got here, we did asanas once a day, before breakfast. "Greet the sun," stuff like that. It was nice at first, you know? I hate getting up early (you know me), but I did feel better after, like it was this gentle transition of moving my body, and I have to admit I felt pretty badass once I mastered all the Warrior poses. Sometimes I even nod off during Shavasana. That one's still my favorite.

Now, we do asanas five times a day. Sometimes they even wake us up in the middle of the night to do more. I say "us", but it's really only a few of us, and last night it was just me and one other girl. Sheila says there are no leaders here, that we are one community of equals, but who's the one making us do this stuff? Who decided we can somehow open the universe and ascend the seven levels by doing these movements in unison at all hours of the day and night?

Yesterday, during afternoon asanas, I swear I saw my fingers lengthening. I was in Warrior III, really concentrating on being strong and engaged and reaching all the way to the far corner of the Temple of Our Perpetual Intention, when I saw my index and middle fingers stretch. One second they were my regular old fingers, and the next they were, like, two feet long, these floppy little sausages boinging in the breeze. It was like that time Brady Heath dislocated his thumb in gym, but, like, times a hundred. Remember that? So I was freaking out about my floppy sausage fingers, but Sister Beth got really excited and said I've broken the third plane. By the time she was done babbling about ascension, my fingers were normal again.

They say it's just yoga, but I don't think so. My mom did yoga. She said it calmed her mind, it balanced her, it made her body stronger. She didn't think it was going to ascend her to some paradise of collective energy and universal knowledge. I mean, I know yoga can also be a spiritual practice that brings people to the self (omg, do I sound like one of them now??) and teaches peace and ethics. I know it's important and good, but I think the people here are doing it wrong. The people at Alderwood are nice enough, but I don't understand what they're trying to do. I don't think they understand either; they're always talking in circles. They can't answer questions to save their lives. Sometimes I think they're just a bunch of idiots in baggy linen and no underwear pretending they're all spiritual and shit.

Sheila says a yogi is silent in doubt. I'd believe it, except she never shuts up. She's always saying I need to believe because I'm special. Yeah, my dad used to say I was special too, until Sheila came around. Why am I special to her, though? She's started putting her hands on my shoulders and trying to get me to breathe in unison with her whenever we pass in the halls. She says an exchange of breath is an exchange of the soul, and my soul is extra super special, apparently. The worst part is, other people in Alderwood have started doing the same thing to me.

You know I don't like to be touched, not by strangers. But of course, when I told my dad, he said there are no strangers here. We're *family*.

Fuck family. You're the only one I need, Jess. Remember that time we camped in my backyard and you got in my sleeping bag because yours wasn't warm enough? I thought there was no way we'd both fit, but you knew where to put your hands and legs and it was perfect, and I slept the best I ever have that night. We fit together as if your fingers were formed from my ribs and my lips were formed from your tongue. You said that's because we were created as one whole so beautiful that the jealous universe separated us. I think about that all the time. You and me, we've already exchanged souls; I have nothing to give these Alderwood people.

They're always staring at me, too. Did I tell you that? Brother Beck says it's because I'm chosen—it's in my blood. They can see my aura, my soul already ascending all the levels, making a path for them. Ha. I guess I'm their fantastical fucking Asian.

Yeah, did I tell you I'm the only Asian person here? Fantastic Francine with her super long sausage fingers piecing the universe's veil. I gotta go to evening asanas now, but I'll let you know if my toes bust through the ceiling or some shit.

Love,

Francine-y Weenie

September 15, 1992

Hey Jess,

Today I asked Sister Beth what I'm supposed to do as their "chosen," how I'm supposed to make this path for everyone when I don't even know where we're going. She went on and on about ascension and higher consciousness again—same circular babble I've been hearing from everyone since my first day here—but then she said what we are striving for is not only enlightenment but knowledge. Only with knowing the self will we fully ascend to a plane of true peace and beauty. Paradise.

I hate to admit it, but it kinda made sense.

So there are seven levels (I don't know what they all are; Sister Beth and Brother Beck say we only know them once we complete them) and I will lead all of Alderwood up every level to Paradise. See, Sister Beth saw what I saw that day during afternoon asanas—she saw my fingers stretch to the far corner of the Temple, same as I did. She said I'm the first one in nine years, and this means Brother Beck is right about me. They need me.

You remember how I'd always get picked last in P.E., but then we did basketball and I made that shot and then everybody wanted me on their team? Even though I hate basketball, it felt so good. I've never been important before, you know? I've never been needed.

What happened to my fingers (and now my toes! It happened last night during our late night movements—I was in Salabhasana when I felt this weird tingling in my feet, so I looked back and the big toes on both my feet were, like, a yard long, off my yoga mat and almost touching the Temple's door) is I'm shedding. As I grow into my consciousness through the movements, the old parts of me—the ignorant, stagnant parts—pull away from my bones and stretch the boundaries of my flesh, like when you push your finger against plastic wrap to see how far it'll stretch before it breaks. Eventually, through the right combination of asanas, these bad parts will push through my skin and fall to the floor as waste (but do I have to clean it up?? haha). Each of the seven levels will strip me of the negativity I've been carrying and center my spiritual focus. They will reveal my light.

After Sister Beth explained it all to me, I asked her what happened to the other chosen people, like the last one nine years ago. If these chosen people had ascended all seven levels, they would've led all of Alderwood to Paradise already, right? They wouldn't need me. She seemed reticent at first, but then she said she had something to show me in the basement.

Jess, it was like a storage room full of mannequins all frozen mid-asana. Freaky, right? Except they're real people. Fucked up people.

There was a woman in Gomukhasana, legs and arms pretzeled like she was trying to scratch an impossible itch, the fingers on both of her hands so long and floppy they looked like fleshy ropes trailing behind her.

A man in Chakrasana, bent backwards like those bridges we did in gymnastics, segments of his spine inverted, dislocated like little fists trying to punch through his ribcage.

A woman in Parsvottanasana (pyramid pose—I remember this one because it was one of my mom's favorites), face over toes, her lips stretched from her mouth and draped over her feet, loose as taffy.

There were a dozen or so of them, all twisted up and stretched out, distorted as if their ignorant and stagnant parts were parasites or rats that died while trying to fight their way out of their flesh. A couple were teens like us. One was even a little girl, maybe nine or ten.

They didn't look decomposed or anything like that, but they were all dead. I touched a man in Garudasana on the shoulder and he didn't flinch. He was so cold. His shoulder should've been hard and bony, but he gave under my touch like a block of congealed fat. When I looked at my fingers, they were oily. The whole room smelled like mildew and congealed pork grease.

Sister Beth said I don't need to be afraid because I've already ascended so much farther than these people, so what happened to them won't happen to me. She started going on about the modesty of sacrifice, but I wasn't really listening. I kept thinking I should scream, but no matter how I tried, I couldn't get any sound out. I was phlegmy, like my throat was filling up with all that congealed fat that dampened the air. My legs were shaking so bad.

I don't think I'll be much of a leader, but I didn't tell Sister Beth that.

xoxo

Your Enlightened Francine

September 18, 1992

Dearest Jess,

I'm so confused.

I need to get out of here, right? I'd be crazy if I don't, right?

After Sister Beth showed me all those poor, twisted dead people, I just froze. These Alderwood people chose them—like they chose me—and they ended up dead in a basement storage room, these monuments to their own failures. That's my fate.

At first I thought it was supposed to be a warning, but I don't think Sister Beth meant it that way. So I've ascended at least part of the way, gotten farther than these poor people ever did, but why do they think I'll make it through all seven levels? Who's to say I won't get stuck at the sixth level, my yard-long fingers and toes all knotted up, another sad specimen in their basement collection?

I don't want to die like that, Jess. I don't want to be frozen there for all eternity when the last time I saw your face you were crying, your mom in your head making you say you were confused and wrong and it would be better if we forgot it all.

I'd call for help, but there are no phones here. Sheila says if we need outside help, we can get one of the Sisters or Brothers to make a call for us when they go into town. They're the only ones with a key to the gate.

I thought I might try climbing the fence anyway, like I could throw a blanket over the barbed wire. I don't know exactly where we are (I fell asleep on the car ride), but I could walk until I found a town or a gas station, or even flag down a car. The asanas have made my body so strong, I think I could walk forever!

Except now the fence is electrified. I took a walk around the border of the community today, and there's a new sign up: DANGER. ELECTRIC FENCE. DO NOT CLIMB. DO NOT TOUCH. MAY CAUSE DEATH.

I thought it might be fake, but I'm too scared to test it.

Do you think you and your mom could come get me? I know she doesn't like me, but you can tell her I know I was wrong and I'm sorry, and whatever else she wants to hear, okay? I remember some landmarks, and I can tell you Alderwood is about two hours or so from my house. You know our PO Box in Pine Grove, so that's got to be the closest town to the community. You're the genius, Jess (are you still tutoring?). You can figure it out.

I know it would be easier for you to call the police, but I don't think these are bad people. I think they're deluded and need help, not jail. Or maybe they deserve to be left alone here, to do whatever it is they're trying to do as long as they're not hurting anybody. I mean, enlightenment is a good thing, right? Shouldn't we all strive for that? Those people in the basement chose to be here, so are they really victims? I'm the only one who isn't 100% sure about being here. Sometimes I think the fence is just for me.

Besides, my dad is one of them. I'm still pissed at him for lying to me, but I don't want him to go to jail either. He's all I have.

God, am I brainwashed, Jess? Is this what it's like—you don't even know it's happening?

Anyway, can you write back as soon as you get this? We can make a plan. I'll figure out a way around the fence. Or, even if I can't, I can at least talk to you through the fence. You can tell me if I'm crazy or not. It would be so good to see your face again.

Love you,

Francine

———◇———

September 26, 1992

Jess,

Are you getting my letters? I haven't heard from you in a long time and I know that's not like you; I know you still care about me. I ask every day, but the Sisters and Brothers always say there was nothing in the PO Box for me.

They're hiding your letters, aren't they? Or tearing them up, trying to make me think you don't care about me anymore. Dad says I should be focusing on the path forward, not the path behind me. Ascension means shedding all the earthly noise. But Paradise wouldn't be Paradise without you, Jess.

Please, I know it's a big ask, but could you come out here? I'll be at the fence every day, every moment I can be there. I'll walk the perimeter until I see you. I just need to see you.

Francine

———◇———

October 14, 1992

Dear Jess,

Something amazing happened last night!

I was thinking about what Brother Beck said during midnight asanas (I'm the only one doing those now; I guess they really do believe I'm "the one", haha): "One cannot pierce the light while carrying the burden of the self. One cannot clear a path for others to follow without the crucifixion of the ego."

It wasn't exactly a crucifixion, but whatever it is that's happening to me, I'm shedding the burden of self. I'm ascending.

So it was just me and Brother Beck, and I'm in Bakasana—a pose I'm terrible at even though I've been practicing for weeks now—when not only was I able to hold my body up with just my hands through Brother Beck's count, but I wasn't shaking. Prana moved through my body then there was a stillness, an emptiness, this moment where I lost myself. Blood filled my head, blocking out all that earthly noise. I suddenly realized I didn't know who I was—who I used to be—or even where I was. In that nothing, I felt my ego fall away.

But, this is the amazing part: I felt my body change. With my body frozen there in Bakasana, my cells began to shift. They purged. The soles of my feet, my elbows, my fingertips, even the crown of my head—they expanded across the Temple, all this dark energy, the ignorant, stagnant parts of myself—shooting from my body and slamming into the walls all around us. I was a perfect five-point star, shedding the veil between self and true enlightenment. I didn't need to see what my body looked like. The look on Brother Beck's face was enough.

Once I was back in my body, aware of myself and my place, I was scared that I'd stay frozen this way, another failure corpse for the Alderwood basement collection. But no, I moved gracefully out of Bakasana, and Brother Beck was so pleased he let me stay in Shavasana until I started to doze off. I did it, Jess. I ascended past all of them.

Back in my room, I was so excited I couldn't sleep, so I decided to practice some of the asanas again, really perfect my movements so I can clear the path, you know? This is where it gets even more amazing, Jess.

I'm really concentrating on my flow, trying to move smoothly between Warrior II and Trikonasana, when I hear a strange sound. Like something heavy and thick slowly dripping onto the floor behind me. It wouldn't be so strange, except this place is really quiet, silent at night.

So I'm in Trikonasana, and I glance up at my arm above my head, and I see it: not only is my hand pushing all the way up to the ceiling, but it's dripping. Dripping this pinkish brown goo in these slow, thick drips like when candle wax starts to cool and congeal. I tried to stay calm and shifted as smoothly as I could into Tadasana (mountain pose—you remember that one). You're supposed to focus straight ahead, but I couldn't help myself—I had to look down. And that's when I saw it. There were pools of that same pink-brown goo encircling me, all over my mat, seeping onto the floor, all slick and sticky under my feet and between my fingers. It smelled foul, the sickly sweet stench of rotten fruit.

That's the bad stuff, the stuff that kept all those people in the basement from ascending.

I know I should've been scared, but it was a relief. To actually *see* my body change and grow and shed this way... Sister Beth was right: I don't need to be afraid.

Do you think I'm crazy, Jess? I know it all sounds crazy—trust me, I would think so too if I were in your position—but once you see it, once it's happening to you... it's a miracle. It's the last step towards Paradise.

This doesn't mean I want to stay here, okay? I gathered up all that rotten goo and shoved it under my bed because I don't want the Sisters and Brothers to know that I've already ascended this far. I'm not even gonna tell my dad. I don't want to lead anyone. These people can find their own way to Paradise.

When I woke up this morning, my limbs were still really long and I felt like Gumby wrapping my arms around my middle, making a straitjacket just for shits and giggles. It takes some getting used to, but what the eye perceives is meaningless. Integrity is in the spirit, and the spirit cannot be contained. I feel so strong now. My bones are hollow, light as air.

You still trust me, right, Jess? I think I can do it now. I'm just sorry it's taking me this long. The way I'm changing... electricity or barbed wire, it doesn't matter. I'll climb that fence. I'll make my way home to you.

Yours,

Francine

———————

October 18, 1992

My Dearest Jess,

I know why you haven't written back.

Your mom's still mad about the last time I slept over, isn't she? She's got you thinking what you feel in your heart is wrong, that I made you lose your way. Maybe she's throwing away these letters before you even get them. There was a time when I would've apologized, told her I was just confused, promised her it wouldn't happen again. But now I know better. When people are forced to confront something that doesn't match their narrow idea of "normal," they lash out. People fear what they don't understand. People are afraid of greatness.

Maybe your mom saw that I'm special and it scared her.

I'm still practicing the asanas in my room from after the midnight session with Brother Beck until our pre-breakfast session in the morning. That's seven sessions a day now, for the seven levels. Get it?

The Brothers and Sisters don't know I've been doing these extra overnight asanas. I've been in such a good headspace after I figured everything out, and now I can't stop. Shedding feels so good, you know? I lose myself in the movements, the organic flow that guides my body and extinguishes my ego as I move into the light. One moment I'm in Matsyasana, then the sun is coming up and I realize I was gone for five or six hours, no more self, only enlightenment. It doesn't matter that my flesh has fallen from my bones, that I've stuffed so much of this stagnant waste under my bed that the odor of decomposition is suffocating—only by releasing the corporeal are we free. I thought I was still tethered to this plane, but guess what? I did it. I ascended.

I went all the way, Jess. Last night, I saw Paradise.

I don't know what pose I was in, whether I was standing or sitting or already reclined in Shavasana. I had no body. No flesh, no bones, no nerves, no brain, yet I could feel everything. My spirit was a five-pointed star and it stretched to every corner of the universe, growing and reaching even as the universe tried to move away from me. If I had skin, it would've been as warm and soft and ungovernable as the sea. If I had a heart, it would've been a slow engine with no limitations, no road to run out of. I was made of the light of stars, and the numbing cold of the night, and layers upon layers of time and knowledge keeping me safe and crystalized and indestructible. Eternal.

Everything I've ever felt was not only validated but cherished. You and me, we were right and everyone who tried to shame us burned below. I have never been more fulfilled, more whole, more at peace.

And here's the crazy thing: after that, when I saw myself in the bathroom mirror with my rubbery arms dragging the floor and my chin scraping my knees, I wasn't afraid. Even my cheeks all loose and draping my shoulders didn't disgust me. Progress is only ugly when our minds are limited.

When the others saw me at morning asanas, they were so overcome they fell to their knees. Some of them even cried. I've learned how to tuck my excess—the parts that haven't fallen to rot yet, my terrible waste—into myself so that I can move freely, but Sister Beth says that's not necessary. They'll come to me because I am their example, their key, their success.

I don't know if I've cleared a path for the others here at Alderwood, but I don't really care. I didn't tell them about the Paradise I saw, and I don't plan to. When I reached the seventh level, I was only thinking of you.

All my love,
Francine

———◈———

October 22, 1992

My Jess,
I can't hide it from the Sisters and Brothers anymore. I can't hide it from my dad and Sheila. My body still drips all that stagnant, evil waste, but they're starting to see the real me underneath. The seventh level me. I'm almost in my true form.

They don't want me to leave because I have yet to reveal the path to them. They've put someone outside my door overnight now, and there is always someone to escort me to meals and asanas. I'm not even alone in the bathroom anymore. They're still taking my letters to the post office in town, or at least they're saying they are. I don't think they're reading them, though; they would've put guards at my door long ago.

It feels selfish and cruel to deny my Sisters and Brothers the path to ascension. I know this is not the yogi way. I have not sufficiently crucified my ego, I suppose. I just don't think they need me. I can't be the only one meant to bathe in Paradise.

I've accepted that you can't come to me. I will come to you. I have a plan.

When I am in the seventh level, I have no physical body. I am free of obstacles, of anything that can contain and hinder my spirit. My overnight asanas transport whatever form I possess, so I can slip out the window and to the fence. With my spirit in Paradise, this earthly form can sling her endless limbs over chain-link and barbed wire to touch the land on the other side. This form absorbs electricity, is propelled by it. There is no pain. I'm not afraid of burning flesh or a shocked-dead heart. You can have my bones; I don't need them anymore.

In one week, once I've made it over the fence and found a way to town, you will see me again. Though you may not recognize my physical form, you will know it's me the same way you always knew it was me by the sound of my fingertips against your window. You'll recognize me because we are still one whole that cannot be separated, not even by the jealous universe.

Promise me you won't be scared. The ruin is leaving me, and remember, what your eyes perceive is meaningless. I cannot be contained.

I love you so much, Jess. And now, I can finally prove it. I can't wait to show you Paradise.

Eternally,

Francine

Afterword

If you told me a year ago I'd be editing a sports and fitness body horror anthology, I wouldn't have believed you.

My history with sports is complicated. Consider my single month on the wrestling team in elementary school. One of the other wrestlers—a beefcake nightmare who would later go on to compete at the national level—scared me so bad that I ran from the mats to the side of the gym where my mom was sitting. Sobbing, I begged her to let me read *National Geographic* instead of returning to practice. That was the end of that.

My later sports experiences weren't much better. The season I played baseball, my parents photographed me crossing home plate with my arms raised in "victory," not realizing I was already out. That photo is still in the family album. Similarly, during a relay race at a swim meet, I secured the "win" for my team without realizing the race had been canceled midway through due to a fast-approaching lightning storm. Back then, these disappointments discouraged me from pursuing sports further, but now I look back at them and laugh.

Even so, the lightning incident reminds me how often athletes brush shoulders with body horror. Sure, I never ended up fried and floating in a swimming pool, but not everyone gets so lucky. Take, for instance, the many student athletes I taught who came to my class with broken collarbones, throbbing concussions, and torn ACLs. Most recovered well enough to play again, but some endured injuries severe enough that they'll be dealing with them for the rest of their lives. Now, *that's* horror.

It might sound like I find sports and fitness repulsive, but my relationship with them has changed over the years. I'm no longer the little boy sobbing and reading *National Geographic* in his mom's lap while the other kids wrestle. These days, I enjoy weightlifting and yoga, and while I'd never want to jump in the Octagon with Francis Ngannou, I love watching MMA from the safety of my couch. Finally, I can appreciate both the horrors *and* joys of sports and fitness. This anthology is the result of that redefined relationship.

Of course, many people helped make this book happen. To them, I express my deepest gratitude. First and foremost, thanks to the writers who brought their muscular prose, sick imaginations, and wildly entertaining storytelling. To Steve Stred for his killer foreword and enthusiasm for this project. To Lynne Hansen whose design skills are unparalleled and who is always a joy to work with. To Anthony Engebretson for suggesting the perfect anthology title. To minicrew for the friendship, advice, and good times. To Kate for the love, support, and joyful embrace of the grotesque.

Finally, a big thank you to everyone who supported the Kickstarter campaign: ABD, Mae Murray, Brandon Applegate, Anthony Engebretson, Eric Netterlund, The Creative Fund by BackerKit, Benjamin Dyer, Dan Bjork, Lor, Alex Ebenstein, Tom Coombe, Patrick Barb, Gordon B. White, MaDonna Flowers, Susan Jessen, Julia Valencia, Arnela Bektas, Graham Scott, Nikki Sherman, AJ Woods, Dylyn, Donyae Coles, Scary Stuff Podcast, Jeff Cilione, Tiffany Brown, Jared Goode, Alice Austin, Maureen Wanket, Cade Eakin, Irena K, Michael Tichy, Jane Holt, Test Pattern Creative (Ben), Nicole Morse, Angel Day, Jeff Raymond, Hailie, Corey Farrenkopf, Tim Meehan, Casanova Funkenstein, Chloe, Samuel Segrist, Bridget Brave, Tyler Welch, Cormack Baldwin, Mike Serritella, Matt Blairstone, Evan Shelton, Charles Austin Muir, Day, Adrienne,

Bec McKenzie, Tala Gallaga, Sam Richard, Ryan, Zackary Stillings, Christopher Wood, Luke W. Henderson, William Jones, John O'Hare, AJ Linscott, Renha, Tom, Kelly Hoolihan, Chris Williams, Jacob Steven Mohr, Evoripclaw, David Swisher, Tim Hoelscher, Cole Turner, Sarah, Zac, Elske van der Werff, Michelle, Loranger, Scott, Sofia, Dave Urban, Bennett, Kari Johnson, Angela Penland, Joshua Hair, S.R. Lewis, Nathan Toby, Sam Sumpter, Rain Corbyn, Kristen Riley, K, Nate Tieman, Rachel Alexander, Richard Leis, Elisa Villani, Keith Reid, Claudia Schloemp Mittelstaedt, Geoff Emberlyn, Xerino, Derek Nason, Mason Hawthorne, Arthur Castro, Giuseppe Lo Turco, Efren, Rais Akbar, and Owen McManus. You all rule!

Keep it spooky and never skip leg day!

Eric Raglin, editor of *SHREDDED*

Author Bios

Nikki R. Leigh is a queer, forever-90s-kid wallowing in all things horror. When not writing horror fiction and poetry, she can be found creating custom horror-inspired toys, making comics, and hunting vintage paperbacks. She reads her stories to her partner and her cat, one of which gets scared very easily.

Tim Meyer dwells in a dark cave near the Jersey Shore. He's written and published over fifteen novels and novellas, including Malignant Summer, The Switch House, Dead Daughters, Limbs, and many other titles. His screenplay adaptation for The Switch House has won two finalist awards (Semifinalist, ScreenCraft Horror Competition 2020 & Semifinalist, Filmmatic Horror Screenplay Awards 5). He exists on coffee and IPAs.

Brandon Applegate lives and writes in a parched suburban hell-scape near Austin, Texas with his wife and two daughters who have, so far, failed to eat him. His debut short fiction collection "Those We Left Behind and Other Sacrifices" is available on Amazon and bapplegate.com, and he's editing the upcoming "It Was All A Dream: An Anthology of Bad Horror Tropes Done Right" for Hungry Shadow Press, where he's the EIC. You can find him on Twitter (@brandonappleg8), and Instagram (@hungryshadowpress).

Red Lagoe is the author of horror collections *Lucid Screams* and *Dismal Dreams*. Her micro-press, Death Knell Press, launched in 2022 and she will be the editor of its debut anthology, *Nightmare Sky*. When Red's not spewing her horror-ridden mind onto the page, she can often be found beside a telescope, enjoying the hobby of amateur astronomy. Find more by Red at www.redlagoe.com.

Caias Ward is a thick-wristed HVAC technician with over two dozen publication credits. A member of SFWA, he currently lives with his wife and daughter in New Jersey where he enjoys terrible movies and agitating for labor. Find him @caias on Twitter.

RW DeFaoite (they & he) is a half-hearted pseudonym meant as a gesture to Googlable modesty. The person behind it can be found on Twitter at @rvlysses and his work is published in Bleed Error #1.

Mae Murray (she/they) is a writer and editor hailing from Arkansas, now living in eerie New England with her spouse and a little gray cat. She contributes essays and criticism to horror-centric publications, including Dread Central and Fangoria. She is the founder of the Horror Writers Support Group, a therapeutic group grounded in the principles of peer support, and writes its accompanying newsletter. Her editing debut The Book of Queer Saints was released March 2022, and her first novel is set to be released in 2023. Find her on Twitter or Instagram at @maemurrayxo or visit her website maemurray.net for news and updates.

D. Matthew Urban grew up in Texas and now lives in Queens, New York, where he reads weird books, watches weird movies, and writes weird fiction. His stories have been published by Bag of Bones Press, Night Terror Novels, and Black Hare Press. He can be found on Twitter @breathinghead.

Charles Austin Muir is a writer and personal trainer living in Portland, Oregon. He is the author of *Slippery When Metastasized* and the Splatterpunk Award-nominated *This Is a Horror Book*. Recently he debuted in the children's book market with *Pug Monster Gallery*, which he wrote with his wife and illustrator, Kara Picante Muir. His short film *A History of Worry*, based on his experiences as a cancer-caregiving spouse, won the Oregon Short Film Festival's Best Experimental Micro Film Award.

Joe Koch (he/they) writes literary horror and surrealist trash. Joe is a Shirley Jackson Award finalist and the author of *The Wingspan of Severed Hands*, *The Couvade*, and *Convulsive*. They've had over fifty short stories published in books and journals like Year's Best Hardcore Horror, The Queer Book of Saints, Three-Lobed Burning Eye, and Not All Monsters. Find Joe online at horrorsong.blog and on Twitter @horrorsong.

Michael Tichy is a writer and nurse practitioner living in the Midwest. Husband of Amy and hoodad of the mad greyhound Sabrina. His work explores his lifelong obsession of finding meaning in the chaos and the absurd. Previously published in Shiver and Into the Crypt of Rays (anthologies), his first novella: Behind Every Tree, Beneath Every Rock, is forthcoming in summer 2022 from Castaigne Publishing.

Rien Gray is a queer, nonbinary author from Chicago, primarily focused on trans/nonbinary stories and experience. Their short stories appear in trans speculative fiction for Neon Hemlock's *Baffling Magazine*, queer erotic horror for Cipher Press' *Unreal Sex*, and ecological horror for the upcoming *Reclamation* anthology by Outland Entertainment.

Robbie Burkhart (he/him) is a queer Chinese American who writes queer sports fiction. He is currently attending college in California with the intent of pursuing a career in veterinary pathology; he enjoys hiking and hanging out with his dogs. He can be found at bobby-hockey.tumblr.com.

Eric Raglin (he/him) is a Nebraska-based speculative fiction writer. He frequently writes about queer issues, the terrors of capitalism, and body horror. His debut short story collection is NIGHTMARE YEARNINGS. He hosts the Cursed Morsels Podcast and is the editor of SHREDDED and ANTIFA

SPLATTERPUNK. Find him at ericraglin.com or on Twitter @ericraglin1992.

Matthew Pritt is the author of The Supes, published by Future House. His work has appeared in Dark Recesses Press, Dread Stone Press, and Bear Creek Gazette. He is a member of the HWA and he lives in West Virginia with his five cats. You can see pictures of them on his Twitter @MatthewTPritt.

Madeleine Sardina is a queer writer of all things weird and magical. She has been published in Psychopomp Magazine, The New Southern Fugitives, 45th Parallel, and elsewhere. She's also the author of the fiction collection *Lonely Creatures*. She can be found in grainy photographs taken in the forests of northern Oregon or online @mgsardina.

Alexis DuBon is a work of fiction. Any resemblance to actual persons, living or dead, is purely coincidental. You can find her in Field Notes From a Nightmare by Dread Stone Press, A Woman Built By Man by Cemetery Gates Media, A Quaint and Curious Volume of Gothic Tales by Brigids Gate Press, on the Horror Oasis YouTube channel, and on twitter at @dubonicplague.

J.A.W. McCarthy is the author of *Sometimes We're Cruel and Other Stories* (Cemetery Gates Media, 2021). Her short fiction has appeared in numerous publications, including *Vastarien*, *LampLight*, *Apparition Lit*, *Tales to Terrify*, and *The Best Horror of the Year Vol 13* (ed. Ellen Datlow). She lives with her husband and assistant cats in the Pacific Northwest, where she gets most of her ideas late at night, while she's trying to sleep. You can call her Jen on Twitter @JAWMcCarthy, and find out more at www.jawmccarthy.com.

Content Warnings

- Nikki R. Leigh's "I Am the Ring, My Heart Is the Mat, My Bones Are the Ropes": substance use

- Tim Meyer's "The Swish Heard 'Round Central Nebraska": animal death (bird)

- Brandon Applegate's "I'm Gonna Make You A Legend": bullying, automobile wreck

- Red Lagoe's "Don't Make It Weird": sexual harrassment, body dysmorphia

- Caias Ward's "Massive Gains": animal death (horse)

- RW DeFaoite's "Testo Hunky, or; FTM Twunk Pounds XL Bear": transphobia, fatphobia, eating disorder and compulsive exercise mentions, explicit sexual content.

- Mae Murray's "That Southern Spirit": fatphobia, misogyny

- D. Matthew Urban's "Flesh Advent": degradation, abuse of power

- Charles Austin Muir's "Blood, Ash & Iron": drug use, suicide, depictions of child abuse, bullying, male violence, emergency rooms, toxic masculinity in fitness culture

- Robbie Burkhart's "Fish, Crusade": animal death - birds (killing not depicted)

- Eric Raglin's "A Pain All My Own": misogyny, self-harm, stalking

- Matthew Pritt's "It All Comes Back": self-harm

- Madeleine Sardina's "Avulsion": child abuse

- Alexis DuBon's "Lucky Like Elena": eating disorder, mention of injured dog (recovers), torture of a minor, mention of cancer, gaslighting

- J.A.W. McCarthy's "Our Perpetual Intention": cults, implied homophobia

Other Cursed Morsels Press Releases

ANTIFA SPLATTERPUNK

Fascism didn't die in 1945. Its grave was only temporary. Rising again, the undead ideology shambles into the present, gathering power and spreading destruction wherever it goes.

This monster stalks the page of *ANTIFA SPLATTERPUNK*, in which sixteen horror writers explore fascism's many terrors: police wielding strange bioweapons against the public, white supremacists annihilating their enemies through dark magic, and TV personalities vilifying all who defy the rising fascist tide.

But these stories are resistance: Nazi-killing demons, Confederate-slaying witches, and everyday people punching fascists in the teeth. Among the gore is a glimmer of hope that one day this monster will return to its grave and never rise again.

Lightning Source UK Ltd.
Milton Keynes UK
UKHW010654210922
409198UK00002B/389